Praise for Robert Crais

'Crais tells a compelling tale that glints with wit, intelligence and expertise'   *Literary Review*

'Far and away the most satisfying private eye novel in years'   Lawrence Block

'A real winner'   *Independent*

'The kind of bravura performance only a pro can give'
                                        Kirkus Reviews

'Terrific . . . should be mentioned in the same breath as Robert B. Parker, Tony Hillerman, Sue Grafton and James Lee Burke'   *Houston Chronicle*

'A big, ambitious book . . . and one that is eminently satisfying'   *Irish Times*

'Robert Crais is a major crime-writing talent, exciting and thought-provoking'   *Sunday Express*

'Crais is in a class by himself – he is quite simply the best'
                                       Eric Van Lustbader

'Robert Crais is shooting for the big time with all guns blazing'   Maxim Jakubowski, *Guardian*

Robert Crais is the author of fourteen novels, including the international bestsellers *The Forgotten Man, The Last Detective, Demolition Angel* and the Edgar-nominated *L.A. Requiem*. He has two additional Edgar nominations as well as Anthony and Macavity awards for his series of Elvis Cole and Joe Pike crime novels. Crais has also written for acclaimed television shows such as *L.A. Law* and *Hill Street Blues*. *Hostage* has been made into a major motion picture featuring Bruce Willis, and *Demolition Angel* is currently in development with Columbia/Tristar. He lives in Los Angeles. Visit his website at www.robertcrais.com.

By Robert Crais

free fall

AN ELVIS COLE NOVEL

ROBERT CRAIS

An Orion paperback

First published in the United States by Bantam in 1993
First published in Great Britain in 1990
by Orion
This paperback edition published in 2000
by Orion Books Ltd,
Orion House, 5 Upper St Martin's Lane,
London WC2H 9EA

An Hachette Livre UK company

Reissued 2008

A CIP catalogue record for this book
is available from the British Library.

Typeset by Deltatype Ltd, Birkenhead, Wirral
Printed and bound in Great Britain by
Clays Ltd, St Ives plc

The Orion Publishing Group's policy is to use papers that
are natural, renewable and recyclable products and
made from wood grown in sustainable forests. The logging
and manufacturing processes are expected to conform to
the environmental regulations of the country of origin.

www.orionbooks.co.uk

free fall

CHAPTER 1

Jennifer Sheridan stood in the door to my office as if she were Fay Wray and I was King Kong and a bunch of black guys in sagebrush tutus were going to tie her down so that I could have my way. It's a look I've seen before, on men as well as women. 'I'm a detective, Ms Sheridan. I'm not going to hurt you. You may even find that you like me.' I gave her my best Dudley Do-Right smile. The one with the twinkle.

Jennifer Sheridan said, 'Is what we say privileged, Mr Cole?'

'As in attorney-client?' I was holding the door, but Jennifer Sheridan couldn't seem to make up her mind whether to come in or leave.

'Yes.'

I shook my head. 'No. My records and my testimony can be subpoenaed, and under California law, I must provide them.'

'Oh.' She didn't like that.

'But there is latitude. I sometimes forget things.'

'Oh.' She liked that better, but she still wasn't convinced. I guess there's only so much you can do with the Dudley.

Jennifer Sheridan said, 'This isn't easy for me, Mr Cole. I'm not sure I should be here and I don't have much time. I'm on my lunch hour.'

'We could talk over sandwiches, downstairs.' There was a turkey and Swiss on a French baguette waiting for me in the deli on the ground floor. I had been thinking about it for most of the morning.

'Thank you, no. I'm engaged.'

'That wasn't a sexual proposition, Ms Sheridan. It was a simple offer to share lunch and perhaps more efficiently use both our times.'

'Oh.' Jennifer Sheridan turned as red as a beating heart.

'Also, Ms Sheridan, I'm getting tired of holding the door.'

Jennifer Sheridan made up her mind and stepped past me into the office. She walked quickly and went to one of the two director's chairs across from my desk. There's a couch, but she didn't even consider it.

Jennifer Sheridan had sounded young on the phone, but in person she looked younger, with a fresh-scrubbed face and clear healthy skin and dark auburn hair. Pretty. The kind of happy, innocent pretty that starts deep inside, and doesn't stop on the way out. That kind of pretty. She was wearing a light blue cotton skirt with a white blouse and a matching light blue bolero jacket and low-heeled navy pumps. The clothes were neat and fit well, and the cuts were stylish but not expensive. She would have to shop and she would have to look for bargains, but she had found them. I liked that. She carried a black imitation leather purse the size of a Buick, and when she sat, she sat with her knees and her feet together, and her hands clutching the purse on her lap. Proper. I liked that, too. I made her for twenty-three but she looked eighteen and she'd still be carded in bars when she was thirty. I wondered if I looked old to her. Nah. Thirty-nine isn't old.

I closed the door, went to my desk, sat, and smiled at her. 'What do you do, Ms Sheridan?'

'I'm a secretary for the law firm of Watkins, Okum, & Beale. We're in Beverly Hills.'

'Is that how you found me?' I work for Marty Beale,

time to time. A little skip-tracing, a little missing persons. That kind of thing.

'I peeked in Mr Beale's reference file. He thinks highly of you.'

'You don't say.'

'They don't know that I'm here and I would appreciate it if you didn't say anything.'

I nodded. 'On the phone you said something about your boyfriend.'

'My fiancé. I think that he's mixed up in some kind of criminal thing. I've asked him, and he denies it, but I know that something's going on. I think he's scared, and that worries me. My fiancé is not scared of very much.'

I nodded again and tucked that away. Fearless Fiancé. 'Okay. What kind of crime are we talking about?'

'I don't know.'

'Is he stealing cars?'

'I don't think so.'

'Is he embezzling?'

'No. It wouldn't be that.'

'How about fraud?'

She shook her head.

'We're running out of choices, Ms Sheridan.'

She glanced into the big purse as if there were something inside it that she was hoping she wouldn't have to show me, as if the purse were somehow a point of no return, and if she opened it and let out whatever was inside, she would never be able to close it again or return the elements of her life to a comfortable or familiar order. Pandora's Purse. Maybe if I had a purse like that, I'd be careful of it, too.

I said, 'I know it's hard, Ms Sheridan. If it was easy, you wouldn't need me. But if you don't tell me about him, or what you think he is up to, I can't help you. Do you see that?'

She nodded and held the purse tighter.

I took out a yellow legal pad, a black SenseMatic pencil, and made as if I were poised to copy the rush of information she was about to provide. I drew a couple of practice marks on the page. Subliminal prompting. 'I'm ready. Fire away.'

She swallowed.

'Anytime.'

She stared at the floor.

I put the pad on the desk and the pencil on the pad. I put my fingertips together and looked at Jennifer Sheridan through the steeple, and then I looked at the Pinocchio clock that I've got on my wall. It has eyes that swing from side to side as it tocks, and it's always smiling. Happiness is contagious. It was twelve twenty-two, and if I could get down to the deli fast enough, the turkey would still be moist and the baguette would still be edible. I said, 'Maybe you should go to the police, Ms Sheridan. I don't think I can help you.'

She clutched the purse even tighter and gave miserable. 'I can't do that.'

I spread my hands and stood up. 'If your fiancé is in danger, it is better to get in trouble with the police than it is to be hurt or killed.' Twelve twenty-three. 'Try the police, Ms Sheridan. The police can help you.'

'I can't do that, Mr Cole.' The misery turned into fear. 'My fiancé *is* the police.'

'Oh.' Now it was my turn. I sat down.

Jennifer Sheridan opened the purse and took out a 3x5 color snapshot of herself and a tall good-looking kid in a navy blue LAPD summer-weight uniform leaning against a squad car. They were smiling. 'His name is Mark Thurman. He doesn't work uniform anymore. Last year he was chosen for a plainclothes position at the Seventy-seventh Division in South Central Los Angeles.'

'What kind of plainclothes?'

'They call it a REACT team. They monitor career

criminals and try to stop them before they hurt people. It's an elite unit, and he was the youngest man chosen. He was very proud of that.' She seemed proud of it, too. 'Everything was fine for the first few months, but then he changed. It happened almost overnight.'

'What kind of change?' I was thinking Kevin McCarthy. *Invasion of the Body Snatchers.*

'He became anxious and scared and secretive. We never keep secrets from each other and now there are things that he won't talk about with me.'

I looked closer at the picture. Thurman had long forearms and a ropey neck and a country boy's smile. He must've been fourteen inches taller than Jennifer Sheridan. I said, 'I know a lot of police officers, Ms Sheridan. Some of them are even my friends. It can be a hard job with unusual hours and you see too much of what's wrong with people. You don't want to go home and chat about it.'

She shook her head, telling me that I didn't get it. 'It isn't just him not talking about the job. He was in uniform for three years and I know to expect that. It's the way he acts. We used to talk about getting married, and having children, but we don't anymore. I ask him what's wrong, he says nothing. I say tell me about your day, he says that there's nothing to say. He was never like that before. He's become irritable and snappish.'

'Irritable.'

'That's right.'

'He's irritable, and that's why you think he's involved in crime?'

She gave me exasperated. 'Well, it isn't just that.'

'Have you seen him perform a criminal act, or heard him speak of it, or seen the results of it?'

'No.'

'Has he exhibited signs of an income other than his police salary?'

5

'No.'

I tapped the desk. 'Sounds like you think he's up to something because he's irritable.'

She gave me more of the impatience. 'You don't understand. Mark and I have known each other since the seventh grade. We fell in love in the ninth grade. That's how long we've been going together. I love him and he loves me and I know him better than anyone else in all the world.'

'All right,' I said. 'Do you have any clues?'

She frowned at me.

'Clues,' I said. 'An overheard snatch of conversation. A subrosa glimpse of a secret bank account. Something that I can use in ascertaining the nature of the crime.' I hadn't used *ascertaining* in three or four weeks.

She said, 'Are you making fun of me?'

I was getting one of those headaches that you get when your blood sugar starts to drop. 'No, I'm trying to make you consider what you want and why you want it. You claim that Mark Thurman is involved in criminal activity, but you have no direction in which to point me. That means that you're asking me to surveil an active-duty police officer. Police officers are paranoid by nature and they move around a lot. This will be expensive.'

She looked uncertain. 'How expensive?'

'Two thousand dollars. In advance.'

You could see her swallow. 'Do you take Visa?'

'I'm afraid not.'

She swallowed a second time. 'That seems an awful lot.'

'Yes,' I said. 'It is.'

She put the photograph of Mark Thurman back in her purse and took out a red doeskin wallet. She dug in the wallet and got a faraway look like she was working with numbers. Then she pulled out two twenties and put them on my desk. 'I can pay you forty dollars now, and forty dollars per month for forty-nine months.'

I said, 'Jesus Christ, Ms Sheridan.'

She clenched her jaw and brought out another ten. 'All right. Fifty dollars.'

I raised my hands, got up, and went to the glass doors that lead out to the little balcony. The doors that came with the office were aluminum sliders, but a couple of years ago I had them changed to a nice set of double-glazed French doors with brass handles. I opened the doors, set them so that the breeze wouldn't blow them closed, and that's when I saw two guys sitting across the street in a brown unmarked sedan four stories below. A tall guy with shaggy, thick-cut hair sat behind the steering wheel and a shorter guy with a ragged face slouched in the passenger's side. The tall guy had long forearms and a ropey neck and looked a lot like Mark Thurman. Sonofagun. I turned away from the doors and looked at Jennifer Sheridan. Nope. She didn't know that they were out there. 'Mark work today?'

She looked surprised that I'd ask. 'That's right. He works Monday through Friday, from eleven until six.'

'He let his hair grow since he went to REACT?'

Jennifer Sheridan smiled, trying to figure me. 'Why, yes. He had to, for the undercover work.'

Thurman, all right.

I walked back to the desk and looked at her. You could see how much she loved him. You could see that she trusted him, and that she'd never think that maybe he was following her. I said, 'Do you and Mark live together?'

She made a tiny headshake and a bit of the red again touched her cheeks. 'We've talked about it, but we decided to wait.'

'Uh-huh. So you believe that he's hiding something, and you want me to find out what.'

'Yes.'

'What if I find out that Mark Thurman isn't who you think he is? What if I look, and I find something that changes the way that you feel about him, and the way that he feels about you?'

Jennifer Sheridan made a little move with her mouth, and then she cleared her throat. 'Mark is a good man, Mr Cole. If he's involved in something, I know it's not because he wants to be. I trust him in that, and I love him. If we find out that he is in trouble, we will help him.' She had thought about these things. Probably lay awake with them.

I went back to the doors and pretended to adjust them. Thurman and the other guy were still in the sedan. Thurman had been looking up, but ducked back when he realized that I had come back onto the balcony. Fast moves are bad. Another couple of years on the job and he'd know better. You just sort of casually look away. Shift the eyes without moving the head. Eye contact can kill you.

I went back into the office and sat, and Jennifer Sheridan said, 'Will you help me, Mr Cole?'

I said, 'Why don't we do this? I'll nose around and see if there is anything worth pursuing. If there is, I will work for you and pursue it. If there isn't, I will return your money, and you won't owe me anything.'

Jennifer Sheridan said, 'That will be fine,' and then she smiled. Her tanned skin dimpled and her white teeth gleamed and there came a quality of warmth to the room as if a small sun had risen from beneath my desk. I found myself returning the smile. I wrote a receipt in her name for the amount of forty dollars, and noted that it was paid against a due balance of one thousand, nine hundred sixty dollars, payable in monthly installments. I gave back the extra ten with her receipt, then put the forty dollars into my wallet. My wallet didn't feel any fatter than it had without the forty. Maybe if I went down to the bank and had the forty changed to ones, it would feel like more.

Jennifer Sheridan took a folded sheet of paper from the huge purse and handed it to me. 'This is where Mark lives, and his home phone number, and his license plate, and his badge number. His partner's name is Floyd Riggens. I've met Floyd several times, but I don't like him. He's a mean-spirited man.'

'Okay.' Riggens would be the other guy in the car.

She took back the paper and scribbled something on the back. 'This is where I live and this is my work number. It's a direct line to Mr Beale's office, and I answer his phone, so I'll be the one who picks up when you call.'

'Fine.'

She stood, and I stood with her. She put out her hand. I took it. I think we were in a contest to see who could smile the most. She said, 'Thank you, Mr Cole. This is very important to me.'

'Elvis.'

'Elvis.' She smiled even wider, and then she gathered her things and left. It was twelve forty-six, and I stopped smiling. I sat at my desk and looked at the paper that she had given me with the information about Mark Thurman and herself, and then I put it into the desk's top right-hand drawer along with my copy of the receipt.

I leaned back and I put my feet up, and I wondered why Mark Thurman and his mean-spirited partner Floyd Riggens were following Jennifer Sheridan while they were on duty. I didn't like the following, but I didn't have very long to wonder about it.

At twelve fifty-two, Mark Thurman and Floyd Riggens came in.

CHAPTER 2

They didn't kick the door off its hinges and they didn't roll into the office with their guns out like Crockett and Tubbs used to do on *Miami Vice*, but they didn't bother to knock, either.

The guy I figured for Floyd Riggens came in first. He was ten years older than Thurman and maybe six inches shorter, with a hard, squared-off build and weathered skin. He flashed his badge without looking at me and crossed to Joe Pike's office. I said, 'It's empty.' He didn't pay attention.

Mark Thurman came in after him and went out onto the balcony, like maybe a couple of Colombian drug lords had ducked out only seconds ago and were hanging off the side of the building with grappling hooks and Thurman wanted to find them. He looked bigger in person than he had in the pictures, and he was wearing faded khaki fatigue pants and a red jersey that said LANCASTER HIGH VARSITY. Number 34. He looked younger, too, with a kind of rural innocence that you rarely find in cops, sort of like *Dragnet* as played by Ronnie Howard. He didn't look like a guy who'd be into crime, but then, what does a criminal look like? Boris Badenov?

Riggens came out of Pike's office and scowled at me. His eyes were red and swollen and I could smell the scotch on his breath even though he was standing on the other side of the chairs. Hmm. Maybe he didn't have the weathered look, after all. Maybe he had the drunk look. Riggens said, 'We need to talk about the girl.'

I gave him innocent. 'Girl?'

Riggens squinted like I'd spit on his shirt and grinned out the corner of his mouth. Mean-spirited. 'Oh, I like it when jerks like you get stupid. It's why I stay on the job.'

'What are you drinking to get eyes like that – Aqua Velva?'

Riggens was wearing a baggy beachcomber's shirt with the tail out, but you could still make out the butt of his piece riding high on his right hip. He reached up under the shirt and came out with a Sig 9-mil and said, 'Get your ass against the goddamned wall.'

I said, 'Come on.'

Mark Thurman came in off the balcony and pushed the gun down. 'Jesus Christ, Floyd, take it easy. He doesn't know what this is about.'

'He keeps dicking with me, he won't make it long enough to find out.'

I said, 'Let me guess. You guys work for Ed McMahon and you've come to tell me that I've won the Publisher's Clearing House sweepstakes for a million bucks.'

Riggens tried to lift his gun but Thurman kept the pressure on. Riggens's face went red to match his eyes and the veins swelled in his forehead, but Thurman was a lot stronger, and sober, so it wasn't much of a problem. I wondered if Riggens acted like this on the street, and if he did, how long he had been getting away with it. Stuff like this will get you killed. Thurman said, 'Stop it, Floyd. That's not why we're here.'

Riggens fought it a little longer, then gave it up, and when he did Thurman let go. Riggens put the Sig away and made a big deal with the hand moves and the body language to let everyone know he was disgusted. 'You want to do it, then do it, and let's get out of here. This asshole says she wasn't even here.' He went to the couch and sat down. Petulant.

Thurman sort of shook his head, like he couldn't figure

Riggens out, like he had tried for a long time and was maybe getting tired of trying. He turned back to me. 'My name is Mark Thurman. This is my partner, Floyd Riggens. We know she was up here because Floyd followed her up.'

I glanced at Floyd again. He was staring at the Pinocchio clock. 'Maybe Floyd got confused. There's an insurance office across the hall. Maybe she went there.'

Floyd said, 'Okay, she wasn't here. We're not here, either, you want to play it that way. You fell asleep and you're dreaming all this.' He got up and went to the clock for a closer look. 'Hurry up, Mark. I don't wanna spend the day.' Like a little kid.

Thurman looked nervous, but maybe he was just uncomfortable. His partner was looking bad and that made him look bad. He said, 'We called in about you and the word is that you're a straight shooter, so I thought we should talk.'

'Okay.'

'Jennifer and I are having some trouble.'

'You mean, this isn't official police business?'

Riggens went back to the couch and sat down. 'It could be, you want. We could have information that you been up to something. We could even find a snitch to back it up. That would look real good for your license.'

Thurman's face went dark and he said, 'Shut up, Floyd.'

Riggens spread his hands. What?

Thurman came to the front of my desk and sat in the right-side director's chair. He leaned forward when he sat and stared at me the way you stare at someone when you're trying to figure out how to say something you don't want to say. 'I'm here for personal reasons, and they have to do with me and Jennifer. You want to pretend she wasn't here, that's fine. I understand that. But we still have to talk. See?'

'Okay.'

Riggens went, 'Jesus Christ, get on with it.'

Thurman's face clouded again and he once more looked at Riggens and said, 'If you don't shut the fuck up, I'm going to clock you, Floyd.' Enough's enough.

Riggens frowned and crossed his arms and drew himself into kind of a knot. Drunk enough to be pissed, but sober enough to know that he'd stepped over the line. These guys were something.

Thurman turned back to me and sat there, his mouth working. He was having trouble with it, and he didn't strike me as a guy who'd have trouble with a lot. He made a little blowing move with his lips, then laced his fingers and leaned forward. 'We followed her because she's been pressing me pretty hard about some stuff, and I knew she'd try something like this. She's pretty strong-willed, and she gets a head on about things, if you know what I mean.'

Riggens made a snorting sound, then recrossed his arms and put his feet up on the little coffee table I have in front of the couch. I didn't like it, but I didn't say anything.

Thurman said, 'Jennifer and I have been going together since we were kids. I've been acting kind of distant with her for the past couple of months and I haven't told her why, and Jennifer has it figured that I'm mixed up in something. I know that's what she talked to you about, because that's what she talks to me about. Only, that isn't it at all.'

'No?'

'No.' Mark Thurman looked down at his feet and worked his jaw harder and then he looked up at me. 'I've got another girlfriend.'

I stared at him.

'I knew that if she hired someone, they'd find out and tell her, and I don't want that. Do you see?'

I said, 'Another woman.'

He nodded.

'You've been seeing another woman and Jennifer knows something is up, but she doesn't know what. And you're trying to head me off so I won't blow the whistle.'

He nodded again.

Riggens uncurled his arms and pushed up from the couch. 'You don't need to know anything else. The word is that you're a straight shooter and we're looking for a break. It was me I'd slap the bitch down and move on, but he doesn't want to play it that way. Why don't you give the kid a hand?'

I said, 'Jesus Christ, Riggens, why'd you come along? Moral support?'

Riggens said, 'No one's trying to muscle you, smart guy. Everyone's playing straight up.' Riggens jerked his head toward Thurman. 'Tell him we're playing straight up.'

Mark Thurman looked back at me, only now there was a lost quality to his eyes. 'I didn't want you telling Jennifer. When it comes, it's got to come from me.' He was leaning forward so far I thought he'd fall out of the chair. 'Do you see?'

'Sure. I see.'

'It's personal. That's how it should stay.'

'Sure.'

Riggens said, 'No one's asking you to turn down the fee. Just play it smart. Do us the favor and someday you'll get a payback.'

'But I can keep the fee.'

'No problem.'

I looked at Thurman. 'Some right guy you've got as a partner, Thurman, saying it's okay for me to stiff your girlfriend.'

Riggens said, 'Fuck you,' and banged out. Thurman sat in the director's chair, not saying anything, and then he pushed himself up. He was twenty-four years old and he looked like a baby. When I was twenty-four I looked a

14

million years old. Vietnam. He said, 'You do what you want, Cole. No one's telling you what to do. But I'm asking you not to tell her what I said. I get ready, I should be the one tells her. Shouldn't I?'

'Sure.'

'I just got to work this out, that's all I'm saying.' Like he was in the principal's office, like he had been caught throwing eggs at the class geek's house, and now he was ashamed of it. He went to the door. Riggens was already down the hall.

I said, 'Thurman.'

He stopped and looked back at me with his right hand on the handle.

'Why don't you just tell her?'

He didn't answer. He stood there, sort of staring, like he didn't know what to say. Maybe he didn't.

I said, 'She didn't say anything to me about crime. She said that she thought you were seeing another woman. She said that she always knew you were that way.'

Mark Thurman went as red as Jennifer Sheridan when I told her that I hadn't been making a pass. He stared at me with the sort of look you'd have if you were in a hurry one day and backed out your drive without looking and ran over a child. Like someone had pushed an ice spike through your heart. He stared at me like that, and then he went out. He didn't close the door.

I went to the little balcony and stood back from the rail and watched the street. Mark Thurman and Floyd Riggens came out of my building, climbed back into the brown sedan, and drove away. Neither of them spoke, as far as I could tell, and neither of them looked particularly happy. It was six minutes after one, and it looked as if my case was solved.

I closed the glass doors, sat on my couch, and thought about what I might say when I was inducted into the Detective's Hall of Fame. Perhaps they would bill me as

Elvis Cole, World's Fastest Detective. Wouldn't Jennifer Sheridan be pleased. She could say *I knew him when.* At six minutes after one, Jennifer Sheridan would be sitting in Marty Beale's outer office, not expecting a phone call in which the detective that she had hired only moments before would crush her heart with one fell blow, service with a smile, *thank you, ma'am, and the bill is in the mail.* Of course, since I had made such a big deal to Jennifer Sheridan about her lack of proof, she might enquire as to mine, and I had none. I had only Mark Thurman's word, and maybe he had lied. People do.

I put aside my thoughts of the Hall of Fame and called a guy I know named Rusty Swetaggen. For twenty-four years he drove a black-and-white in and around the city of Los Angeles, then his wife's father died and he inherited a pretty nice restaurant in Venice, about four blocks from the beach. He likes it better than being a cop. He said, 'Rusty's.'

I made hissing and cracking noises into the phone. 'I'm calling from the new car phone. Pretty good, huh?'

Rusty Swetaggen said, 'Bullshit, you got a car phone.' Then he yelled at someone in the background. 'It's the big-time op, making like he's got a car phone.' Someone said something and then he came back on the line. 'Emma says hey.'

'Hey back. I need to find out about an officer and I don't want him to know.'

'This guy active duty?'

'Yeah. His name is Mark Thurman. He works a REACT team out of the Seventy-seventh.'

Rusty didn't say anything. I guess he was writing. Then he said, 'Is this guy dirty?' He didn't like asking. You could hear it in his voice. You ride the black-and-white for twenty-four years and you don't like asking.

'I want to find out. Can you do this for me?'

'Sure, Elvis. I'd do anything for you. You know that.'

'I know. I'll be by in a couple of hours. That okay?'

'Fine.'

Rusty Swetaggen hung up, and then I hung up.

I took the shoulder holster out of my bottom left drawer and put it on. It's a nice brushed-leather Bianchi rig that cost a fortune, but it's comfortable, and it's made for the Dan Wesson .38 revolver that I carry. Stylish detectives often carry automatics, but I have never been a slave to fashion.

I took the Dan Wesson out of its drawer and seated it into the shoulder holster and then I covered the works with a light gray cotton sport coat. It looks great over my black-and-maroon Hawaiian beach shirt, and is ideal for hiding firearms in L.A.'s summer weather. I took the Watkins, Okum, & Beale stationery out of my desk, put it in the inside pocket of the sport coat, then called the deli and asked them if they still had my turkey and Swiss on baguette. They did.

I walked the four flights down to the deli, ate my sandwich at a little table that they have by the door, then left to find out whether or not LAPD Officer Mark Thurman was telling the truth, or telling a lie.

Either way, Jennifer Sheridan wouldn't like it.

CHAPTER 3

Driving along Santa Monica Boulevard through West Hollywood and Beverly Hills is a fine thing to be doing in late March, just at the end of the rainy season. It was warmer than it should have been, with highs in the mid-eighties and mare's-tail cirrus streaking the sky with feathery bands, and there were plenty of men in jogging shorts and women in biking pants and Day-Glo headbands. Most of the men weren't jogging and most of the women weren't biking, but everyone looked the part. That's L.A.

At a traffic light in Westwood I pulled up next to a woman in pristine white biking pants and a white halter workout top sitting astride a white Japanese racing bike. I made her for Jennifer Sheridan's age, but maybe she was older. The line of her back was clean and straight, and she leaned to the right, her right toe extended down to kiss the street, her left toe poised on its pedal. Her skin was smooth and tanned, and her legs and body were lovely. She wore a ponytail and bronze-tinted sunglasses. I gave her the big smile. A little Dennis Quaid. A little Kevin Costner. She stared at me through the bronze lenses and said, 'No.' Then she pedaled away. Hmm. Maybe thirty-nine is older than I thought.

At the western edge of UCLA, I climbed the ramp onto the 405 freeway and headed north into the San Fernando Valley. In another week the smog and haze would build and the sky would be bleached and obscured, but for now the weather was just right for boyfriends tailing girl-friends and girlfriends hiring private eyes to check up on boyfriends and private eyes spending their afternoons on long drives into the valley where they would risk life and limb snooping around police officers' apartments. If Randy Newman were here, he'd probably be singing *I Love L.A.*

I edged off the 405 at Nordhoff and turned west, cruising past the southern edge of Cal State, Northridge, with its broad open grounds and water-conscious land-scaping and remnants of once-great orange groves. In the prewar years before freeways and super-highways the valley was mostly orange trees, but after the war the orange groves began to vanish and the valley became a bedroom community of low-cost family housing tracts. When I came to L.A. in the early seventies, there were still small bits of orchard dotted around Encino and Tarzana and Northridge, the trees laid out in geometric patterns, their trunks black with age but their fruit still sweet and brilliant with color. Little by little they have melted away into single-family homes and minimalls with high vacancy rates and high-density apartment complexes, also with high vacancy rates. I miss them. Minimalls are not as attractive as orange trees, but maybe that's just me.

Mark Thurman lived in a converted garage apartment in the northwestern part of the San Fernando Valley, about a mile west of Cal State, Northridge, in an older area with stucco bungalows and clapboard duplexes and mature landscaping. Though the structures are old, the residents are not, and most of the apartments are rented to college students or junior faculty from the university or kids out on their own for the first time. Lots of bikes around. Lots of small foreign cars. Lots of music.

I parked across the street from a flat-topped duplex and looked down the drive. The sheet of Watkins, Okum stationery said that Thurman drove a 1983 blue Ford Mustang as his personal car, but the Mustang wasn't around, and neither was the dark brown cop-mobile. Still out fighting crime, no doubt. Or tailing Jennifer Sheridan. A chain-link fence ran parallel to the drive along a row of eight-foot hedges. About halfway back, a little wrought-iron gate ran from the fence to the duplex, cutting the drive in half. Thurman's converted garage was in the rear yard behind the gate, snuggled against the hedges. A set of sliding glass doors had been installed where the garage door used to hang and someone had built a little sidewalk out of stepping-stones that ran around the side of the place by the hedges. A curtain of vertical blinds was drawn across the glass doors and pulled closed. It was a nice, neat, well-kept place, but it didn't look like the kind of place a cop taking down heavy graft would keep. Of course, maybe Mark Thurman was smart, and the outward appearance of his home was just a dodge to throw off unsuspecting PIs. Maybe the inside of the place looked like Uncle Scrooge's money bin and the walls were lined with cash and bricks of gold. Only one way to find out.

I got out of the Corvette, strolled up the drive, and let myself through the little wrought-iron gate. A young German shepherd was lying by the gate beneath the hedges next door. He watched me come and when I let myself through the gate he lifted his head. I said, 'Woof.' He got up and walked with me. Police dog. If Thurman came home I'd have to go over the fence. Hope he didn't bite.

There were three young women lying on towels in the little yard that separated the duplex from the guest house. One was on her belly, the other two were on their backs, and the one nearest to me was up on an elbow, adjusting a radio. U-2. Nobody was wearing very much in the way of clothes, and you could smell the suntan oil. The one with the radio saw me first and made a little gasping noise. I said, 'Hi, ladies. Is Mark around?' Elvis Cole, the Smooth Detective.

The one with the radio relaxed and the other two looked over. The one without the radio was wearing little round sunglasses and the one on her belly smiled. The two on their backs were brunette, the one on her belly a blonde.

The one with the radio said, 'He's at work.'

I glanced at my watch and made a big deal out of looking disappointed. 'He said he'd meet me here. I guess he got hung up.'

The one on her belly said, 'Are you a cop, too?'

I said, 'Do I look like a cop?'

The three of them nodded.

I spread my hands. 'I'd do great undercover, hunh?'

The one on her belly said, 'I don't know. You might.'

The other two laughed.

The one with the little round glasses covered her mouth and said, 'Ohmygod, do you know who he looks like? He looks like Mel Gibson in *Lethal Weapon*. Don't you think so?'

I was liking the one with the glasses just fine. Maybe thirty-nine wasn't so old after all.

The one with the radio said, 'If Mark told you he'd be here, he's probably on his way. He's pretty good about that kind of stuff.'

I said, 'I've just got to drop something off. You think he'd mind?'

Radio said, 'You could leave it with us.'

'Couldn't do that. It's business-related. And it's sort of a surprise.'

The one on her belly looked interested. 'Evidence.'

The one with the little round sunglasses said, 'Allie likes cops. She wants to see your gun.'

Allie slugged Sunglasses in the leg, and all three of them laughed.

The one with the radio said, 'Go ahead. Mark's cool. He keeps a spare key in a little Sucrets box to the left of the landing behind a plant pot.'

'Thanks.'

The German shepherd was waiting for me when I went around the side of the guest house, and followed me to the door. The Sucrets box and the key were exactly where Radio said they'd be. Some neighbors, hunh? I took out the key and let myself in. The German shepherd sat on his haunches and stared after me and whined. Helluva police dog, too.

Mark Thurman's garage had been converted into a pretty nice apartment. The side door opened into a living room, and from the door you could see the kitchen and another door that led to a bedroom and a bath. A brown cloth couch rested against the west wall and a shelving unit stood against the north. The east wall was the glass doors. A CD player and a Sony TV and a VCR and about a zillion CDs were in the wall unit, but the CD player and the VCR were low-end Pioneer and neither was a bank breaker, even on a police officer's take-home. There was an overstuffed chair at either end of the couch, and a coffee table of bright white pine that matched the wall unit. He would've bought the set from one of those discount places. Imported, they would have told him. Danish. There wasn't a sea of gold coins that you could dive into, or mounds of money bags scattered around, but I hadn't yet seen the bedroom. One shouldn't jump to conclusions.

I glanced through the kitchen, then went into the bedroom. It was small, with a single window and a door that led into the bath, and it wasn't any more lavishly appointed than the living room. I went into the bath first, then came back into the bedroom. There was a king-sized bed without a headboard, a nightstand, and a dresser with a large curved mirror that didn't match any of the other furniture. Garage sale. The bed was made and neat, and the spread was pulled tight across its surface. I went through the dresser drawers and then I looked under the bed. Under the bed there was a red Lily of France brassiere. Thirty-six C. I pulled it out and looked at it, but there was nothing to suggest the owner. Jennifer Sheridan might be a thirty-six C, but I hadn't asked and I hadn't thought about it. I put the brassiere back where I had found it, and then I looked in the nightstand. There was a New Balance shoe box in the large cabinet at the bottom of the nightstand with Mark Thurman's diploma from the police academy, a couple of letters from someone named Todd, and Thurman's credit card and banking receipts. Thurman held a checking account and savings account with Cal Fed, one MasterCard, one Visa card, plus gas cards from both Chevron and Mobil. He kept the billing statements from the Visa and MasterCard in a legal-sized envelope marked *VISA*. Neither card showed recent purchases for anything out of the ordinary, but the most recent bill was three weeks old. His savings account held $3,416.28. I copied the account numbers for the Visa and the MasterCard and then I put the box back as I had found it and went to the closet.

A summer-weight LAPD uniform and a set of navy winters hung with the sport shirts and the jeans and the slacks. They hadn't been worn in a while. A single blue suit looked like it didn't get worn much, either. There were shoes and a spinning rod and a set of golf clubs that looked so old they had probably been handed down from father to son. Above the clothes, a high shelf ran around the perimeter of the closet, weighted down with old issues of *Sports Illustrated*, a motorcycle helmet that looked like it had never been used, and a cardboard box containing an outsized scrapbook with yellowed clippings of Mark Thurman playing football and baseball and basketball and track for the Lancaster Wildcats. Four letter man. Mark had played fullback and strong side linebacker, going both ways for sixty minutes a game. There were newspaper photos of Mark in action, and Mark celebrating with teammates, but there were also snapshots of Mark alone and Mark with Jennifer and Jennifer alone, here Mark eating ice cream at the Tastee Freeze, here Jennifer posing shyly in the empty bleachers, here the two of them at the Sophomore Prom and the Junior-Senior and at graduation. I don't know how old they were in the earliest photographs, but they looked like babies. You got the feeling that Jennifer had taken the photos of Mark and Mark had taken the photos of Jennifer, and that there had never been anyone else in their lives, that they had been complete and whole since that moment when they'd fallen in love in the ninth grade, and, in some wonderful way, always would be. But maybe not. The clippings and the photographs began in ninth grade and ended with graduation. Maybe all those years of oneness had become oppressive to Mark and he had decided that there had to be more and, like the photos in the scrapbook, the oneness had to end. Maybe he had told me the truth. Maybe, after all those years, it was finally over.

I put the scrapbook back as I had found it and finished going through his things, but there were no keys to a newly purchased Porsche, no hastily scrawled map to bags of money buried in the high desert, and no unexplained series of numbers for the Swiss accounts. There was only the thirty-six C. That's the way it goes, sometimes.

I made sure the rooms were like I had found them, then I let myself out, locked the door, and went around to the drive. The German shepherd was gone. So was Allie. The other two were still on their backs. I said, 'Allie get bored?'

The one with the radio said, 'She said she was hot. She went in to cool off.'

The one with the little round glasses said, 'What took you so long?'

'Pit stop.' Elvis Cole, Man of a Thousand Lies. 'You guys know Mark's friend, Jennifer?'

'Sure.'

'She come around lately?'

'Not for a couple of weeks, but she used to.'

The one with the glasses said, 'She's so flat. I don't know what he sees in her.'

The one with the radio said, 'Puh-lease, Brittany.' Brittany. Whatever happened to the women's movement?

I said, 'Mark said he's got another friend. Have you met her?'

The one with the radio said, 'We haven't seen her.'

Brittany sat up and wrapped her arms around her knees. 'You mean he's available?'

I shrugged.

Michael Bolton started singing about how much being in love hurt and the one with the radio turned it up. Brittany lay back and stretched, making a thing out of lifting her ribs and showing her body. She looked thoughtful. Making plans, no doubt. Devising strategies.

The one with the radio said, 'Let me get Allie. She wanted to say good-bye.' Then she got up and went into the house. Brittany was mumbling to herself and Allie was probably mumbling, too. I left before they got back.

Women in heat are frightening to behold.

CHAPTER 4

I let myself out through the little gate, walked back to my car, and drove two blocks to a 7-Eleven where I used their pay phone to call a friend of mine who works in the credit department of Bank of America. I gave her Mark Thurman's name, social security number, and account numbers from both his Visa and MasterCard. I told her that I wanted to know if the charge totals for the month exceeded two thousand dollars and, if they did, how many separate purchases exceeded five hundred dollars and where and when they had been made. I also told her that I wanted to know if Thurman had applied for or received any additional credit cards during the past year. She asked me who the hell did I think I was, calling up out of the blue and asking for all of that? I told her that I was the guy who was going to take her to see Sting at the Greek Theater, then take her to dinner at Chinois on Main afterwards. She asked if tomorrow was okay, or did I want the information later tonight? She called me Chickie when she said it.

I drove back to the 405, then went south, back across the floor of the valley, then through the Sepulveda Pass and into the basin, heading toward Venice and Rusty Swetaggen's place. I left the freeway at Wilshire and turned west to San Vicente Boulevard in Brentwood. It would've been faster to stay on the 405, but San Vicente was nicer, with interesting shops and elegant cafes and palatial homes that somehow seemed attainable, as if the people within them got there by working hard, and were still the type of folks who would give you a smile if you passed them on the sidewalk. Sort of like the Cleavers or the Ricardos.

Bike paths bordered the east- and westbound lanes, and an expansive center island with a row of mature coral trees divided the traffic. Bicyclists and joggers and power walkers flock to San Vicente for its pleasant surroundings and two-mile straightaway from Brentwood to the ocean. Even at midday, the bike paths were crowded and runners pounded along the center island. A man who might've been Pakistani ran with a dust mask, and a red-haired woman with a Rottweiler stopped to let the dog piddle on a coral tree. The woman kept her legs pumping as she waited for the dog. Both of them looked impatient.

Brentwood became Santa Monica and the nice homes became nice apartment buildings, and pretty soon you could smell the ocean and pretty soon after that you could see it. Santa Monica has rent control, and many of the apartment buildings had little signs fastened to their walls that said PEOPLE'S REPUBLIC OF SANTA MONICA. Protest by the apartment owners.

San Vicente ended at Ocean, which runs along a sixty-foot bluff separating Santa Monica proper from the sand and the water and Pacific Coast Highway. Most of the joggers turned back at Ocean, but most of the riders turned left to continue on the bike paths that run along the top of the bluff. I turned with the riders. The top of the bluff sports green lawns and roses and a comfortable parklike setting. There are benches, and some of the time you can sit and watch the ocean and the volleyball games down below on the beach. The rest of the time the benches are used by the thousands of homeless who flock to Santa Monica because of its mild climate. Santa Monica encourages this. The People's Republic.

A block and a half up from the Venice boardwalk I aced out a flower delivery van for a parking spot, fed the meter, and walked two blocks inland to Rusty Swetaggen's place between a real estate office and an architectural firm where they specialized in building houses on unbuildable building sites. You could eat at Rusty's during the day, and people did, but mostly they went there to drink. The real estate salespeople were all politically correct women who believed in Liz Claiborne and the architects were all young guys in their thirties who dressed in black and wore little round spectacles. Everyone was thin and everyone looked good. That's the way it is in Venice. Rusty Swetaggen is a short, wide guy with a body like a bulldog and a head like a pumpkin. If you didn't know that he owned the place, you'd think he was there to rob it. Venice is like that, too.

Six years ago, Rusty and Emma's fifteen-year-old daughter, Katy, took up with a guy from the Bay Area who introduced her to the joys of professional loop production and crack-inspired public sex performance. Katy ran away and Rusty asked me to help. I found her in the basement of a three-bedroom house in the San Francisco hills, sucking on a crack bong to kill the pain of the beating that her Bay Area hero had just given her because she wasn't quite enthusiastic enough in the multiple-partner sex she'd just been forced to have in front of a Hitachi 3000 Super-Pro video camera. I got Katy and all copies of the fourteen sex loops she'd made in the previous three days. None of her performances had as yet been distributed. I destroyed the tapes and brought Katy to a halfway house I know in Hollywood. After eight months of hard family therapy, Katy moved back home, returned to high school, and began to put her life on track. She met a guy named Kevin in a support group during her second year of college, and fourteen months later they were married. That was seven months ago, and now she was finishing a business degree at Cal State, Long Beach. Rusty Swetaggen cried for a week after I brought her back, said he'd never be able to repay me, and refused to let me or anyone who was with me pay for a drink or for anything else that he might provide. I stopped going to Rusty's because all the free drinks were embarrassing.

Rusty was sitting at the bar, reading a copy of *Newsweek*, when I walked in. It was twenty-six minutes past two, but the place was still crowded with the lunch-hour rush. The real estate salespeople and the architects were vying for bar space with a lot of businessmen sporting bow ties and very short hair. The real estate people were getting the best of it. More practice, I guess. I pushed in beside Rusty and said, 'I can't believe a guy with your money hangs around the job. I had your bucks, I'd be on the beach in Maui.'

Rusty squinted at the kid who worked the bar and said, 'It's a cash business, Hound Dog. You don't watch'm, they'll rob you blind.'

The kid showed Rusty his middle finger without looking up. 'I don't have to steal it. I'm going to own it one day.' The kid's name was Kevin. Rusty's son-in-law.

Rusty shook his head and looked back at me. 'The day I get any respect around here I'll drop dead and be buried.'

I said, 'Eat the food around here and it'll happen sooner rather than later.'

Rusty Swetaggen laughed so hard that an architect looked over and frowned.

Kevin said, 'You want a Falstaff, Elvis?'

'Sure.'

Rusty told him to bring it to the table and led me to an empty window booth where someone had put a little *Reserved* sign. People were waiting by the maitre d', but Rusty had saved the booth.

After Kevin had brought the beer, I said, 'You get anything on my guy?'

Rusty hunkered over the table. 'This guy I talked to, he says the people from the Seventy-seventh like to hang at a bar called Cody's over by LAX. It's a shitkicker place. They got dancers in little chicken-wire cages. They got secretaries go in to get picked up. Like that.'

'Is Thurman a regular?'

'He didn't give it to me as a fact, but a REACT unit is a tight unit, sort of like SWAT or Metro. They do everything together, and that's where they've been hanging.'

'You got the address?'

He told me and I wrote it down.

'Your guy know if Thurman is mixed up in anything dirty?'

Rusty looked pained, like he was letting me down. 'I couldn't push it, Hound Dog. Maybe I could've gotten more, but you want Mr Tact. The rest is going to take a couple days.'

'Thanks, Rusty. That's enough for now.'

I finished the Falstaff and took out my wallet. Rusty covered my hand with his. 'Forget it.'

I said, 'Come on, Rusty.'

Rusty's hand squeezed. 'No.' The squeeze got harder and Rusty's jagged teeth showed and suddenly the pumpkin head looked like a jack-o'-lantern from hell and you could see what had kept Rusty Swetaggen alive and safe for twenty-four years in a black-and-white. It was there for only a second and then it was gone, and he gently pushed my wallet toward me. 'You don't owe me anything, Elvis. I'm glad to help you, and I will always help you in any way I can. You know that.' There was something in his voice and his eyes and the way he held his hand that said that my not paying was profoundly important, as profound as anything had been or ever would be in his life.

I put the wallet away and stood. 'Okay, Rusty. Sure.'

He looked apologetic. 'I've got a couple more calls to make, and I'm waiting to hear from a guy. You want tact.'

'Sure.'

'You hungry? We got a pretty good halibut today.' Like nothing would make him happier than to feed me, to give to me.

'I'll see you around, Rusty. Thanks.'

One hour and forty minutes later I parked in a McDonald's lot about three-quarters of a mile from LAX and walked across the street to Cody's Saloon. Mid-afternoon was late for lunch and early for quitting time, but a dozen men were lining the bar and sipping cold beer out of plain glasses. There weren't any female real estate agents and none of the guys at the bar looked like architects, but you never know. Maybe they were politically incorrect and wanted to keep it a secret. There was a big sign on the roof of a neon cowgirl riding a bucking horse. The cowgirl looked sort of like a cheerleader from Dallas. Maybe she was politically incorrect, too.

A young guy with a lot of muscles was behind the bar, talking with a couple of women in skimpy cheerleader outfits who were hanging around at the waitress station. A red-haired woman in an even skimpier outfit danced without enthusiasm in a chicken-wire cage behind the bar. Neither the bartender nor the waitresses were looking at the dancer, and neither were most of the guys lining the bar. Guess it's tough to get motivated with the chicken wire. They were playing Dwight Yoakam.

I went to a little table across from the dancer's cage and one of the waitresses came over with her little pad. I ordered another Falstaff. When you've got a forty-dollar retainer, the sky's the limit.

When she came back with it, I said, 'What time do things pick up?' I gave her the nice smile. The Kevin Costner.

She smiled back and I saw her eyes flick to my hands. Nope. No wedding ring. I made the smile wider. She said, 'Mostly after dinner. We get a lot of cops in here and they don't get off until later.'

31

I nodded. 'You know an officer named Mark Thurman?'

She tried to remember. 'What's he look like?'

'Big. Like a jock. He probably comes around with a guy named Floyd Riggens. They work together.'

Now she remembered and her face grew hard. 'I know Floyd.' Floyd must be a real pip all the way around.

I grinned like it was an old joke. 'That Floyd is something, isn't he?'

'Uh-huh.' She wasn't seeing much humor in it.

'What time do they usually get here?'

'I don't know. Maybe eight. Something like that.' Like she was getting tired of talking about it. Maybe even pissed. Floyd must be something, all right. 'Look, I've got to get back to work.'

'Sure.'

She went back to the bar and I sipped the beer and pretty soon I ordered another. There didn't seem to be a lot to do until eight o'clock, so sipping Falstaff seemed like a good way to pass the time.

Dwight Yoakam stopped and Hank Williams, Jr, came on and pretty soon the day-shift waitresses left and the night shift cranked up the Garth Brooks and the Kentucky Headhunters. The night-shift dancers were younger and moved better in the cage, but maybe that was because of the music. Or maybe it just seemed that way because of the Falstaff. Maybe if you drank enough Falstaff your personal time scale would grind to a stop and everyone around you would move faster and faster until they looked like a Chip'n Dale cartoon running at fast forward and you looked like a still picture frozen in time. Maybe they would continue to age but you would stay young and pretty soon they'd be dead and you'd have the last laugh. That Falstaff is something, isn't it? Maybe I was just drunk. Occupational hazard.

By seven o'clock the crowd had grown and I didn't want to be there if Riggens or Thurman walked in early, so I paid for the beer, went back to the McDonald's, and bought a couple of cheeseburgers to eat in the car.

At fourteen minutes after eight, Mark Thurman's blue Ford Mustang turned into Cody's parking lot. There were three other people in the car. A brown-haired woman was sitting in the front passenger seat beside Thurman. Riggens and an overweight blonde were shoehorned into the back. The overweight blonde was loud and laughing and pulling at Riggens's pants as they got out of the car. The brown-haired woman was tall and slender and looked like a thirty-six C. They walked across the parking lot, Riggens and the blonde together, Thurman and the brunette together, and then the four of them went into the bar.

I sat in my car for a long time after they disappeared, smelling the McDonald's and tasting the beer and watching the neon cowgirl blink. My head hurt and I was tired from all the sitting, but I wasn't anxious to get home. Getting home meant going to bed and sleep wouldn't come easy tonight. Tomorrow I would have to speak with Jennifer Sheridan and tell her what I had found.

Sleep never comes easy when you're going to break someone's heart.

CHAPTER 5

I woke the next morning with a dull ache behind my right eye and the sound of finches on my deck. I have a little A-frame off Woodrow Wilson Drive in Laurel Canyon, in the hills above Hollywood. I don't have a yard because the A-frame is perched on a hillside, but I've got a deck, and a nice view of the canyon. A woman I know gave me a build-it-yourself bird-feeder kit for Christmas, so I built it, and hung it from the eve of my roof high enough to keep the birds safe from my cat. But the birds scratch the seed out of the feeder, then fly down to the deck to eat the seed. They know there's a cat, but still they go down to pick at the seed. When you think about it, people are often like this, too.

I rolled out of bed, pulled on a pair of shorts, then went downstairs and out onto the deck. The finches flew away in a gray, fluttery cloud.

I did twelve sun salutes from the hatha-yoga to loosen my muscles, then moved to the tai chi, and then to the tae kwon do, first the Tiger and Crane *katas*, and then the Dragon and Eagle. As I worked, the finches returned to eat and watch as if I were now elemental to their world and no longer a threat. I worked for the better part of an hour, driving through the *katas* faster and faster, breathing deep to well my energy, then unloading that energy with long explosive moves until my muscles burned and the sweat spotted the deck as if there had been a passing rain shower. I finished with another twelve sun salutes, and then I went in. Penance for the Falstaff. Or maybe just client avoidance.

My cat was staring at the finches. He's large and he's black and he carries his head sort of cocked to the side from when he was head-shot by a .22. He said, 'Naow?'

I shook my head. 'Not now. Got a call to make.'

He followed me into the kitchen and watched while I called my friend at B of A. You know you're serious when you call after an hour's worth of *katas* before you shower. Good thing we don't have smell-o-phones.

I said, 'You get anything out of the ordinary on Mark Thurman?' The detective makes a desperate last-ditch attempt at linking Mark Thurman to Criminal Activity.

'Doesn't look like it. Thurman's outstanding credit charges on both Visa and MasterCard appear typical. Also, he has not applied for higher credit limits nor additional credit cards through any facility in the state of California.' The desperate attempt fails.

'That's it, huh?'

'You sound disappointed.'

'What's disappointment to a hard guy like me?'

'Tell me about it. Are these good seats for Sting, or are we going to camp in the back of the house like last time?'

'Did I mention that you're not aging well?'

She hung up. So did I. These dames.

I took a deep breath, let it out, and then I called Jennifer Sheridan at Marty Beale's office. She answered on the second ring. 'Watkins, Okum, & Beale. Mr Beale's office.'

'This is Elvis Cole. I have uncovered some things, and we should speak.' The cat came over and head-bumped me.

'Well. All right.' She didn't sound happy about it, like maybe she could hear something in my voice. 'Can you tell me now?'

'It's better if we meet for lunch. Kate Mantilini's is very nice.'

More of the pause. 'Is it expensive?'

'I'll pay, Ms Sheridan.'

'Well, I only have the hour.' Nervous.

'I could pick up a couple of cheeseburgers and we could sit on the curb.'

'Maybe the restaurant would be all right. It's only a few blocks from here, isn't it?'

'Three blocks. I'll make a reservation. I will pick you up in front of your building or we can meet at the restaurant.'

'Oh, I don't mind walking.'

'Fine.'

I put the receiver down and the cat looked up at me. He said it again. 'Naow?'

I picked him up and held him close. He was warm against me and his fur was soft and I could feel his heart beat. It was good to hold him. He often doesn't like it, but sometimes he does, and I have found, over the years, that when I most need to hold him, he most often allows it. I like him for that. I think it's mutual.

I scrambled two eggs, put them in his bowl, then went upstairs to shower and dress. At seven minutes after twelve, I walked into Kate Mantilini's and found Jennifer Sheridan already seated. The waiters were smiling at her and an older woman at the next table was talking to her and all the lights of the restaurant seemed focused on her. Some people just have lives like that, I guess. She was wearing a bright blue pant suit with a large ruffled tie and black pumps with little bows on them, and she looked even younger than the first time I'd seen her. Maybe she wasn't twenty-three. Maybe she was seventeen and the people around us would think I was her father. If she looked seventeen and I looked thirty-eight, that would work out. Bummer.

She said, 'I hope this won't take long.'

'It won't.'

I motioned to the waiter and told him that we were in a

hurry and would like to order. He said fine and produced a little pad. I ordered the niçoise salad with sesame dressing and an Evian water. Jennifer Sheridan had a hamburger and french fries and a diet Coke. The waiter smiled at me when she ordered. Probably thought I was a lecher. When the waiter had gone, Jennifer Sheridan said, 'What have you found out, Mr Cole?' The mister.

'What I have to tell you will not be pleasant, and I want you to prepare yourself for it. If you'd rather leave the restaurant so that we might go someplace private, we can do that.'

She shook her head.

I said, 'Typically, when an officer is profiting from crime, it shows up in his lifestyle. He'll buy a boat or a time-share or maybe a high-end sound system. Something like that.'

She nodded.

'Mark hasn't. In fact, I checked his bank balances and his credit card expenses and there is no indication that he has received any undue or inordinate sums of money.'

She looked confused. 'What does that mean?'

'It means that he has not been acting strangely because he's involved in crime. There's a different reason. He's seeing another woman.'

Jennifer Sheridan made a little smile and shook her head as if I'd said three plus one is five and she was going to correct me. 'No. That's not possible.'

'I'm afraid that it is.'

'Where's your proof?' Angry now. The older woman at the next table looked over. She frowned when she did. She had a lot of hair and the frown made her look like one of those lizards with the big frill.

I said, 'Five minutes after you left my office yesterday, Mark came to see me. He had been following you. He explained to me that he was seeing someone else, and that he had not been able to bring himself to tell you. He asked me not to tell you this, but my obligation and my loyalty are to you. I'm sorry.' The detective delivers the death blow.

Jennifer Sheridan didn't look particularly devastated, but maybe that was just me.

The waiter brought our food and asked Jennifer Sheridan if she'd like catsup for her french fries. She said yes and we waited as he went to the counter, found a bottle, and brought it back. Neither of us said anything and Jennifer Sheridan didn't look at me until he had gone away. He seemed to know that something was wrong and frowned at me, too. The woman with the big hair was keeping a careful eye on our table.

When the waiter was gone, Jennifer Sheridan ate two french fries, then said, 'For Mark to come to you and make up a story like this, he must be in bigger trouble than I thought.'

I stared at her. 'You think he's making it up?'

'Of course.'

I put down my fork and I looked at the niçoise. It was a good-looking salad with freshly grilled ahi tuna, and I think I would've enjoyed eating it. Jennifer Sheridan had asked me for proof and I told her about my visit from Mark Thurman, but I hadn't told her the rest of it and I hadn't wanted to. I said, 'He's not making this up.'

'Yes, he is. If you knew Mark, you'd know that, too.' Confident.

I nodded, and then I looked at the salad again. Then I said, 'What size bra do you wear?'

She turned a deep shade of crimson. 'Now you're being ugly.'

'I put you at a thirty-four B. I went into Mark's apartment to look through his bank papers and I found a thirty-six C-cup brassiere.'

She looked shocked. 'You broke into his apartment? You went through his things?'

'That's what private detectives do, Ms Sheridan.'

She put her hands in her lap. 'It isn't real.'

'It was a red Lily of France brassiere. I held it. It was real.'

She shook her head. 'That's not what I mean. They knew you would look so they planted it there to make you think he was seeing another woman. What do they call it? A false lead?'

'Later that evening, I staked out a country-and-western bar called Cody's. It's a place where the police officers who work with Mark tend to gather. At a little bit after eight last night, Mark and his partner Floyd Riggens arrived. Mark was with a tall woman with dark brown hair.' I felt bad telling her and the bad feeling was oily and close, but there didn't seem to be any other way.

'And?'

'I wish I had better news, but there it is. I have looked into the matter and this is what I have found. I think my work here is done.'

'You mean you're quitting?'

'The case is solved. There's nothing left to do.'

Jennifer Sheridan's eyes welled and her mouth opened and she let out a long loud wail and began to cry. The woman with the big hair gasped and looked our way and so did most of the other people in the restaurant.

I said, 'Maybe we should leave.'

'I'm all right.' She made loud whooping sounds like she couldn't catch her breath and the tears rolled down her cheeks, making dark tracks from the mascara. The waiter stormed over to the maitre d' and made an angry gesture. The woman with the big hair said something to an elderly man at an adjoining table and the elderly man glared at me. I felt two inches tall.

'Try to see it this way, Jennifer. Mark being involved with another woman is better than Mark being involved

39

in crime. Crime gets you in jail. Another woman is a problem you can work out together.'

Jennifer Sheridan wailed louder. 'I'm not crying because of that.'

'You're not?'

'I'm crying because Mark's in trouble and he needs our help and you're *quitting*. What kind of crummy detective are you?'

I spread my hands. The maitre d' said something to the waiter and the waiter came over.

'Is everything all right, sir?'

'Everything is fine, thank you.'

He looked at Jennifer Sheridan.

She shook her head. 'He's a quitter.'

The waiter frowned and went away. The woman with the big hair made a *tsk*ing sound like she thought they should've done something.

Jennifer said, 'I want to be sure, that's all. If he's seeing this other woman, then who is she? Do they work together? Does he love her? Did you follow them home?'

'No.'

'Then you don't know, do you? You don't know if they slept together. You don't know if he kissed her good night. You don't even know if they left the bar together.'

I rubbed my brow. 'No.'

The woman with the big hair whispered again to the elderly man, then stood and went to three women sitting in a window booth. One of the women stood to meet her.

Jennifer Sheridan was crying freely and her voice was choking. 'He needs us, Mr Cole. We can't leave him like this, we *can't*. You've *got* to help me.'

The woman with the big hair shouted, 'Help her, for God's sake.'

The three women at the window booth shouted, 'Yeah!'

I looked at them and then I looked back at Jennifer Sheridan. She didn't look seventeen anymore. She looked fifteen. And homeless. I dropped my napkin into the niçoise. I'd had maybe three bites. 'You win.'

Jennifer Sheridan brightened. 'You'll stay with it?'

I nodded.

'You see how it's possible, don't you? You see that I'm right about this?'

I spread my hands. The Defeated Detective.

She said, 'Oh, thank you, Mr Cole. Thank you. I knew I could depend on you.' She was bubbling now, just like Judy Garland in *The Wizard of Oz*. She used her napkin to dry her eyes, but all she did was smear the mascara. It made her look like a raccoon.

The woman with the big hair smiled and the elderly man looked relieved. The waiter and the maitre d' nodded at each other. The three women in the window booth resumed their meal. The restaurant returned to its normal course of lunchtime events, and Jennifer Sheridan finished her hamburger. Everybody was happy.

'Jesus Christ,' I said.

The waiter appeared at my elbow. 'Is something wrong with the niçoise, sir?'

I looked at him carefully. 'Get away from me before I shoot you.'

He said, 'Very good, sir,' and he got.

CHAPTER 6

At twelve fifty-five, I gave Jennifer Sheridan a lift the three blocks back to her office and then I headed back toward mine, but I wasn't particularly happy about it. I felt the way you feel after you've given money to a panhandler because the panhandler has just dealt you a sob story that both of you knew was a lie but you went for it anyway. I frowned a lot and stared down a guy driving an ice cream truck just so I could feel tough. If a dog had run out in front of me I probably would've swerved to hit it. Well, maybe not. There's only so much sulking you can do.

The problem was that Jennifer Sheridan wasn't a panhandler and she wasn't running a number on me. She was a young woman in pain and she believed what she believed, only believing something doesn't make it so. Maybe I should spend the rest of the afternoon figuring out a way to convince her. Maybe I could rent one of those high-end, see-in-the-dark video cameras and tape Mark Thurman in the act with the brown-haired woman. Then we could go back to Kate Mantilini's and I could show everyone and what would the woman with the big hair think then? Hmm. Maybe there are no limits to sulking, after all.

I stopped at a Lucky market, bought two large bottles of Evian water, put one in my trunk, then continued on toward my office. Half a block later two guys in a light blue four-door sedan pulled up behind me and I thought I was being followed. A Hispanic guy in a dark blue

Dodgers cap was driving and a younger guy with a light blond butch cut was riding shotgun. His was the kind of blond that was so blond it was almost white. I looked at them, but they weren't looking at me, and a block and a half later they turned into a Midas Muffler shop. So much for being followed.

When I got up to my office I opened the French doors off the little balcony, then turned on the radio, and lay down on my couch. KLSX on the airwaves. Howard Stern all morning, classic rock all afternoon. We were well into classic rock and I liked it just fine. Lynyrd Skynyrd. What could be better than that?

It was a cool, clear afternoon and I could be at the beach but instead I was here. Portrait of a detective in a detective's office. When a detective is in a detective's office, shouldn't he be detecting? One of life's imponderables. The problem was that I didn't suspect Mark Thurman of a crime, and crime still didn't look good to me as the answer to Jennifer Sheridan's problems. If you're talking cops and crime, you're talking motive, and I didn't see it. I had been in Thurman's home and I had talked to his fiancée and his neighbors, and the crime part just didn't fit. When you're talking cops and crime, you're talking conspicuous consumption. Cops like to buy cars and they like to buy boats and they like to buy vacation homes and they explain it all by saying that the wife came into a little money. Only Thurman didn't have a wife and, as near as I could tell, he didn't have any of the other things, either. Of course, there could always be something else. Debt and dope are popular motives, but Thurman didn't seem to fit the profile on those, either. I had witnessed events and gathered evidence, and an examination of same had led to certain conclusions which seemed fair to me but not to the client. Maybe the client was crazy. Maybe I was crazy. Maybe the client was just confused and maybe I should have done more to alleviate

43

her confusion, but I had not. Why? Maybe she should be the detective and I should be the client. We couldn't be any more confused than we were now.

Sometime later the phone rang. I got up, went to my desk, and answered it. 'Elvis Cole Detective Agency. We never lie down on the job.'

'Caught you sleeping, huh?' It was Rusty Swetaggen.

'Ha. We never sleep.'

Rusty said, 'I talked to a guy who knows about REACT.'

'Yeah?' I sat in the chair and leaned back and put my feet up. It was quiet in the office. I looked at the water cooler and the couch and the two chairs opposite my desk and the file cabinet and the Pinocchio clock and the closed door to Joe Pike's office. The water machine hummed and little figures of Jiminy Cricket and Mickey Mouse stared back at me and the coffee machine smelled of old coffee, but something was missing.

Rusty said, 'Maybe I shouldn't even mention this.'

'You've rethought our friendship and you want me to pay for lunch?'

'Nothing that important. This guy I talked with, he said something that's maybe a little funny about the REACT guys down at Seventy-seven.'

'Funny.' I have seen these things in my office ten thousand times, and today something was different.

'Yeah. It's like he wouldn't've even mentioned it if I hadn't pushed him, like it's one of those things that doesn't matter unless you're looking, and it probably doesn't matter even then.'

'Okay.' I was only half listening. I picked up the phone and carried it around to the file cabinet and looked back at my desk. Nope. Nothing was off with the desk.

'He says their arrest pattern is maybe a little hinky for the past few months, like maybe these guys aren't making the arrests that they should be, and are making a lot of arrests that they shouldn't.'

'Like what?' I looked at the file cabinet. I looked at the Pinocchio clock.

'REACT was always big on dope and stolen property, and they've always posted high arrest rates, but the past couple of months they haven't been making the big numbers. They've mostly been booking gang-bangers and stickup geeks. It's a different level of crime.'

'We're not just talking Thurman? We're talking the team?'

'Yeah. It's a team thing. What I hear, Thurman's got a great record. That's why he got the early promotion.' I looked at the French doors. I looked at the little refrigerator. Nope.

Rusty said, 'Hell, Elvis, maybe it's just the off-season. I hear anything else, I'll let you know.'

'Sure, Rusty. Thanks.' I looked back at the Pinocchio clock.

Rusty Swetaggen hung up and then I hung up and that's when I saw it. The Pinocchio clock was still. Its eyes weren't moving. It wasn't making the tocking sound. The hands were stopped at eleven-nineteen.

I followed the cord to where it plugs into the wall behind the file cabinet. The plug was in the socket, but not all the way, as if someone had brushed the cord and pulled it partway out of the wall and hadn't noticed. I stood very still and looked around the office and, in the looking, the office now felt strange, as if an alien presence were a part of it. I went back to my desk, opened each drawer and looked at it without touching it. Everything appeared normal and as I had left it. Ditto the things on the desk top. I got up again and opened the file cabinet and looked at the files without touching them and tried to recall if they were positioned as I had last seen them, but I couldn't be sure. I keep all active files in the office cabinet as well as all cases in the current quarter. At the end of every quarter I box the closed files and put them in storage. There were twenty-seven files in the cabinet drawer. Not much if you're the Pinkertons but plenty if you're me. Each file contains a client sheet and day book entries where I've made notes along the way, as well as any photographs or paperwork I accumulate, and a conclusion sheet, which is usually just a copy of the letter I write to the client when the job is over. I hadn't yet made a file for Jennifer Sheridan. I fingered through the twenty-seven files that were there, but nothing seemed to be missing. I closed the cabinet and looked at the little figurines of Jiminy Cricket and Mickey Mouse and Pinocchio on my desk and on top of the file cabinet. Jiminy doffing his top hat had been moved, but Mickey and Minnie riding in a Hupmobile had not. Sonofagun. Someone had searched my office.

I put Jiminy in his proper place, plugged in the Pinocchio clock and set it to the correct time, then went back to my desk and thought about Mark Thurman. The odds were large that whoever had come into my office wasn't Mark Thurman or anyone who knew Thurman, and that the timing had just been coincidental, but the timing still bothered me. I had thought the case was over, but apparently it wasn't. I wasn't exactly sure that the case was still on, but maybe that's what I had to prove. Hmm. Maybe I should ask Jennifer Sheridan to be a partner in the firm. Maybe she gave detective lessons.

I called this reporter I know who works for the *Examiner* named Eddie Ditko. He's about a million years old and he loves me like a son. He said, 'Jesus Christ, I'm up to my ass in work. What the fuck do *you* want?' You see?

'I need to find out about the REACT unit deployed out of the Seventy-seventh Division down in South Central L.A.'

Eddie said, 'You think I know this shit off the top of my head?' Isn't Eddie grand?

'Nope. I was thinking maybe you could conjure it in your crystal ball.'

'You got crystal balls, always imposing like this.' Eddie went into a coughing fit and made a wet hacking noise that sounded like he was passing a sinus.

'You want I should call 911?'

'That's it. Be cute.' I could hear keys tapping on his VDT. 'This'll take some time. Why don'tchu swing around in a little while. I might have something by then.'

'Sure.'

I put on my jacket, looked around my office, then went to the door and locked up. I had once seen a James Bond movie where James Bond pasted a hair across the seam in the doorjamb so he could tell if anyone opened the door while he was gone. I thought about doing it, but figured that someone in the insurance office across the hall would come out while I was rigging the hair and then I'd have to explain and they'd probably think it was stupid. I'd probably have to agree with them.

I forgot about the hair and went to see Eddie Ditko.

CHAPTER 7

The *Los Angeles Examiner* is published out of a large, weathered red-brick building midway between downtown L.A. and Chinatown, in a part of the city that looks more like it belongs in Boston or Cincinnati than in Southern California. There are sidewalks and taxis and tall buildings of cement and glass and nary a palm tree in sight. Years ago, enterprising developers built a nest of low-rise condominiums, foolishly believing that Angelenos wanted to live near their work and would snap the places up to avoid the commute. What they didn't count on is that people were willing to work downtown but no one wanted to live there. If you're going to live in Southern California, why live in a place that looks like Chicago?

I put my car in the lot across the street, crossed at the light, then took the elevator up to the third floor and the pretty black receptionist who sits there. 'Elvis Cole to see Eddie Ditko. He's expecting me.'

She looked through her pass list and asked me to sign in. 'He's in the city room. Do you know where that is?'

'Yep.'

She gave me a peel-and-stick guest badge and went back to talking into the phone. I looked at the badge and felt like I was at a PTA meeting. *Hello! My name is Elvis!* I affixed the badge to my shirt and tried not to look embarrassed. Why risk the hall police?

I went through a pair of leather upholstered swinging doors, then along a short hall that opened into the city room. Twenty desks were jammed together in the center of the room, and maybe a dozen people were hanging around the desks, most of them typing as fast as they could and the rest of them talking on the phone. Eddie Ditko had the desk on the far left corner, about as close to the editors' offices as you could get without being one of the editors. A woman in her late twenties was working at a terminal next to him. She was wearing huge round glasses and a loud purple dress with very wide shoulders and a little purple pillbox hat. It was the kind of clothes you wore when you were establishing your identity as a retro-hip urban intellectual. Or maybe she was just odd. She glanced up once as I approached, then went on typing. Eddie was chewing on an unlit Grenadiers cigar and scowling at his VDT when I got there. He had to be forty years older than her. He didn't bother glancing up. 'Hey, Eddie, when are they going to make you an editor around here and get you off the floor?'

Eddie jerked the cigar out of his mouth and spit a load of brown juice at his wastebasket. He never lit them. He chewed them. 'Soon's I stop saying what I think and start kissing the right ass, like everybody else around here.' He said it loud enough for most of the room to hear. The purple woman glanced over, then went on with her typing. Tolerant. Eddie grimaced and rubbed at his chest. 'Jeez, I got chest pains. I'm a goddamned walking thrombo.'

'Lay off the fats and exercise a little.'

'What're you, my fuckin' mother?' Eddie leaned to the side and broke wind. Classy.

I pulled up a chair and sat on it backwards, hooking my arms over its back. 'What'd you find on the REACT guys?'

Eddie clamped the wet cigar in his teeth, leaned toward the VDT, and slapped buttons. The little VDT screen filled with printing. 'I put together some stuff from our morgue files, but that's about it. REACT is an elite

49

surveillance unit, and that means the cops block their files. They can't do their jobs if everybody knows who they're surveilling.'

'How many guys we talking about?'

'Five. You want the names?'

'Yeah.'

He hit a couple of buttons and a little printer beside his VDT chattered and spit out a page. He handed it to me. Five names were listed in a neat column in the center of the page.

> LT. ERIC DEES
> SGT. PETER GARCIA
> OFF. FLOYD RIGGENS
> OFF. WARREN PINKWORTH
> OFF. MARK THURMAN

I looked over the names. They meant nothing. 'They any good?'

Eddie grinned like a shark with his eye on a fat boy in baggy shorts. 'They wouldn't be a REACT team if they weren't any good. They target felons and they've got a ninety-nine-point-seven per cent conviction rate. Dees has been down there almost six years, along with Garcia and Riggens. Pinkworth joined a couple of years back and they picked up Thurman a year ago. He's the baby.'

'How'd Thurman make the squad?'

Eddie hit more buttons and the printing on the screen changed. 'Same as everybody else. Top ten of his academy class, a string of outstandings in his quarterly evaluations, Officer of the Month four times. You remember that nut pulled a gun on the RTD bus and threatened to start killing people unless Madonna gave him a blow job?'

'Sort of.'

The purple woman looked over. Interested.

'Hell, I wrote about that one. Guy stops the bus in the

middle of Hollywood Boulevard, and Thurman and a guy named Palmetta were the first cops on the scene. Thurman was, what, maybe twenty-two, twenty-three years old?'

The purple woman shrugged.

'Yeah, he was just a kid. That was part of the story. Anyway, the nut shoots this fat guy in the leg to make his point, then grabs this nine-year-old girl and starts screaming he's going to do her next. He wants Madonna, right? Palmetta puts the call in for a hostage negotiator and the SWAT team but Thurman figures there ain't time. He takes off his gun and goes into the bus to talk to the guy. The nut tries to shoot him twice but he's shaking so bad both shots miss, so he puts the gun to the girl's head. You know what happened then?'

The purple lady was leaning forward, frowning because she wanted to know.

Eddie said, 'Thurman tells the guy he's had Madonna and Madonna's a lousy lay, but he knows Rosanna Arquette and Rosanna Arquette is the best blow job in town. Thurman tells the guy if he puts down the gun, as soon as he's out on bail, he'll set it up with Rosanna Arquette 'cause she owes him a couple of favors.'

The purple woman said, 'And he went for that?'

Eddie spread his hands 'Here's a nut believes he's gonna get Madonna, why not? The guy says only if she blows him *twice*. Thurman says, okay, she'll do it twice, but not on the same day, she's got a thing about that. The nut says that's okay with him 'cause he's only good for once a week anyway, and puts down the gun.'

The purple lady laughed, and she didn't look so odd anymore.

Eddie was smiling, too. 'That was, what, a couple years ago? Thurman gets the Medal of Valor and six months later he wins the early promotion to plain-clothes and the REACT team. They're top cops, pal. Every one of those guys has a story like that in his file else he wouldn't be on the team.'

'Eddie, what if I didn't want the good stuff? What if I was a reporter and I was looking for something that maybe had a smell to it?'

'Like what?'

'Like maybe I'm looking to see if they've crossed over.'

Eddie shook his head and patted the VDT. 'If it's in here, it's already public record. Someone would've had to lodge the complaint, and it would've had to come out through LAPD PR or one of the news agencies or the courts. It wouldn't be a secret and no one would be trying to hide it.'

'Okay. Could you check for allegations?'

'Substantiated or otherwise?'

I looked at him.

'Reporter humor. It's probably over your head.' Eddie hit more keys and watched the screen, and then did it again. When he had filled and wiped the screen three times, he nodded and leaned back. 'I had it search through the files keying on the officers' names for every news release during the past year, then I threw out the junk about them saving babies and arresting the Incredible Hulk and just kept the bad stuff. This is pretty neat.'

I leaned forward and looked at the screen. 'What's it found?'

'Excessive-force complaints. "Suspect injured while resisting arrest." "Suspect filed brutality charges." Like that. 'Course, these guys are busting felons and felons tend to get nasty, but check it out, you've got twenty-six complaints in the past ten months, and eleven of them are against this guy Riggens.'

'Any charges brought?'

'Nada. IAD issued letters of reprimand twice, and dealt a two-week suspension, but that's it.'

I read the list. Twenty-six names ran down the left side

of the page, and next to each name there was a booking number and the arresting charge and the claims levied by the defendants and the accused officer or officers. Riggens had all or part of eleven of the charges, and the remainder were divided pretty evenly between Pinkworth and Dees and Garcia and Thurman. Thurman had part of three.

Eddie said, 'You've got to understand, cops on these special tac squads get charges filed all the time, so most of these really are garbage, but if I'm looking for tuna I'm looking for losers, and that's Riggens.'

'Thanks, Eddie.'

Eddie stuck the cigar in his mouth and rolled it around and looked at me. 'What you got going here, kid? It any good?'

'I don't know. I'm still just running down the leads.'

He nodded and sucked on the cigar, and then he gazed at the editors' offices. He wasn't getting any younger. 'If there's a story here, I want it.'

'You bet, Eddie.'

Eddie Ditko spread his hands, then hacked up something phlegmy and spit it into the basket. No one looked and no one paid any mind. I guess seniority has its privileges.

I went back the way I came, took the elevator down to the lobby, then used the pay phone there to call Jennifer Sheridan in Marty Beale's office. I asked her for Floyd Riggens's address. She said, 'Which one?'

'What do you mean, which one?'

'He's divorced. He used to live in La Cañada, but now he's got a little apartment somewhere.'

I told her that if she had them both, I'd take them both. She did. She also told me that Riggens's ex-wife was named Margaret, and that they had three children.

When I had the information that I needed, I said, 'Jennifer?'

'Yes?'

'Did Mark ever complain to you about Floyd?'

There was a little pause. 'Mark said he didn't like having Floyd as a partner. He said Floyd scared him.'

'Did he say why?'

'He said Floyd drank a lot. Do you think Floyd is involved in this?'

'I don't know, Jennifer. I'm going to try to find out.'

We hung up and I went out of the building and across the street to my car.

CHAPTER 8

Floyd Riggens was living in a small, six-unit stucco apartment building on a side street in Burbank, just about ten blocks from the Walt Disney Studio. There were three units on the bottom and three on top, and an L-shaped stair at the far end of the building. It was a cramped, working-class neighborhood, but working class was good. Working class means that people go to work. When people go to work, it makes things easier for private eyes and other snoopers who skulk around where they shouldn't.

I parked three houses down, then walked back. Riggens had the front apartment, on top. Number four. None of the units seemed to belong to a manager, which was good, but the front door was open on the bottom center unit, which was bad. Light mariachi music came from the center unit and the wonderful smells of simmering *menudo* and fresh-cut cilantro and, when I drew closer, the sound of a woman singing with the music. I walked past her door as if I belonged, then took the stairs to the second level. Upstairs, the drapes were drawn on all three units. Everybody at work. I went to number four, opened the screen, and stood in Riggens's door with my back to the street. It takes longer to pick a lock than to use a key, but if a neighbor saw me, maybe they'd think I was fumbling with the key.

Floyd Riggens's apartment was a single large studio with a kitchenette and a closet and the bath along the side wall. A sleeping bag and a blanket and an ashtray were lined against the opposite wall and a tiny Hitachi portable television sat on a cardboard box in the corner. A carton of Camel Wides was on the floor by the sleeping bag. You could smell the space, and it wasn't the sweet, earthy smells of *menudo*. It smelled of mildew and smoke and BO. If Floyd Riggens was pulling down graft, he sure as hell wasn't spending it here.

I walked through the bathroom and the closet and the kitchenette and each was dirty and empty of the items of life, as if Riggens didn't truly live here, or expect to, any more than a tourist expects to live in a motel. There was a razor and a toothbrush and deodorant and soap in the bathroom, but nothing else. The sink and the tub and the toilet were filmed with the sort of built-up grime that comes of long-term inattention, as if Riggens used these things and left, expecting that someone else would clean them, only the someone never showed and never cleaned.

There were four shirts and three pants hanging in the closet, along with a single navy dress uniform. Underwear and socks and two pairs of shoes were laid out neatly on the floor of the closet, and an empty gym bag was thrown in the far back corner. The underwear and the socks were the only neat thing in the apartment.

An open bottle of J&B scotch sat on the counter in the kitchenette, and three empties were in a trash bag on the floor. The smell of scotch was strong. A couple of Domino's pizza boxes were parked in the refrigerator along with four Styrofoam Chicken McNuggets boxes and half a quart of lowfat milk. An open box of plastic forks and a package of paper plates sat on the counter beside the sink. The sink was empty, but that's probably because there were no pots or pans or dishes. I guess Riggens had made the choice to go disposable. Why clutter your life with the needless hassle of washing and cleaning when you can use it and throw it away?

It had taken me all of four minutes to look through

Riggens's apartment. I went back into the main studio and stood in the center of the floor and felt oily and somehow unclean. I don't know what I expected, but it wasn't this, and it left me feeling vaguely depressed, as if this wasn't a place where someone lived, but more a place where someone died. I went to the sleeping bag and squatted. A photograph had been pushpinned to the wall. It was an older picture and showed Riggens with a plain woman about his age and three kids. A boy and two girls. The boy looked maybe fourteen and sullen. The oldest girl was maybe twelve, and the youngest girl was a lot younger. Maybe four. She was tiny compared to the others, with a cute round face and a mop of curly hair and she was holding up a single bluegill on a nylon cord. She looked confused. Riggens was smiling and so was his wife. Margaret. They were standing in front of the bait shop at Castaic Lake, maybe twenty miles north of L.A. in the Santa Susana Mountains. The picture looked worn around the edges, as if it had been handled often. Maybe it had. Maybe Riggens lived here but maybe he didn't. Maybe he brought his body here, and drank, and slept, but while the body was here he looked at the picture a lot and let his mind go somewhere else. Castaic, maybe. Where people were smiling.

I closed the apartment as I had found it, went down the stairs, and picked up the Ventura Freeway east through the Glendale Pass and into La Cañada in the foothills of the Verdugo Mountains.

It was mid-afternoon when I got there, and knots of junior high school kids were walking along the sidewalks with books and gym bags, but no one looked very interested in going home or doing homework.

Margaret Riggens lived in a modest ranch-style home with a poplar tree in the front yard in the flats at the base of the foothills. It was one of those stucco-and-clapboard numbers that had been built in the mid-fifties when a developer had come in with one set of house plans and an army of bulldozers and turned an orange grove into a housing tract to sell 'affordable housing' to veterans come to L.A. to work in the aerospace business. The floor plan of every house on the block would be the same as every other house. The only differences would be the colors and the landscaping and the people within the houses. I guess there is affordability in sameness.

I parked at the curb across the street as a girl maybe thirteen with limp blonde hair walked across the Riggenses' front lawn and let herself into their home without knocking. That would be the older daughter. A white Oldsmobile Delta 88 was parked in the drive. It needed a wash. The house looked like it needed a wash, too. The stucco was dusty and the clapboard part was peeling and needed to be scraped and painted. I crossed the street, then went up the drive to the front door and rang the bell. It would have been shorter to cut across the lawn, but there you go.

A tired woman in a sleeveless sun shirt and baggy shorts opened the door. She was smoking a Marlboro. I said, 'Hello, Ms Riggens. Pete Simmons, Internal Affairs, LAPD.' I took out my license and held it up. It would work, or it wouldn't. She would read the ID, or she wouldn't.

Margaret Riggens said, 'What'd that sonofabitch do now?' Guess she didn't bother to read it.

I put the license away. 'I'd like to ask you a couple of questions. It won't take long.'

'Ain't that what they all say.' She took a final pull on the Marlboro, then flipped it into the front yard and stepped out of the door to let me in. I guess visits by guys like Pete Simmons were an inevitable and expected part of her life.

We went through the living room into an adjoining dining area off the kitchen. The girl who had come in before me was sitting cross-legged on the living room floor, watching *Geraldo* and reading a copy of *Sassy* magazine. There was a hard pack of Marlboros beside her and a green Bic lighter and a big clay ashtray that looked like she'd made it in pottery class. She was smoking. Loud music came from the back of the house, but there was a muffled quality to it as if a door was closed. The music suddenly got louder, and a boy's voice screamed, 'I told you to stay out of my room, you little shit! I don't want you here!' Then the boy came out of the back hall, pulling the younger girl by the upper arm. He was maybe sixteen now, with most of his father's growth, and she was maybe six. The little girl's face was screwed up and she was crying. The boy shouted, 'Mom, make her stay out of my room! I don't want her back there!'

Margaret Riggens said, 'Jesus Christ, Alan.'

I said, 'You're holding her too tight. Let go.'

Alan said, 'Who in the hell are you?'

The little girl was staring at me. 'You're hurting her,' I said. 'Let go.'

Margaret Riggens said, 'Hey, I don't need any help with my kids.'

I was looking at Alan and Alan was looking at me, and then he suddenly let go and bent over the little girl and screamed, 'I *hate* you!' He stomped back down the hall and the music went soft as the door closed. The little girl didn't seem too upset by what had happened. Guess it happened so often she was used to it. Probably even a game by now. She rubbed at her arm and ran back down the hall. The music didn't change pitch, so I guess she went into her own room.

Margaret Riggens said, 'These kids,' then stooped down, took a cigarette from her older daughter's pack, and turned away to sit at the dining room table.

I said, 'Maybe it'd be better if we had a little privacy.'

Margaret Riggens used a book of paper matches to light

the Marlboro, and put the spent match in a little beanbag ashtray she had on the table. 'Is Floyd going to get fired?' Guess the privacy didn't matter.

'No, ma'am. This is just follow-up on a couple of things.'

'That alimony is all I have. He pays it on time. Every month.'

I took out the little pad I keep in my jacket and made a big deal out of taking that down. 'That's good to hear. The Department frowns on a man if he ducks his responsibility.'

She nodded and sucked on the cigarette. Out in the living room, the oldest girl was sucking on a cigarette, too.

I tried to look sly. 'We hear enough good things like that, and it makes it easy to overlook a bad thing. Do you see?'

She squinted at me through the smoke. 'I don't understand.'

I made a little shrugging move. Conversational. 'Everybody thinks we're looking to chop heads, but that's not true. We hear a guy does right by his family, we don't want to throw him out in the streets. We find out he's gotten himself into trouble, we'll try to counsel him and keep him on the payroll. Maybe suspend him for a while, maybe demote him, but keep him employed. So he can take care of his family.'

She drew so hard on the Marlboro that the coal glowed like a flare. 'What kind of trouble?'

I smiled. 'That's what I want you to tell me, Ms Riggens.'

Margaret Riggens turned toward her older daughter. 'Sandi. Shut off the TV and go to your room for a little while, okay?'

Sandi gathered up her things, then went down the same

hall the other kids had used. Margaret turned back to me.
'I don't know what you're talking about.'

'You and Floyd talk?'

'Maybe once a week. There's always something with one of the kids.'

'He's supporting two households, Ms Riggens. Kids need things. So do adults.'

'Jesus Christ, have you seen where he lives?'

I spread my hands. 'Has money seemed a little easier to come by?'

'Ha.'

'Has Floyd maybe hinted around that he has something going?'

'Absolutely not.'

I leaned forward and I lowered my voice. 'If an officer crosses the line and someone aids and abets in that crossing, they can be charged. Did you know that, Ms Riggens?'

She drew on the cigarette and now her hands were trembling. 'Are you telling me that Floyd has stepped over the line?'

I stared at her.

She stood up, dribbling cigarette ash. 'I've had enough with that sonofabitch. I really have. I don't know anything about this. I don't know what the hell you're talking about.'

'Sit down, Ms Riggens.'

She sat. Breathing hard.

'I'm making no accusations. I'm just curious. Floyd has a problem with the drinking. Floyd has a problem with the excessive-force complaints. Floyd has money problems. Pretty soon problems become a way of life. You see how these things add up?'

She crushed out the cigarette in the little beanbag ashtray and lit another. The first continued to smolder.

'I'm not accusing Floyd, and I'm not accusing you. I'm

just wondering if maybe you've heard anything, or noticed a change in Floyd's behavior, that's all.'

She nodded. Calmer, now, but with eyes that were still frightened and weak. The look in her eyes made me feel small and greasy, and I wanted to tell her it had all been a mistake and leave, but you don't learn things by leaving. Even when the staying smells bad.

She said, 'He's been out of his mind ever since that guy died. The past couple of years have been tough, but since then has been the worst. That's when he went back to the bottle.'

I nodded like I knew what she was saying.

'He was in AA before that, and he was getting better, too. He'd come over sometimes, we'd have dinner, like that.'

'But then the guy died?'

She rolled her eyes. 'Well, everyone's still thinking about Rodney King and this black guy dies when they're trying to arrest him and then the family files a lawsuit and it was awful. Floyd started drinking worse than ever. He was angry all the time, and he'd blow up over the tiniest thing. They told me it was a stress reaction.'

'About how long ago was that?'

She gestured with the cigarette. 'What was it? Three or four months?'

I nodded. 'Did Floyd feel responsible?'

She laughed. 'Floyd doesn't feel responsible for hitting the bowl in the morning. I thought he was worried about the suit, but then the suit went away and I thought he'd relax. You know those suits cost a fortune. But he still stayed drunk all the time. Eric would call and check on him to make sure he was holding it together. Things like that. Eric was a godsend.' Eric Dees.

I nodded.

'Floyd hasn't been acting right since then. If he's gotten

himself mixed up in something, I'll bet that's why. I'll bet it's all part of the stress reaction.'

'Maybe so.'

'That should qualify for disability, shouldn't it?'

There were about ten million questions I wanted to ask, but I couldn't ask them without tipping her that I wasn't from LAPD. I patted her hand and tried to look reassuring. 'That'll be fine, Ms Riggens. You've been a big help, and that will be in the record.'

'Why don't you people make him go back to AA? When he was in AA he was doing a lot better.'

'Let's just keep this our little secret, all right, Ms. Riggens? That way it looks better for you all the way around.'

She crushed out the cigarette into the over-full ashtray and pushed ashes out onto the table. 'Look, I don't know what Floyd's mixed up with, and I don't want to know. I'm not aiding and abetting anything. I got enough to worry about.'

'Sure. Thank you for your time.'

I got up and went to the door. Margaret Riggens stayed at the table and lit another Marlboro and drew the smoke deep off the match and stared out through the windows into her shabby backyard. You could hear the kids screaming over the loud bass throbbing of the music and I imagined that it went on without end, and that her living hell wasn't a whole lot different from Floyd's.

Out in the living room there was an upright Yamaha piano that looked like it hadn't been played in a long time. A schoolbag was sitting on one end of it, and half a dozen wilting yellow roses were floating in a glass jar on the other end. Between the two was a framed picture of Floyd and Margaret Riggens standing together at his police academy graduation. They were fifteen years younger, and they were smiling. It was a photograph very much like the one that Jennifer Sheridan had, only

63

Jennifer and Mark still looked like the people in their picture, and Floyd and Margaret didn't.

I guess romance isn't for everyone.

CHAPTER 9

When I pulled away from the house that Floyd Riggens once shared with his wife and children, the sun was low in the west and the ridgeline along the Verdugo Mountains was touched with orange and pink. I worked my way across the valley, letting the rush hour traffic push me along, and enjoyed the darkening sky. I wondered if Margaret Riggens found much in the mountains or the sky to enjoy, but perhaps those things were too far away for her to see. When you're hurting, you tend to fix your eyes closer to home.

I cut across the northern edge of Burbank and Pacoima, and then dropped down Coldwater to a little place I know called Mazzarino's that makes the very best pizza in Los Angeles. I got a vegetarian with a side of anchovies to go and, when I pulled into my carport fifteen minutes later, the pizza was still warm.

I opened a Falstaff and put out the pizza for me and the anchovies for the cat, only the cat wasn't around. I called him, and waited, but he still didn't come. Off doing cat things, no doubt.

I ate the pizza and I drank the beer and I tried watching the TV, but I kept thinking about Margaret Riggens and that maybe I had come at all of this from the wrong direction. You think crime, and then you think money, but maybe that wasn't it. Maybe Mark Thurman had gotten himself involved in another type of crime. And maybe it wasn't Mark alone. Maybe it was Mark and Floyd. Maybe it was the entire REACT team. For all I knew, it was the full and complete population of the state of California, and I was the only guy left out of the loop. Me and Jennifer Sheridan. I was still thinking about that when I fell asleep.

At ten oh-six the next morning I called this cop I know who works in North Hollywood. A voice answered the phone with, 'Detectives.'

'Is that you, Griggs?' It was this other cop I know, Charlie Griggs.

'Who's this?'

'Guess.'

Griggs hung up. Some sense of humor, huh?

I called back and Griggs answered again. I said, 'Okay, I'll give you a hint. I'm known as the King of Rockin' Detectives, but I wasn't born in Tupelo, Mississippi.'

'I knew it was you. I just wanted to see if you'd call back. Heh-heh-heh.' That's the way Griggs laughs. Heh-heh-heh.

'Lemme speak to Lou.'

'What's the magic word?'

'C'mon, Charlie.'

'What do you say, wiseass? You wanna speak to Lou, tell me what you say? Heh-heh-heh.' This guy's an adult.

'I'm going to get you, Griggs.'

'Heh-heh-heh.' Griggs was killing himself.

'I'm going to give your address to Joe.'

The laughing stopped and Griggs put me on hold. Maybe forty seconds later Lou Poitras picked up. 'I don't pay these guys to goose around with you.'

'Griggs hasn't done a full day's work in fifteen years.'

'We don't pay him to work. We keep'm around because he's such a scream. Sort of like you.' Another comedian.

I said, 'Four months ago, a guy died during a REACT arrest down in South Central. You know anyone I can talk to about it?'

'Hold on.' Poitras put me on hold again and left me

there for maybe eight minutes. When he came back he said, 'Suspect's name was Charles Lewis Washington.'

'Okay.' I wrote it down.

'There's a guy working Hollywood named Andy Malone used to be a partner of mine. He's a uniform supervisor on the day shift. He just came out of the Seventy-seventh. You wanna go down there now?'

'Yeah.'

'I'll call him and set it up.'

'Thanks, Lou.'

'You got that twelve bucks you owe me?'

I made a staticky noise and pretended we had been cut off. Works every time.

Forty minutes later I parked in a diagonal parking place outside the glass front door of the Hollywood Police Division, and went past three black women who were standing on the sidewalk into a trapezoidal public room with a high ceiling and a white tile floor. There was a pay phone on the wall up by the front glass and padded chairs around the perimeter of the wall for your waiting comfort. The walls were aqua, the glass was bulletproof. A Formica counter cut off the back third of the room, and three uniformed officers sat on stools behind the counter. Two women and a man. One of the women and the man were talking on telephones, and the other woman was writing in a small black notebook. A Hispanic man and woman sat in the chairs under the pay phone. The Hispanic man sat with his elbows on his thighs and rocked steadily. He looked worried. The Hispanic woman rubbed his back as he rocked and spoke softly. She looked worried, too.

I went past them to the officer writing in the little black notebook and said, 'Elvis Cole to see Sergeant Malone.'

'He expecting you?'

'Yes.'

'Have a seat.'

She left the counter and went back through a door into the bowels of the station house. There was another door on the customer side of the counter. It was heavy and dense and if no one buzzed you through it'd probably take a rocket launcher to get past it. I sat opposite the door and waited. In a couple of minutes the female officer reappeared behind the counter and said, 'He's finishing up a couple of things. He'll be with you in a minute.'

'Sure.'

I waited some more.

A well-dressed black woman came in and asked the people behind the counter if Officer Hobbs was in. The same officer who had gone to see Malone said something into a phone, and a couple of minutes later a tall muscular black officer came through the heavy door. He smiled when he saw the woman and she smiled when she saw him. He offered his hand and she took it and they went out through the glass door to hold hands in the privacy of the sidewalk. Love at the station house. Two Pakistani men came in past the lovers. One of them was maybe in his fifties and the other was maybe in his forties. The older one looked nervous and the younger one wore a loud pink shirt and leather sandals. The younger one went to the counter and said, 'We would like to speak with the chief of police.' He said it so loud the Hispanic man stopped rocking. The two desk officers glanced at each other and smiled. The desk officer on the phone kept talking like it was nothing. Guess you work the desk at Hollywood, nothing surprises you. The male desk officer leaned back on his stool and looked through the doorway behind the counter and yelled, 'We got a citizen out here wants to see the chief.' A uniformed lieutenant with silver hair came out and stared at the Pakistanis, then frowned at the desk officer. 'Knock off the shit and take care of these people.'

The younger Pakistani said, 'Are you the chief?'

The lieutenant said, 'The chief's busy with the city council. How can I help you?'

Just as he said it the heavy door opened and a hard-shouldered uniformed sergeant looked out at me. 'You Cole?'

'Yeah.' He had sandy hair and thick, blocky hands and a deep tan because most of his time would be spent on the street. He wore a little red and green and gold Vietnam service ribbon beneath the badge on his left breast and a marksmanship pin beside the ribbon.

'Andy Malone,' he said. 'We can talk back here.' He put out his hand and I stood and took it, and then I followed him through the door.

We went down a long hall past three candy machines and a soft-drink machine and a couple of rest rooms for people who weren't cops to use. At the far end of the hall there was a booking desk where a couple of cops were processing a tall skinny black kid. The kid's hands were cuffed. One of the cops was white and the other was black, and they both were thick across the chest and back and arms, like they spent a lot of time in the gym. Guess you work in a war zone, you want to be as threatening as possible. The white cop was trying to unlock the cuffs and the black cop was shaking his finger about two inches from the kid's nose, saying, 'Are you listening to me?' The kid was giving with attitude and you knew he wasn't listening and wasn't going to. Your bad guys are often like that.

There were a couple of varnished wood benches in the hall opposite a door that said SERGEANT'S OFFICE. We went into the office and Malone closed the door. 'You want coffee?'

'Sure. Thanks.'

Malone filled a couple of paper cups, handed one to me, then went behind a cluttered desk and sat. He didn't offer cream or sugar. Maybe they didn't have any.

I sat across from him in a hard chair, and we looked at each other and sipped our coffee. He said, 'My buddy Lou Poitras says you want to know about Charles Lewis Washington.'

'Uh-huh.'

'You're a private investigator.'

'That's it.' The coffee was hot and bitter and had probably been made early this morning.

'Make any money at it?'

'No one's getting rich.'

He took more of the coffee and made a little smile. 'The wife's been after me to leave the force since the riots. All this time, she's still after me.' He made a shrugging move with his head, then set the cup on his desk. 'So tell me why you're digging around Charles Lewis.'

'His name came up in something I'm working on and I want to run it down.'

Malone nodded and had more of his coffee. He didn't seem to mind the taste, but then, he was used to it. 'How do you know Poitras?'

'Met on the job. Got to know each other.'

He nodded again and leaned back. When he did, the old swivel squealed. 'Lou says you pulled time in Vietnam.'

'Yep.'

He put down his coffee and crossed his arms. 'I was there in sixty-eight.'

'Seventy-one.'

The chair squealed again. The nod. 'People think the Nam they think the sixties. Lot of people forget we still had guys there till March twenty-nine, 1973.'

'Lot of people don't care.'

He made a little smile. 'Yeah. We kicked ass in Saudi. That sort of makes up for things.'

'Don't forget Panama and Grenada.'

The smile got wider. 'Kick enough ass, and pretty soon

you forget the losers. Who wants to remember losers when you got so many winners running around?'

I said, 'Hell, Malone, we're not that damned old, are we?'

Malone laughed, uncrossed his arms, and said, 'What do you want to know about Washington?'

I told him.

Malone went to a battered gray cabinet, took out a manila folder, and brought it back to the desk. He skimmed through it for a couple of minutes, then he closed it. He didn't offer to let me see. 'Washington worked in a pawnshop over on Broadway, down in South Central. We had information that the shop was being used as a fence drop for some of the guns looted during the riots, so REACT put eyes on the place, then went in with a sting.'

'And it went bad.'

'That's a way to say it. Washington thinks he's making a buy on ten thousand rounds of stolen ammo, the officers think it's under control, but when they flash the badges he goes a little nuts and decides to resist. Washington dives behind a counter, and comes up with a piece, but our guys are thinking Rodney King, so they don't shoot him. There's a scuffle and Washington hits his head and that's it.'

'I hear it was controversial.'

'They're all controversial. This one less than most.'

'What do you have on Washington?'

Malone checked the report again. 'Twenty-eight. A longtime Double-Seven Hoover Crip with multiple priors.'

'He there alone in the store?'

'Sure. The family went nuts. We had the pickets, the wrongful-death suit, all of that, but they backed off.'

'Did the city settle?'

'Nope. They dropped it.'

'Can I read the report?'

Malone stared at me for a while and you could tell he didn't like it, then he shrugged and shoved it across the desk at me. 'Here in my presence. I can't let you copy it and I can't let you take it.'

'Sure.'

I read the report. It told me what Malone had told me, only with more words. Lieutenant Eric Dees, the REACT team leader, had written the report. Garcia and Pinkworth and Riggens had gone in to front the sale, and Thurman and Dees were the outside men. When it was clear that the transaction would be consummated, Garcia identified himself as a police officer, told Washington that he was being placed under arrest, and Dees and Thurman entered the premises. As the cuffs were being applied, Washington broke free from Pinkworth and Riggens and lunged for a weapon. The officers attempted to subdue the suspect without the use of deadly force, and Pinkworth and Riggens received substantial injuries. Washington was struck repeatedly by all officers involved, but refused to succumb, and died when team leader Eric Dees tackled him, causing his head to strike the corner of a metal display case. Dees assumed full responsibility. There were copies of the IAD investigation report and a letter of final disposition of the case. The letter of disposition released the officers involved from any wrongdoing. Copies of the death report, the coroner's findings, and Charles Lewis Washington's arrest record were appended to the finding.

'What about Riggens?'

'What can I say? Riggens has his problems, but you read the report. It was a team effort.'

I said, 'Does it seem odd to you that five officers couldn't apprehend this guy without letting him kill himself?'

'Hell, Cole, you know what it's like out there. Shit

happens. This kid was a felon gangbanger and he picked the wrong time to pull a gun. Our guys tried to do the right thing, but it went wrong. That's all there is to it. Nobody wants another Rodney King.'

I nodded. 'Mind if I copy down Washington's address?'

'No problem.'

'Any idea why they dropped the suit?'

Malone shrugged. 'People down there are tired. I spent four years in South Central. God knows I can tell you *we* are.' He made the shrug again. 'Nobody ever drops a wrongful death against LAPD. Too many shysters are willing to take the case on a contingency, and the city council's always ready to settle out, but who can tell.'

'Yeah. Who can tell. Thanks, Malone. I appreciate it.'

I handed back the file and went to the door. He said, 'Cole.'

'Yeah?'

'I know the kind of press South Central gets, but the people down there, most of the people down there are good people. That's why I stayed the four years.'

'Most folks everywhere are good people.'

He nodded. 'I don't know what you're doing, or where you're going, but watch yourself around the gangs. LAPD owns the streets, but the gangs keep trying to take'm away. You understand?'

'More than I want.'

I showed myself out, picked up my car, and took the long drive down to South Central Los Angeles.

Home of the body bag.

CHAPTER 10

I dropped down through West Hollywood and the southwest corner of Beverly Hills through La Cienega Park to the 1-10 freeway, then picked up the 10 east to the Harbor, then went south on the Harbor past USC and Exposition Park, and into South Central.

Even on the freeway, the world begins to change. The cinderblock sound walls and ramp signs show more graffiti, and, if you know how to read it, you can tell that it isn't just young Hispanic taggers out to get famous all over town, it's gangbangers marking turf and making challenges and telling you who they've killed and who they're going to kill. Just the thing you want to see when you're looking for an exit ramp.

I left the freeway at Florence, looped under to Hoover, then turned south to Eighty-second Street. Broadway and Florence show liquor stores and neighborhood groceries and gas stations and other businesses, but Hoover and the cross streets are residential. Up by the businesses you get out-of-work men hanging around and a lot of graffiti and it looks sort of crummy, but the residential streets will surprise you. Most of the houses are stucco or clapboard bungalows, freshly painted and well maintained, with front yards as neat and pretty as anything you'd find anywhere.

Elderly people sat on porches or worked in yards trimming roses and, here and there, small children played on tricycles. Satellite dishes sprouted from poles like black aluminum mums and clean American cars sat in the drives. There were a lot of the dishes, and they looked identical, as if a satellite-dish salesman had gone door-to-door and found many takers.

There was no graffiti on the houses and there was no litter in the streets or the yards, but every house had heavy metal bars over windows and door fronts and sometimes the bars encircled a porch. That's how you knew there was a war on. If there wasn't a war, you wouldn't need the protection.

According to the police report, Charles Lewis Washington had lived with his mother in a rose-colored bungalow on Eighty-second Street, just west of Hoover. His mother, Ida Leigh Washington, still lived there. It was a nice-looking place, with a satellite dish on a tower in their backyard and a well-kept Buick LeSabre in the drive. An open-air front porch was boxed in by a redwood trellis and bright yellow vine roses. The vine roses were healthy and vibrant.

I parked at the curb in front of their home, went up the narrow walk, and onto the porch. The roses threw off a heavy scent and smelled wonderful. The front door opened before I got there, and a slender young black man looked out at me. I could hear music, but it was coming from another house, not this one. He said, 'May I help you?'

I gave him the card. 'My name is Elvis Cole. I'm a private investigator, and I was hoping to speak with Mrs Ida Leigh Washington.' He was wearing a plain white crewneck tee shirt and blue Navy work pants and white sneakers and an imitation gold watchband. The band was bright against his dark skin. He read the card and then he looked back at me.

'About what?'

'Charles Lewis Washington.'

'Lewis is dead.'

'I know. That's what I want to talk about.'

He stared at me a couple of seconds longer, like he had to make up his mind, but like he was making it up about things that had nothing to do with me. After a little of that, he stepped back out of the door and held the screen. 'All right. Please come in.'

I went past him into a small, neat living room. An old man maybe three hundred years old and a young woman who couldn't have been more than sixteen were watching TV. The girl was sitting on a burgundy velveteen couch and the old man in a hardwood rocker. He was holding a can of Scrapple. They both looked at me with a sort of curious surprise. The white man comes to call. A little boy maybe three years old pulled at the girl's legs, but she ignored him. Crocheted doilies were spread on the arms of the couch and the headrest, but you could make out the worn spots through the gaps in the doilies. The girl didn't look a whole hell of a lot older than the baby, but there you go. Toys appropriate to a three-year-old were scattered about the floor. I smiled at them. 'Hi.'

The old man nodded and the girl picked up a remote control and clicked off the TV.

The younger man said, 'Go tell Mama we got company.'

The girl slipped off the couch and went down a little hall into the back of the house. I said, 'Your wife?'

'Lewis's girlfriend, Shalene. This is their son, Marcus, and this is my grandfather, Mr Williams. Say hello, Marcus.'

Marcus covered his eyes with his fingers and sat down on the floor, then rolled over onto his belly. He giggled as he did it. The old man started rocking.

Lewis's girlfriend came back with a heavy, light-skinned woman in her fifties. Ida Leigh Washington. There was a friendly half smile on her face, and a fine film of perspiration as if she'd been working.

The younger man held the card toward her. 'Man wants to ask you about Lewis.'

76

The older woman froze as if someone had put a gun to her head, and the half smile died. 'Are you with the police?'

'No, ma'am. I'm a private investigator, and I had some questions about what happened to Charles Lewis Washington. I was hoping you could help me.'

She looked at the card, and then she looked at me, and then she looked at her son. He crossed his arms and stared at her with the sort of look that said you're on your own. She shook her head. 'I'm very sorry, but you've come at a bad time.'

'Please, Mrs Washington. This won't take long, and it would be terribly inconvenient to come back later.' I thought about saying *aw, shucks*, but I figured that would be overboard.

She fingered the card and looked at the younger man. 'James Edward, did you offer the man a cool drink?'

James Edward said, 'You want a Scrapple?'

'No, thank you. I won't take any more of your time than necessary.'

Mrs Washington offered me a seat in the overstuffed chair. It was worn and comfortable and probably had belonged to Mr Washington. She sat on the couch with the girl and the baby. James Edward didn't sit.

I said, 'Was Lewis in a gang, Mrs Washington?'

Her foot began to move. Nervous. 'No, he was not. The police said he was, but that wasn't so.'

'I saw his arrest record. He was arrested for stealing electronics equipment with three other young men when he was sixteen years old. All four kids, including Lewis, admitted to being members of the Double-Seven Hoover Crips.'

'When he was a baby.' The foot stopped moving and she made an impatient gesture. 'Lewis got out of all that. That Winslow Johnston was the troublemaker. They put him in the penitentiary and he got killed there and Lewis gave it up. He joined the Navy and got away from all this. When he came back he found Shalene.' Mrs Washington reached out and patted Shalene on the thigh. 'He was trying to make something of himself.'

Shalene was staring at me the way you stare at someone when you're thinking that a good time would be punching little holes in their head with an ice pick.

'The report also said Lewis owned the pawnshop.'

'That's right.'

'Where'd he get the money to buy an ongoing business like that, Mrs Washington?'

There were lovely crocheted doilies on the couch's arms. She straightened the one nearest her, then began to twist it. 'He had money from the Navy. And I co-signed some papers.'

Marcus climbed down off the couch and toddled out of the living room and into the kitchen. Mrs Washington leaned forward to see where he was going but Shalene didn't. Mrs Washington straightened and looked at her. 'You'd better see where he's going.'

Shalene went into the kitchen after him.

I said, 'Mrs Washington, I don't want to offend you, and I promise you that nothing you say to me will be repeated to police or to anyone else. Was Lewis fencing stolen goods?'

Her eyes filled. 'Yes,' she said. 'I believe that he was. But that gave them no call. Lewis didn't carry no gun. Lewis wouldn't have done what they said.'

'Yes, ma'am.'

'I know my boy. I know him the way only a mother can know a son. They had no call to hurt my boy.' Jennifer Sheridan knowing Mark Thurman.

'Yes, ma'am.' She was twisting the crocheted doily into a high, tight peak.

I said, 'If you believe that, then why did you drop the wrongful-death suit against the officers who killed him?'

Mrs Washington closed her eyes against the tears, and the old man spoke for the first time. He said, 'Because Lewis was always looking for trouble and he finally found it. There's nothing else to it, no reason to keep it alive.' His voice was deep and gravelly, and more like a bark than a voice. His eyes blinked rapidly as he said it. 'It was right to let it go, just let it go and walk away. Let the dead lie. There's nothing more to say to it.' He put the Scrapple can carefully on the floor, then, just as carefully, he pushed himself up and walked from the room. He took very short steps, and used first the couch and then the wall to steady himself. Shalene had come back with Marcus in her arms to stand in the door to the kitchen, staring at me and hating me. Mrs Washington was staring into the folds of her lap, eyes clenched, her body quivering as if it were a leaf in the wind. I sat there in the warm living room and looked at them and listened and I did not believe them. Mrs Washington said, 'You should go. I'm sorry, now, but you should go.'

'You really, truly believe he was murdered.'

'You have to go.'

I said, 'Did the officers threaten you?'

'Please, go.'

'The officers who shot Lewis. Did they come here and threaten you and make you drop the suit?'

'Please leave.'

James Edward said, 'What're you going to tell him, Mama?'

'Don't you say anything, James Edward. There's nothing more to say.' Ida Leigh Washington pushed to her feet and waved me toward the door. 'I want you out of my house. You're not the police and you have no paper that says you can be here and I want you out.'

Marcus began to wail. For a moment, everything was still, and then I stood. 'Thank you for your time, Mrs Washington. I'm sorry about your son.'

James Edward went to the door and followed me out. Mrs Washington hurried after us, but stopped in the door. 'Don't you go out there with him, James Edward. They'll see you, out there.'

James Edward said, 'It's all right, Mama.'

He pushed her gently back into the house and closed the door. It was cooler on the porch, and the rose smell was fresh and strong. We stood like that for a moment, then James Edward went to the edge of the porch and peered out between the roses and looked at his neighborhood. He said, 'I wasn't here when it happened.'

'The Navy?'

He nodded. 'Missed the riots, too. I was away for four years, first in the Med, then the Indian.'

'How long have you been out?'

'Five weeks, four days, and I gotta come back to this.' He looked at me. 'You think it's the cops, huh?'

I nodded.

He gave disgusted, and moved into the shade behind the trellis. 'The cops killed my brother, but a nigger named Akeem D'Muere made'm drop the suit.'

I gave him stupid. 'Who's Akeem D'Muere?'

'Runs a gang called the Eight-Deuce Gangster Boys.'

'A black gang made your family drop the suit?' I was taking stupid into unexplored realms.

'You're the detective. I been away for four years.' He turned from the street and sat on the glider and I sat next to him.

'So why's a black gang force a black family to drop a wrongful-death suit against a bunch of white cops?'

He shook his head. 'Can't say. But I'm gonna find out.'

'There has to be some kind of connection.'

'Man, you must be Sherlock fuckin' Holmes.'

'Hey, you get me up to speed, I'm something to watch.'

He nodded, but he didn't look like he believed it.

I said, 'This is your 'hood, James Edward, not mine. If

there's a connection between these guys, there's going to be a way to find out, but I don't know what it is.'

'So what?'

'So they don't have a detective's-mate rating in the Navy, and maybe I can help you find out. I find out, and maybe we can get your mother out from under this thing.'

James Edward Washington gave me a long, slow look, like maybe he was wondering about something, and then he got up and started off the porch without waiting for me. 'C'mon. I know a man we can see.'

CHAPTER 11

We walked out to the Corvette and James Edward Washington gave approval. I got in, but James Edward took a slow walk around. 'Sixty-five?'

'Sixty-six.'

'I thought private eyes were supposed to drive clunky little cars like Columbo.'

'That's TV.'

'What about if you follow somebody? Don't a car like this stand out?' James Edward was liking my car just fine.

'If I was living in Lost Overshoe, Nebraska, it stands out. In L.A., it's just another convertible. A lot of places I work, if I drove a clunker it'd stand out more than this.'

James Edward smiled. 'Yeah, but this ain't those places. This is South Central.'

'We'll see.'

James Edward climbed in, told me to head east toward Western, and I pulled a K-turn and did it.

We drove north on Western to Slauson, then turned east to parallel the railroad tracks, then turned north again. James Edward told me that we were going to see a guy he knew named Ray Depente. He said that Ray had spent twenty-two years in the Marine Corps, teaching hand-to-hand down at Camp Pendleton before tendering his retirement and opening a gym here in Los Angeles to work with kids and sponsor gang intervention programs. He also said that if anyone knew the South Central gang scene, Ray did. I said that sounded good to me.

Four blocks above Broadway I spotted the same two

guys in the same blue sedan that I'd suspected of following me two days ago. They stayed with us through two turns, and never came closer than three cars nor dropped back farther than six. When we came to a 7-Eleven, I pulled into the lot and told James Edward that I had to make a call. I used the pay phone there to dial a gun shop in Culver City, and a man's voice answered on the second ring. 'Pike.'

'It's me. I'm standing in a 7-Eleven parking lot on San Pedro about three blocks south of Martin Luther King Boulevard. I'm with a black guy in his early twenties named James Edward Washington. A white guy and a Hispanic guy in a dark blue 1989 sedan are following us. I think they've been following me for the past two days.'

'Shoot them.' Life is simple for some of us.

'I was thinking more that you could follow them as they follow me and we could find out who they are.'

Pike didn't say anything.

'Also, I think they're cops.'

Pike grunted. 'Where you headed?'

'A place called Ray's Gym. In South Central.'

Pike grunted again. 'I know Ray's. Are you in immediate danger?'

I looked around. 'Well, I could probably get hit by a meteor.'

Pike said, 'Go to Ray's. You won't see me, but I'll be there when you come out.' Then he hung up. Some partner, huh?

I climbed back into the car, and fourteen minutes later we pulled into a gravel parking lot on the side of Ray Depente's gymnasium. James Edward Washington led me inside.

Ray's is a big underground cavern kind of place with peeling paint and high ceilings and the smell of sweat pressed into the walls. Maybe forty people were spread around the big room, men and women, some stretching, some grinding through *katas* like formal dance routines, some sparring with full-contact pads. An athletic woman with strawberry hair was on the mats with a tall black man with mocha skin and gray-flecked hair. They were working hard, the woman snapping kick after kick at his legs and torso and head, him yelling c'mon, get in here, c'mon, I'm wide open. Every time she kicked, sweat flew off her and sprayed the mat. Each of them was covered with so many pads they might've been in space suits. James Edward said, 'That's Ray.'

I started fooling around with the martial arts when I was in the Army and I got pretty good at it. Ray Depente was good, too, and he looked like an outstanding teacher. He snapped light punches and kicks at the woman, making her think defense as well as offense. He tapped them on the heavy pad over her breasts and taunted her, saying stop me, saying Jesus Christ protect yourself, saying you mine anytime I want you. She kicked faster, snapping up roundhouse kicks and power kicks, then coming in backwards with spin kicks. He blocked most of the kicks and slipped a few and taunted her harder, saying he ain't never had a white woman but he was about to get one now. As fast as he said it she hooked his left knee and he stumbled to catch himself and when he did she got off a high fast spin kick that caught him on the back of the head and bowled him over and then she was on him, spiking kicks hard at his groin pad and his spine and his head and he doubled into a ball, covering up, yelling that he gives, he gives, he gives, and laughing the big deep laugh. She helped him up and they bowed to each other, both of them grinning, and then she gave a whoop and jumped up to give him a major league hug. Then she hopped away to the locker rooms, pumping her fist and yelling 'Yeah!' Ray Depente stepped off the mat, unfastening the pads, and then he saw us standing on the hardwood at the edge of the mat. He grinned at James

Edward and came over, still pulling off the pads. He was two inches taller than me and maybe fifteen pounds heavier. 'Welcome back, Admiral. I've missed you, young man.'

He grabbed James Edward in a tight hug, and the two men pounded each other on their backs. When James Edward stepped back, he said, 'You ain't never had a white woman but you're about to get one now?'

Ray grinned. 'Thirteen months ago two assholes followed her into a parking lot in Rancho Park. One of them raped her in the backseat of her MB. The second one was just getting ready to mount up when a couple of women came along and scared'm off. What you think would happen if those guys came back today?'

'Testicular transplant?'

'Uh-huh.'

I said, 'She's come along fast.'

'Motivation, baby. Motivation is all.'

James Edward said, 'Ray, this is Elvis Cole. He's a private investigator.'

'Do tell.' We shook. Ray Depente had a hand like warm steel. 'What do you investigate?'

'I'm working with something that's bumped up against a gang called the Eight-Deuce Gangster Boys. James Edward says that you know about those guys.'

Ray peeled away the rest of his body pads and used his sweatshirt to wipe his face and neck. Everybody else in the place was wearing heavy canvas karate *gies*, but not Ray. Ray wore desert-issue combat pants and an orange Marine Corps tee shirt. Old habits. 'Bumping up against the Crips isn't something you want to do if you can help it. Crips got sharp edges.'

I gave him shrug. 'Occupational hazard.'

'Uh-huh. Be tough and see.'

'The Gangster Boys a Crip set?' People hear Crips or Bloods and they think it's just two big gangs, but it isn't.

85

Both the Crips and the Bloods are made up of smaller gang sets. Eight-Deuce Gangster Boys, Eight-Trey Swan Crips, Rolling Sixties Crips, Double-Seven Hoover Crips, East Coast Crips, like that.

Ray nodded. 'Yeah. From down around Eighty-second and Hoover. That's where they get the name. You want to be a Gangster Boy, you got to do a felony. You want to be OG, you got to pull the trigger. It's as simple as that.'

James Edward said, 'O.G. means Original Gangster. That's like saying you're a made man in the Mafia.'

'Okay.'

Ray said, 'What are you messing around with that's got you down here in South Central with a goddamned Crip set?'

'Charles Lewis Washington.'

Ray's smile faded and he looked at James Edward. 'How's your mama doing, son?'

'She's okay. We got a little problem with the Eight-Deuce, though.'

Ray looked back at me. 'You working for the family?'

'Nope. But maybe what I'm doing gets us to the same place.'

Ray looked at James Edward and James Edward nodded. Ray said, 'I hadn't seen Lewis for a couple years, but when I heard about him dying, I didn't like it, and I didn't like how it happened. I worked with that boy out of youth services. It was a long time ago and he didn't stay with it, but there it is. Once you're one of my young men, you're one of my young men. Just like this one.' Ray Depente put a warm steel hand on James Edward's shoulder and gave him a squeeze. 'I tried to point this one toward the Marines but he liked the idea of ships.' Ray and James Edward grinned at each other, and the grins were as warm as the hand.

I said, 'The cops say that Lewis was a Double-Seven gangbanger. His mother says no.'

Ray frowned. 'Lewis used to mess around with the Double-Sevens, but that was years ago. That's how he came to me.'

'He ever have anything to do with the Eight-Deuce Gangster Boys?'

'Not that I know.'

'The family filed a wrongful death after Lewis was killed, but James Edward here tells me that a guy named Akeem D'Muere made them back off.'

Ray looked at James Edward again. 'You sure?'

James Edward nodded.

I said, 'Why would Akeem D'Muere go to bat for a bunch of white LAPD officers?'

Ray shook his head. 'I know Akeem. Akeem D'Muere wouldn't go to bat for anybody unless there's something in it for him.'

'When Lewis Washington died, every news service in town was looking into it, smelling Rodney King all over again. Maybe Akeem D'Muere wanted all the looking to stop. Maybe there was something going on at the Premier Pawn Shop that he didn't want anyone to find out.'

'You think?'

I shrugged. 'I think there's a connection. I just don't know who to ask to find out.'

James Edward said, 'That's why I brought him here, Ray. Figured you'd be the guy to know.'

Ray Depente smiled at James Edward. 'You want me to ask around, young mister, I can do that. Know a man who'll probably be able to help. But you stay away from those Eight-Deuce. The Navy doesn't teach you what you need to know to mess with that trash.'

James Edward said, 'Hell Ray.'

The strawberry-haired woman came out of the dressing room, showered and changed, and gave Ray a ten-megawatt smile as she bounced out of the gym and into the sunshine. I said, 'Pretty.'

Ray said, 'Uh-huh.'

An older woman pushed her head out of a little glass cubicle that served as an office at the rear of the gym. She called, 'Ray, it's somebody from Twentieth Century-Fox. They say it's some kind of emergency and they need you to come over and show Bruce Willis how to do something for a movie they're making.'

James Edward grinned. 'Bruce Willis. Damn.'

Ray didn't look as thrilled with Bruce Willis as did James Edward. 'Now?'

'They said right away.'

James Edward said, 'These studio dudes hire Ray to set up fight scenes and teach his moves to their actors. Arnold been here, man. Sly Stallone useta come here.'

Ray shook his head. 'I can do it tonight, but I can't do it now. I've got a class coming in, now.'

The woman said, 'They said right away.'

Ray shook his head. 'Movie people.' He called back to her. 'Tell'm I gotta pass.'

James Edward Washington gave impressed. 'Is this fuckin' righteous or what? Tellin' Bruce Willis to pass.'

The older woman went back into the glass cubicle.

Ray said, 'Jesus Christ, James Edward. It ain't no big thing.' Ray Depente looked my way and gave embarrassed. 'These kids think this movie stuff is a big deal. They don't know. A client's a client.'

'Sure.'

'I've got a class.'

'Sure.'

A dozen little girls came in, shepherded by a tall erect black woman in a neat dress suit. Most of the little girls were black, but a couple were Hispanic. They all wore clean white karate *gies* and tennis shoes. They took off their shoes before they stepped onto the mat. Ray uncrossed his arms and smiled. 'Here they are, now.'

James Edward Washington laughed and said, 'Damn.'

Ray Depente squeezed James Edward's shoulder again, then told me that it had been a pleasure to meet me, and that if he learned something he would give James Edward a call. Then he turned away and walked out onto the mat to face his class.

The little girls formed a neat line as if they had done it a thousand times before and bowed toward Ray Depente and shouted *kun hey* with perfect Korean inflection. Ray said something so quietly that I could not hear, and then he bowed to them.

Ray Depente gets five hundred dollars an hour from movie stars, but some things are more important.

CHAPTER 12

James Edward Washington wanted to chill with Ray for a while, so he stayed, and I walked out to my car, making a big deal out of taking off my jacket so that I could look up and down the street and across the intersections. Joe Pike drives an immaculate red Jeep Cherokee, and I was hoping to spot him or the blue sedan, but I saw neither. Of course, maybe they weren't there. Maybe the blue sedan hadn't really been following me and I was making a big deal with the jacket for nothing. Elvis Cole, Existential Detective. On the other hand, maybe the guys in the blue sedan were better than me and I wasn't good enough to spot them.

Not.

I climbed the ramp to the I-10 freeway and went west, changing lanes to avoid slower traffic and speeding up when the traffic allowed and trying to play it normal. Just another Angeleno in the system. It paid off. A quarter mile past the La Brea exit I spotted the blue sedan hiding on the far side of a Ryder moving van, two lanes over. The guy with the Dodgers cap was still driving and the guy with the butch cut was still riding shotgun.

I took the La Cienega exit and went north, timing the lights to get a better view, but always just missing. They were good. Always three or four cars back, always with plenty of separation, and they didn't seem worried that they'd lose me. That meant they knew they could always pick me up again, or that they were working with a second car. Cops always use a second car.

La Cienega is four lanes, but Caltrans was at it again, and as La Cienega approached Pico, the two northbound lanes became one. There's a 20/20 Video in a large shopping center on the northeast corner, and the closer I got to the 20/20, the slower I drove. By the time I cleared the work in the intersection, a guy behind me in a Toyota 4x4 had had enough and roared past, giving me the finger. I stayed in the right lane as I crossed Pico, and the remaining two cars behind me turned. Then there was just me and the blue sedan. The driver swung right, making the turn with the two other cars as if they had never intended anything else, and that's when I picked up the slack car. Floyd Riggens was driving his dark brown sedan two cars back, sitting in traffic behind a couple of guys on mopeds. My, my.

I stayed north on La Cienega and three blocks later the blue sedan sat at a side street ahead of me, waiting. As soon as they made the turn onto Pico they must've punched it like an F-16 going into afterburner, then swung north on a parallel side street to come in ahead of me. Floyd would've radioed that he still had me in sight, and that we were proceeding northbound, and that's how they'd know where to wait. Floyd hung back, and after I passed, the blue sedan pulled in behind me again. Right where I wanted them.

I turned east on Beverly, then dropped down Fairfax past CBS Television City to the Farmer's Market. The Market is a loose collection of buildings surrounded on all sides by parking lots used mostly by tour buses and people from Utah, come to gawk at CBS.

I turned into the north lot and made my way past the buses and about a million empty parking spots toward the east lot. Most of the traffic stays in the north lot, but if you want to get from the north lot to the east, you have to funnel through a cramped drive that runs between a couple of buildings where people sell papayas and framed pictures of Pat Sajak. It's narrow and it's cramped and it's lousy when you're here on a Saturday and the place is jammed with tourists, but it's ideal for a private eye looking to spring an ambush.

When I was clear of the little drive, I pulled a quick reverse and backed my car behind a flower truck. A teenaged girl in a white Volkswagen Rabbit came through the gap after me, and, a few seconds later, the blue sedan followed. It came through at a creep, the guy in the passenger seat pointing to the south and the driver sitting high to see what he was pointing at. Whatever he saw he didn't like it, because he made an angry gesture and looked away and that's when they saw me. I jumped the Corvette into their path and got out of the car with my hands clear so they could see I had no gun. The kid with the butch bounced out and started yelling into a handi-talkie and the Hispanic guy was running toward me with his badge in one hand and a Browning 9mm in the other. Floyd Riggens was roaring toward us from the far end of the lot. Thurman wasn't with him. Thurman wasn't anywhere around.

The Hispanic guy yelled, 'Get your hands up. Out and away from your body.' When the guns come out there's always a lot of yelling.

The guy with the butch ran over and patted me down with his free hand. I made him for Pinkworth. The other guy for Garcia. While Pinkworth did the shakedown, some of the people from the tour buses began to gather on the walk and look at us. Most of the men were in Bermuda shorts and most of the women were in summer-weight pant suits and just about everyone held a camera. Tourists. They stood in a little group as they watched, and a fat kid with glasses and a DES MOINES sweatshirt said, 'Hey, neat.' Maybe they thought we were the CBS version of the Universal stunt show.

Garcia said, 'Jesus Christ, we've got a goddamned crowd.'

I smiled at him. 'My fans.'

Pinkworth looked nervous and lowered his gun like someone might see it and tell. Garcia lowered his, too.

Riggens's car screeched to a stop and he kicked open the door. His face was flushed and he looked angry. He also looked drunk. 'Stay the fuck away from my wife.'

Garcia yelled, 'Floyd,' but Floyd wasn't listening. He took two long steps forward, then lunged toward me with his body sort of cocked to the side like he was going to throw a haymaker and knock me into the next time zone.

He swung, and I stepped outside of it and snapped a high roundhouse kick into the side of his head that knocked him over sideways.

The fat kid said, 'Look at that!' and the fat kid's father aimed a Sony video camera at us.

When Riggens fell, Garcia's gun came up and Pinkworth started forward, and that's when Joe Pike reared up from behind their car, snapped the slide on a 12-gauge Ithaca riot gun, and said, 'Don't.'

Garcia and Pinkworth froze. They spread their fingers off their pistol grips, showing they were out of it.

The crowd went, 'Ooo.' Some show, all right.

Joe Pike stands six-one and weighs maybe one-ninety, and he's got large red arrows tattooed on the outside of each deltoid, souvenirs from his days as a Force Recon Marine in Vietnam. He was wearing faded blue jeans and Nike running shoes and a plain gray sweatshirt with the sleeves cut off and government-issue sunglasses. Angle the sun on him just right, and sometimes the tattoos seem to glow. I think Pike calls it his apparition look.

I said, 'Gee, and I thought you'd got lost in traffic.'

Pike's mouth twitched. He doesn't smile, but sometimes he'll twitch. You get a twitch out of Pike, he's gotta be dying on the inside. In tears, he's gotta be.

I took Garcia's and Pinkworth's guns, and Pike circled the blue sedan, finding a better angle to cover Riggens. When he moved, he seemed to glide, as if he were flowing over the surface of the earth, moving as a panther might move. To move was to stalk. I'd never seen him move any other way.

Garcia said, 'Put down that goddamned gun. We're LAPD officers, goddamn it.'

Pike's shotgun didn't waver. An older woman with a lime green sun hat and a purse the size of a mailbag looked at the other tourists and said, 'Does the bus leave after this?'

I pulled Riggens's gun and then I went back to Pinkworth and Garcia and checked their IDs. Pinkworth said, 'You're marked fuck for this, asshole. You're going down *hard*.'

'Uh-huh.'

Riggens moaned and sort of turned onto his side. His head was bleeding where it had bounced on the tarmac, but it didn't look bad. I took the clips out of the three police guns, tossed them into the blue sedan's backseat, then went back to Riggens. 'Let me see.'

Riggens pushed my hand off and tried to crab away, but he didn't do much more than flop onto his back. 'Fuck you.'

Pinkworth said, 'You're in a world of shit. You just assaulted a Los Angeles police officer.'

I said, 'Call it in and let's go to the station. Maybe they'll give Riggens a Breathalyzer while you guys are booking me.' You could smell it on him a block away.

Garcia said, 'Quiet, Pink.'

A green four-door sedan identical to the other two cop sedans came toward us across the lot. Riggens was still trying to get up when the green car pulled in behind him and a tall guy with short gray hair got out. He was wearing chino slacks and a striped short-sleeve shirt tucked neatly into his pants and short-topped Redwing trail shoes. He was tanned dark, like he spent a lot of time in the sun, and his face was lined. I made him for his mid-forties, but he could've been older. He looked at Riggens, then the two cops by the blue sedan, and then at Joe Pike. He wasn't upset and he wasn't excited, like he knew what he'd find when he got here and, when he got here, he knew that he could handle it. When he saw Joe Pike he said, 'I didn't know you were in on this.'

Pike nodded once.

I gave them surprised. 'You guys know each other?'

Pike said, 'Eric Dees.'

Eric Dees looked at me, then looked back at Pike. 'Pike and I rode a black-and-white together for a couple of months maybe a million years ago.' Pike had been a uniformed LAPD officer when I'd met him. 'Put away the shotgun, Joe. It's over, now. No one's going to drop the hammer.'

Pike lowered the shotgun.

Pinkworth craned around and stared at Pike. 'This sonofabitch is Joe Pike? *The* Joe Pike?' Pike had worn the uniform for almost three years, but it hadn't ended well.

Riggens said, 'Who?' He was still having trouble on the ground.

Dees said, 'Sure. You've just been jumped by the best.'

Pinkworth glowered at Pike like he'd been wanting to glower at him for a long time. 'Well, fuck him.'

Joe's head sort of whirred five degrees to line up on Pinkworth and Pinkworth's glower wavered. There is a machine-like quality to Joe, as if he had tuned his body the way he might tune his Jeep, and, as the Jeep was perfectly tuned, so was his body. It was easy to imagine him doing a thousand pushups or running a hundred miles, as if his body were an instrument of his mind, as if his mind were a well of limitless resource and unimaginable strength. If the mind said start, the body would start.

When the mind said stop, the body would stop, and whatever it would do, it would do with precision and exactness.

Dees said, 'Long time, Joe. How's it going?'

Pike's head whirred back and he made a kind of head shrug.

'Talkative, as always.' Dees looked at the people from Des Moines. 'Pink, move those people along. We don't need a crowd.' Pinkworth gave me tough, then pulled out his badge and sauntered over to the crowd. The fat kid's father didn't want to move along and made a deal out of it. Dees turned back to me. 'You're this close to getting stepped on for obstruction and for impersonating an officer, Cole. We drop the hammer, your license is history.'

I said, 'What's your connection with Akeem D'Muere and the Eight-Deuce Gangster Boys?'

Dees blinked once, then made a little smile, like maybe he wasn't smiling at me, but at something he was thinking. 'That's an official police investigation. That's what I'm telling you to stay away from. I'm also telling you to stay the hell out of Mark Thurman's personal life. You fuck with my people, you're fucking with me, and you don't want to do that. I'm a bad guy to fuck with.'

Riggens made a sort of a coughing sound, then sat up, squinted at me, and said, 'I'm gonna clean your ass, you fuck.' He got most of his feet under himself but then the feet slipped out and he sort of stumbled backwards until he rammed his head into the green sedan's left front wheel with a *thunk*. He grabbed at his head and said, 'Jesus.'

Dees stared hard at me for another moment, then went to Riggens. 'That's enough, Floyd.'

Floyd said, 'He hit me, Eric. The fuck's takin' the ride.' There was blood on Riggens's face.

Dees bunched his fingers into Riggens's shirt and gave a

single hard jerk that almost pulled Riggens off the ground and popped his head back against the sedan. 'No one's going in, Floyd.'

Riggens got up, took out a handkerchief, and dabbed at his head. The handkerchief came back red. 'Shit.'

I said, 'Better get some ice.'

'Fuck you.'

Dees made a little hand move at Garcia. 'Pete, take Floyd over there and get some ice.'

Floyd said, 'I don't need any goddamn ice. I'm fine.'

Dees said, 'You don't look fine. You look like a lush who got outclassed.' When he said it his voice was hard and commanding and Floyd Riggens jerked sideways as if he had been hit with a cattle prod. Garcia went over to him and took him by the arm. Floyd shook his hand off but followed him into the Market.

Joe Pike said, 'Elite.'

Eric Dees's face went hard. 'They're good, Joe. They didn't cut and walk away.'

Pike's head whirred back to lock onto Eric Dees.

I said, 'That's the second time I've seen Riggens and the second time I've seen him drunk. Your people always get shitfaced on duty?'

Dees came close to me. He was a little bit taller than me, and wider, and maybe six or eight years older. He reminded me of a couple of senior NCOs that I had known in the Army, men who were used to leading men and taking care of men and exercising authority over men. He said, 'I take care of my people, asshole. You'd better worry about taking care of you.'

Joe Pike said, 'Easy, Eric.'

Eric Dees said, 'Easy what, Joe?' He looked back at me. 'This is your wake-up call, and you're only going to get one. The little girl's problems with Mark are going to be solved. She's not going to need you anymore. That means you're off the board.'

'Is that why four LAPD officers have nothing better to do than follow me around?'

'We followed you to talk to you. It was either talk to you or kill you.'

'I'm shaking, Dees.' The detective plays it tough. 'What did Akeem D'Muere have to do with Lewis Washington's death?'

When I said *Lewis Washington*, Dees's eyes went hard and I wondered if I'd pushed too hard. 'I'm trying to play square with you, Cole. Maybe because of Joe, or maybe because I'm a square guy, but if you're not smart enough to listen, there are other ways I can solve the problem.'

'Where's Mark Thurman? You give him the day off?'

Dees looked at the ground like he was trying to think of the magic word, and then Pinkworth came back with Riggens and Garcia. As soon as Pinkworth turned away, the crowd came back. The fat kid's father was smiling. Riggens got into his sedan and Pinkworth and Garcia went back to the blue. Dees looked up at me with eyes that were profoundly tired. 'You're not helping the girl, Cole. You think you are, but you're not.'

'Maybe she has nothing to do with it anymore. Maybe it's larger than her. Maybe it's about Lewis Washington and Akeem D'Muere and why five LAPD officers are so scared of this that they're living in my shorts.'

Dees nodded. Like he knew it was coming, but he wasn't especially glad to see it arrive. 'It's your call, bubba.'

Then he went back to his car and drove away.

Riggens cranked his sedan and took off after him with a lot of tire squealing. Garcia fired up the blue, and as they pulled out after Riggens, Pinkworth gave me the finger. When he gave me the finger the fat kid in the DES MOINES sweatshirt laughed and shook his dad's arm so that his dad would see.

A Kodak moment.

CHAPTER 13

Thirty-five minutes later I pulled up the little road to my house and saw Pike's red Jeep Cherokee under the elm by the front steps. I had left the Farmer's Market before Pike, and I had made good time, but when I got home, there he was, as if he had been there for hours, as if he had been both here and there at the same time. He does this a lot, but I have never been able to figure out how. Teleportation, maybe.

Pike was holding the cat and the two of them were staring at something across the canyon. Looking for more cops, no doubt. I said, 'How'd you beat me?'

Pike put down the cat. 'I didn't know it was a race.' You see how he is?

I turned off the alarm and let us into the kitchen through the carport. I was uncomfortable moving into and through the house, as if I expected more cops to be hiding in a closet or behind the couch. I looked around and wondered if they had been in the house. People have been in my house before. I didn't like it then, and I liked it even less, now.

Pike said, 'We're clear.'

One minute he's across the room, the next he's right behind you. 'How do you know?'

'Went down to the end of the road. Checked the downslope and the upslope. Walked through the house before you got here.' He made a little shrug. 'We're clear.'

A six-thousand-dollar alarm, and it's nothing to Pike. He said, 'You want to tell me about this?'

I took two Falstaffs out of the refrigerator, gave one to Pike and kept one for myself, and then I told him about Jennifer and Thurman and Eric Dees's REACT team. 'Four months ago Dees's team was involved in an arrest in which a man named Charles Lewis Washington died. Washington's family filed a suit against Dees and the city, but they dropped it when a street gang called the Eight-Deuce Gangster Boys pressed them.'

Pike took some of the Falstaff and nodded. 'So what's the connection between a street gang and Eric Dees?'

'That's the question, isn't it?'

I went upstairs, got the notes I had made on the case, and brought them down. 'You hungry?'

'Always.'

'I've got some of the venison left.'

Pike made a face. 'You got something green?' Two years ago he had gone vegetarian.

'Sure. Tuna, also, if you want.' He'll sometimes eat fish. 'Read the notes first, then we'll talk after.'

Pike took the notes, and I went into the freezer for the venison. In the fall, I had hunted the hill country of central California for blacktail deer and had harvested a nice buck. I had kept the tenderloins and chops, and had the rest turned into smoked sausage by a German butcher I know in West L.A. The tenderloins and the chops were gone, but I still had three plump sausage rings. I took two of the rings from the freezer, put them in the microwave to thaw, then went out onto the deck to build the fire. The cat was sitting out there, under the bird feeder. I said, 'Forget the birds. We're making Bambi.'

The cat blinked at me, then came over and sat by the grill. Venison is one of his favorite things.

I keep a Weber charcoal grill out on the deck, along with a circular redwood picnic table. The same woman who had given me the bird feeder had also helped me build the picnic table. Actually, she had done most of the building and I had done most of the helping, but that had probably worked out better for the table. I scraped the grill, then built a bed of mesquite coals in the pit and fired them. Mesquite charcoal takes a while, so you have to get your fire going before you do anything else.

When the coals were on their way, I went back into the kitchen.

Pike looked up from the report. 'We're squaring off against five LAPD officers, and all we're getting paid is forty bucks?'

'Nope. We're also getting forty dollars per month for the next forty-nine months.'

Pike shook his head.

'Think of it as job security, Joe. Four years of steady income.'

Pike sighed.

I opened another Falstaff, drank half of it on the way upstairs to the shower, and the other half on the way back down. When I got back down, Pike had built a large salad with tuna and garbanzo beans and tomatoes and onions. We brought the salad and the venison out onto the deck.

The sky had deepened, and as the sun settled into a purple pool in the west, the smells of budding eucalyptus and night-blooming jasmine mingled with the mesquite smoke. It was a clean, healthy smell, and made me think, as it always does, of open country and little boys and girls climbing trees and chasing fireflies. Maybe I was one of the little boys. Maybe I still am. There are no fireflies in Los Angeles.

I put the venison on the grill, then sat with Pike at the table and told him about Charles Lewis Washington and the Washington family and what I had learned from Ray Depente about Akeem D'Muere and the Eight-Deuce Gangster Boys.

Pike sipped his beer and listened. When I finished he

said, 'You think the family was telling the truth about Charles Lewis going straight?'

'They believed it.'

'Then where'd a guy like that get the cash to buy a solvent business?'

'There is that, yes.'

'Maybe he had a partner.'

I nodded. 'D'Muere funds the pawnshop to front a fence operation, and Lewis's working for D'Muere. I can see that, but why does D'Muere front off the Washington family from pressing their lawsuit? The pawnshop is shut down. The fence operation is history.'

'If there's a suit, there's an investigation. There was something else there that he wants to hide.'

'Something that Eric Dees knows?'

Pike shrugged.

'If Dees knows about it, it's not hidden.'

Pike angled his head around and stared at me. 'Unless it's something Eric wants hidden, too.'

'Ah.' I turned the sausages. Fat was beginning to bubble out of the skin and they smelled wonderful. 'Akeem D'Muere and Eric Dees are sharing a secret.'

Pike nodded.

'The question arises, how far will they go to protect it?'

Pike stared at me for a moment, then got up and went into the house. I heard the front door open, then I heard his Jeep's door, and then he came back out onto the deck. When he came back, he was wearing his pistol. It's a Colt Python .357 with a four-inch barrel. Eternal vigilance is the price of freedom. I said, 'Guess that means they'll go pretty far.'

Pike said, 'If five cops are on you, then it's important to them. If they're with you, then they're not doing the work they're supposed to be doing, and that's not easy to cover. Dees's people can't just go to the beach. He has to account for their time to his boss, and he has to produce results with whatever cases they're working.'

'And all five guys have to be on board with it.'

Pike nodded. 'Everybody has to be on board.'

I turned the sausages again. The skins were taking on a crunchy texture and the cat had hopped up on the rail that runs around the edge of the deck so he could be as close to the sausage as possible. Any closer and we could serve barbecued cat.

Pike said, 'Eric was nervous. That's not like him. Maybe even scared, and that's not like him, either.'

'Okay.'

'Scared people do atypical things. He was thinking maybe that he could scare you off. Now that he knows that I'm in, it will change what he thinks. He knows that I won't scare.'

'Great. That will make him all the more dangerous.'

'Yes,' Pike said. 'It will.'

'Maybe Dees is telling the truth. Maybe we're just stepping on a case and he's pissed.'

Pike shook his head. 'He wants you out, it's easy. He tells his boss and his boss calls you in and you sit down together. You know that.' The sky darkened and the hillside below us grew speckled with lights. Pike adjusted his sunglasses, but did not remove them. He never removes them. Even at night. 'If he's not playing it straight, then he can't play it straight. That's the first rule every cop learns.'

I turned the sausage rings a last time, then took them off the grill and put them onto a maple cutting board. I sliced them at an angle, then put half the meat on my plate and a serious portion on a saucer for the cat. I blew on his to cool it. Pike went into the house and came out with two more Falstaffs and what was left of a loaf of rosemary bread. I took some of the salad and tasted it.

Pike had made a dressing of soy sauce, rice vinegar, and minced garlic. I nodded. 'Good.'

He nodded back.

We ate without speaking for several minutes, and Pike didn't look happy. Of course, since Pike never smiles, it's sometimes tough to tell when he is happy, but there are ways. I said, 'What?'

Pike picked up a piece of tuna with his fingers, took a small bite, then held out the rest to the cat. The cat stepped forward and ate with enthusiasm. Pike said, 'I haven't seen Eric in many years.'

'Was he good?'

'Yes.'

'Was he honest?'

Pike turned his head and the dark lenses angled toward me. 'If I saw it any other way, I wouldn't have ridden with him.'

I nodded. 'But people change.'

Pike wiped his fingers on his napkin, then turned back to his meal. 'Yes. People change.'

We ate the rest of the meal in silence, and then we brought the dirty dishes into the kitchen and flipped a nickel to see who would wash. I lost. Midway through the load the phone rang and Joe Pike answered. He said, 'Jennifer Sheridan.'

I took the phone and said, 'Elvis Cole, Personal Detective to Jennifer Sheridan.'

Jennifer Sheridan said, 'Floyd Riggens just left me. He was here with another officer. They said that I was going to get Mark killed. They said that if I didn't make you stop, something bad would happen.' Her voice was tight and compressed and the words came quickly, as if she were keeping a close rein, but just.

'Are you all right?'

'I called Mark, but he's not home.'

'What about you? Are you all right?'

I could hear her breathe. She didn't say anything for a time, and then she said, 'I'd like someone with me, I think. Would you mind?'

'I'm leaving now.'

I hung up. Pike was staring at me, his glasses reflecting the kitchen lights. 'Riggens paid her a visit. I'd better go over there.'

Pike said, 'This isn't going to work out the way she wants it to.'

I spread my hands. 'I don't know. Maybe we can make it work out that way.'

'If Dees and Thurman and these guys are mixed up with Akeem D'Muere, it'll be ugly. She may find out something about him that she wished she didn't know.'

I spread my hands again. 'Maybe that's the price for being in love.'

Pike said, 'I'll finish the dishes.'

I told him thanks, then I put on the Dan Wesson and drove to see Jennifer Sheridan.

CHAPTER 14

Twenty-six minutes later I parked on the street across from Jennifer Sheridan's apartment building and buzzed her number on the security phone. The speaker came to life and Jennifer Sheridan said, 'Who is it?'

'Elvis Cole.'

The door lock buzzed open and I went in and took the elevator to the third floor.

Jennifer Sheridan lived in one of those stucco ant farms just off the freeway in Woodland Hills that caters to attractive young singles, attractive young couples, and the not-so-young-but-almost-as-attractive newly divorced. There would be a lot of grabass around the pool and something called a 'fitness room' where men and women would watch each other work out, but I guess it was a fair trade for a secure building at an affordable price in a low-crime area. Unless the cops were doing the crime.

Apartment 312 was down a long hall with a lot of shag carpeting and textured wallpaper and cottage-cheese ceilings. Jennifer Sheridan was peeking out of a two-inch crack in her door, waiting for me. When she saw me, she closed the door to unhook the chain, then opened it again. 'I'm sorry for calling you like that, but I didn't know what else to do. I feel so silly.'

I gave her the benevolent detective smile. 'It's no trouble and you did the right thing by calling me.' Maybe it was the six-pack-of-Falstaff smile.

She stepped out of the door and led me through an entry past her kitchen and into the living room. She was wearing an oversized white sweatshirt that hung low over black tights and white Keds tennis shoes. Comfortable. Just the kind of thing to be lounging around in in the apartment when Floyd Riggens came to call. She said, 'I tried calling Mark again, but there's still no answer. I left a message on his machine.'

'Okay.'

'There was another man with Floyd, but I don't know his name. He was a police officer, also.'

'What did he look like?'

'Bigger than Floyd, with very short hair. Blond.'

'Pinkworth.'

She nodded. 'Yes, that's right. Floyd called him Pink but I didn't realize that was a name.' She was trying to be brave and she was doing a good job.

'Did Floyd threaten you?'

She nodded.

I said, 'Did they hurt you?'

'Not really.' She made an uneasy smile, as if she didn't want to say anything that would cause trouble. 'He sort of grabbed me a little, that's all. I think he'd been drinking.' When she said it, she sort of brushed at her right arm. She wore the sweatshirt with the sleeves pushed above her elbows and on her forearm where she brushed there were angry red marks, the way there might be if someone grabbed hard and twisted.

I touched her forearm and turned it to look at the marks and a sharp pain throbbed behind my eyes. I said, 'Floyd.'

She took her arm back, and made a sort of dismissive laugh. 'I don't think he meant to. It just surprised me, that's all.'

'Of course.' The throbbing pain was worse.

It was a nice apartment, with inexpensive oak furniture and the kind of large overstuffed couch and matching chairs that you would buy on sale at Ikea or Home Club. A Sony television sat on a long white Formica table opposite the couch, along with a lot of plants and a portable CD player. A little forest of photographs stood between the plants and Mark Thurman was in most of the photographs. Many of the shots were duplicates of ones I had seen in Mark Thurman's album but many were not. An enormous stuffed Garfield stood sentry by the dining room table and a half-dozen smaller stuffed animals rested on the couch. Everything was neat and clean and in its proper place. I said, 'Why don't you sit, and I'll get something for us to drink, and then we can figure out what to do.'

She shook her head. 'I'm not helpless. Besides, the activity is good. Would you like a diet Coke or a glass of wine? I've got a Pinot Grigio.'

'The Pinot.'

She said, 'You sit, and I'll be right back.'

'Yes, ma'am.'

She smiled and went into the kitchen.

There was a pass-through between the kitchen and the living room so you could see from one into the other. I sat in the overstuffed chair at the far end of the living room and watched her get the wine. Jennifer Sheridan stood on her toes to reach two flute glasses out of her cupboard, then put them on the counter beside her sink. She opened the fridge, took out the bottle of Pinot, and worked out the cork. The Pinot had been opened earlier and was missing maybe a glass. She worked with her back to me. I watched the shape of her calves when she went up onto her toes and the line of her thighs and the way the oversized sweatshirt hung low over her bottom and draped from her shoulders. She didn't look so young from the back and I had to turn away to make myself stop looking at her. Jesus Christ, Cole. Portrait of the detective as a lecher. I looked at the pictures on the white table instead. Mark Thurman. Watching me. I crossed my eyes and made a face at him. Screw you, Mark. I looked at the

Garfield, instead. Maybe you shouldn't drink a six-pack of Falstaff before you visit a client.

Jennifer Sheridan came out with the two glasses of wine, handed one of them to me, and went to the couch. She must've seen me looking at the Garfield. 'Mark won that for me. Isn't it cute?'

'How nice.' I smiled. 'Tell me about Riggens and Pinkworth. Tell me everything they said. Don't leave anything out.'

She shook her head. 'The other guy didn't say very much. He just stood by the door, and every once in a while said something like "You oughta listen to him" or "We're only trying to help."'

'Okay. Then tell me about Floyd.'

She sipped her wine and thought about it, as if she wanted to be very careful and get it right. As she told me she picked up a stuffed lion from the couch and held it. 'He told me that Mark didn't know they were here, but that he was Mark's partner and he said that someone had to straighten me out because I was going to get Mark killed. I asked him to tell me what was going on but he wouldn't. He said that I didn't love Mark and I said that I did. He said I had a funny way of showing it. I told him to get out, but he wouldn't. He said that I never should have hired you because all you're doing is making trouble.'

'Floyd and I had a run-in today.' I told her about the Farmer's Market.

She blinked at me. 'You hit him?'

'No. I kicked him.'

She said, 'Kicked?'

'Yeah. Like Bruce Lee. You know.'

'You can get your foot up that high?'

I spread my hands. 'I am a man of profound talents.'

She touched her left cheek between the ear and the eye. 'He had a bruise right here.' Sort of awed.

I spread my hands again and she smiled, maybe

thinking how he had grabbed her. When she smiled I wanted to drop one wing and run in a circle. Guess we aren't so mature, after all.

I said, 'You don't get four active-duty REACT cops on your tail unless they're very scared of what you're doing. They didn't want me to know that they were on me, and now they know that I do, and they didn't want you to know that something is going on, and now Riggens has come here and threatened you. They've been trying to control the program but that isn't working, and things are beginning to fall apart. The gloves are coming off.'

She nodded, and looked thoughtful, like maybe whatever she was thinking wasn't easy to think about. She said, 'Was Mark there? At the Market?'

'No.' I was watching her. The thing that was hard to think about was even harder to say.

'He said Mark was in trouble. He said that they've been trying to help Mark, but that I was messing everything up and Mark was going to be hurt. He started yelling. He said maybe somebody ought to show me what it was like. I got scared then, and that's when he grabbed me.' She suddenly stopped speaking, went into the kitchen, and came back with the bottle of Pinot. She added more to her glass, then put the bottle on the table. 'Do you think Mark knew that Floyd was coming here?'

'I don't know. Probably not.' The detective answers a cry for support with a resounding maybe.

'I asked him why he was doing this. I asked him to tell me what had happened or what was going on. I told him I would help. He thought that was funny. He said that I didn't want to know. He said that Mark had done bad things and now they were fucked. I said Mark wasn't like that and he said I didn't know anything about Mark.' She stopped as if someone had pulled her plug, and stared into the forest of photographs.

I said, 'And you're scared he's right?'

She nodded.

'You're scared that you don't know anything about Mark, and that if you find out, you might not love him anymore.'

She pursed her lips and shook her head, then looked directly at me. 'No. I will always love him. No matter what. If he did something, it's because he believed he had to. If I can help him, then I will help him. I will love him even if he no longer loves me.' She blinked hard several times, and then took more wine. I watched her drink, and I wondered what it would be like to have someone love me with that commitment and that intensity, and, in that moment, I wished that it were me.

I said, 'Jennifer, did Mark ever mention someone named Lewis Washington?'

'No.'

'It might've been three or four months ago.'

'Maybe he said the name in passing and I wasn't paying attention, but I don't think so.'

I said, 'Four months ago, Mark's REACT team went into a place called the Premier Pawn Shop to arrest Lewis Washington for fencing stolen goods. There was a struggle, and Lewis Washington died of massive head injuries.'

She stared at me.

'The REACT team statement is that Washington pulled a gun and the head injuries resulted accidentally when team members tried to subdue Washington without the use of firearms. Washington's family said that Lewis didn't own a gun and was trying to go straight. The Washingtons sued the city and the LAPD, claiming wrongful death. The LAPD investigated, but found that there had been no wrongdoing.'

Jennifer Sheridan didn't move. She was staring at the far pictures. Mark and Jenny at the prom. Mark and Jenny after the big game. See them smile. See them laugh. 'Was it Mark?'

'The REACT team statement was that it was a combination of all five officers present, though Eric Dees, the team leader, took responsibility.'

She took a deep breath. 'Mark never told me any of that.'

'How about the name Akeem D'Muere?'

'No.'

'Akeem D'Muere is a gangbanger in South Central Los Angeles. He bosses a street gang called the Eight-Deuce Gangster Boys. Lewis Washington's family dropped their lawsuit because Akeem D'Muere told them that he'd kill them if they didn't.'

'He didn't tell me any of this. You think Mark has something to do with these people?'

'I don't know if these two things are connected or not. Maybe they're not. Maybe Mark didn't tell you about Akeem D'Muere because he doesn't know.'

'He didn't tell me about any of this.' She was shaking her head.

'This isn't going to be easy, Jennifer. What we find out about Mark might be a bad thing, just like Riggens said. It might be something that you'll wish you didn't know, and what you find out might change forever what you feel about Mark and about you with Mark. Do you see that?'

'Are you telling me that we should stop?'

'I'm not telling you one way or the other. I want you to know what you're dealing with, that's all.'

She turned away from me and looked at the pictures on the white Formica table, the pictures that had charted her life from the ninth grade until this moment. Her eyes turned pink and she rubbed at them. 'Damn it, I didn't want to cry anymore. I'm tired of crying.' She rubbed her eyes harder.

I leaned forward and touched her arm. The arm that Riggens had hurt. I said, 'Crying is dangerous. It's wise of you to avoid it this way.'

She said, 'What?' Confused.

'First, there's the dehydration, and then the lungs go into sob lock.'

She stopped the rubbing. 'Sob lock?'

I nodded. 'A form of vapor lock induced by sobbing. The lungs lose all capacity to move air, and asphyxiation is only moments away. I've lost more clients to this than gunshot wounds.'

'Maybe,' she said, 'that doesn't so much speak to the clients as to the detective.'

I slapped a hand over my chest. 'Ouch.'

Jennifer Sheridan laughed, forgetting about the tears. 'You're funny.'

'Nope. I'm Elvis.' You get me on a roll, I'm murder.

She laughed again and said, 'Say something else funny.'

'Something else funny.'

She laughed again and made a big deal out of giving me exasperated. 'No. I meant for you to *say* something funny.'

'Oh.'

'Well?' Waiting.

'You want me to say something funny.'

'Yes.'

'Something funny.'

Jennifer Sheridan threw the stuffed lion at me but then the laughter died and she said, 'Oh, my God. I am so scared.'

'I know.'

'I've got a college education. I have a good job. You're supposed to go out a lot, but I don't do that. You're supposed to be complete and whole all by yourself, but if I can't have him I feel like I'll die.'

'You're in love. People who say the other stuff are saying it either before they've been in love or after the love is over and it hasn't worked out for them, but no one says it when they're in the midst of love. When you're in love, there's too much at stake.'

She said, 'I've never been with anyone who makes me feel the way that he makes me feel. I've never tried to be. Maybe I should've. Maybe it's all been a horrible mistake.'

'It's not a mistake if it's what you wanted.' I was breathing hard and I couldn't get control of it.

She stared down into her flute glass, and she traced her fingertip around its edge, and then she stared at me. She didn't look sixteen, now. She was lean and pretty, and somehow available. She said, 'I like it that you make me laugh.'

I said, 'Jennifer.'

She put down the flute glass. 'You're very nice.'

I put down my glass and stood. She went very red and suddenly looked away. She said, 'Ohmygod. I'm sorry.'

'It's all right.'

She stood, too. 'Maybe you should go.'

I nodded, and realized that I didn't want to go. The sharp pain came back behind my eyes. 'All right.'

'This wine.' She laughed nervously, and still didn't look at me.

'Sure. Me, too.'

I backed away from her and went into the entry hall by the kitchen. I liked the way the tights fit her calves and her thighs and the way the sweatshirt hung low over her hips. She was standing with her arms crossed as if it were cold. 'I'm sorry.'

I said, 'Don't be.' Then I said, 'You're quite lovely.'

She flushed again and looked down at her empty glass and I left.

I stood in the street outside her apartment for a long time, and then I drove home.

Pike was gone and the house was cool and dark. I left it that way. I took a beer from the refrigerator, turned on the radio, and went out onto my deck. Jim Ladd was conning the air waves at KLSX. Playing a little George Thorogood. Playing a little Creedence Clearwater Revival. When you're going to listen to radio, you might as well listen to the best.

I stood in the cool night air and drank the beer and, off to my left, an owl hooted from high in a stand of pine trees. The scent of jasmine now was stronger than it had been earlier in the evening, and I liked it. I wondered if Jennifer Sheridan would like smelling it, too. Would she like the owl?

I listened and I drank for quite a long while, and then I went in to bed.

Sleep, when it finally came, provided no rest.

CHAPTER 15

At ten-forty the next morning I called my friend at B of A. She said, 'I can't believe this. Two calls in the same week. I may propose.'

'You get that stupid, I'll have to use the Sting tickets on someone else.'

'Forget it. I'd rather see Sting.' These dames.

'I want to know who financed the purchase of a place called the Premier Pawn Shop on Hoover Street in South Central L.A.' I gave her the address. 'Can you help me on that?'

'You at the office?'

'Nope. I'm taking advantage of my self-employed status to while away the morning in bed. Naked. And alone.' Mr Seduction.

My friend laughed. 'Well, if I know you, that's plenty of company.' Everybody's a comedian. 'Call you back in twenty.'

'Thanks.'

She made the call in fifteen. 'The Premier Pawn Shop was owned in partnership between Charles Lewis Washington and something called the Lester Corporation. Lester secured the loan and handled the financing through California Federal.'

'Ah ha.'

'Is that "ah ha" as in this is important, or "ah ha" as in you're clearing your throat?'

'The former. Maybe. Who signed the papers?'

'Washington and an attorney named Harold Bellis.

Bellis signed for Lester and is an officer in that corporation.'

'Bellis have an address?'

'Yeah. In Beverly Hills.' She gave it to me, then I hung up, showered, dressed, and charged off to deepest, darkest Beverly Hills. Portrait of the detective in search of mystery, adventure, and a couple of measly clues.

The Law Offices of Harold Bellis were on the third floor of a newly refurbished three-story office building a half block off Rodeo Drive and about a million light-years from South Central Los Angeles. I found a parking space between a Rolls-Royce Corniche and an eighty-thousand-dollar Mercedes two-seater in front of a store that sold men's belts starting at three hundred dollars. Business was brisk.

I went into a little glass lobby with a white marble floor and a lot of gold fixtures and took the elevator to the third floor. Harold Bellis had the front half of the building and it looked like he did very well. There was a lot of etched glass and glossy furniture and carpet about as deep as the North Atlantic. I waded up to a receptionist seated behind a semicircular granite desk and gave her my card. She was wearing one of those pencil-thin headphones so she could answer the phone and speak without having to lift anything. 'Elvis Cole to see Mr Bellis. I don't have an appointment.'

She touched a button and spoke to someone, then listened and smiled at me. There was no humor in the smile, nor any friendliness. She said, 'We're sorry, but Mr Bellis's calendar is full. If you'd like an appointment, we can schedule a time next week.'

I said, 'Tell him it's about the Premier Pawn Company. Tell him I have a question about the Lester Corporation.'

She said it into the microphone, and a couple of minutes later a rapier-thin woman with prominent cheeks and severely white skin came out and led me through a long common office where secretaries and aides and other people sat in little cubicles, and then into her office, and then into his. Her office held a bank of designer file cabinets and fresh-cut tulips and the entrance to his office. You want to see him, you've got to get past her, and she wouldn't be easy to beat. She'd probably even like the fight.

Harold Bellis had the corner office and it was big. She said, 'This is Mr Cole.'

Harold Bellis stood up and came around his desk, smiling and offering his hand. He was short and soft with pudgy hands and a fleshy face and thinning gray hair that looked as soft as mouse fur. Sort of like the Beverly Hills version of Howdy Doody. 'Thanks, Martha. Harold Bellis, Mr Cole. Martha tells me you're interested in the Premier Pawn Shop. Would you like to buy it?' He sort of laughed when he said it, like it was an obvious joke and we both knew it. Ha ha.

'Not today, Mr Bellis, thanks.'

Martha looked down her nose at me and left.

Harold Bellis's handshake was limp and his voice was sort of squeaky, but maybe that was just confidence. An original David Hockney watercolor and two Jésus Leuus oils hung on the walls. You don't get the Hockney and the Leuus by being sissy in the clinches. 'I'm working on something that brought me across the Premier and I learned that you're an officer in the company that owns it.'

'That's correct.' Bellis offered me a seat and took the chair across from me. The decor was Sante Fe, and the seating was padded benches. Bellis's chair looked comfortable, but the benches weren't. He said, 'I have a meeting with a client now, but she's sorting through records in the conference room, so we can squeeze in a few minutes.'

'Great.'

'Does this involve Mr Washington's death?'

'In part.'

Bellis gave me sad and shook his head. 'That young man's death was a tragedy. He had everything in the world going for himself.'

'The police say he was fencing stolen goods. His family suspects that, too.'

'Well, that was never established in a court of law, was it?'

'Are you saying he wasn't?'

'If he was, it was unknown to the co-owners of the shop.' Bellis's smile grew tighter and he didn't look so much like Howdy Doody now.

I smiled at him. 'Who are the co-owners, Mr Bellis?'

Harold Bellis looked at my card as if, in the looking, something had been confirmed. 'Perhaps if you told me your interest in all of this.'

'Mr Washington's family implied that he was the sole owner of the Premier, but upon checking, I found that something called the Lester Corporation arranged the financing and carried the paper.'

'That's right.'

'Since Mr Washington had no credit history, and was working at a minimum-wage job at the time, I was wondering why someone would co-sign a loan with him for such a substantial sum of money.'

Harold Bellis said, 'The Lester Corporation provides venture capital for minority businessmen. Lewis Washington made a proposal, and we agreed to enter into partnership. That's all there is to it.'

'To the tune of eighty-five thousand dollars.'

'Yes.'

'You co-signed a loan for a man with no formal education, a criminal record, and no business experience, because you like to help underprivileged entrepreneurs?'

'Someone has to, don't you think?' He leaned forward

out of the Sante Fe chair and the Howdy Doody eyes were as hard as a smart bomb's heart. Nope, he wouldn't be sissy in the clinches.

I said, 'Does Akeem D'Muere own the Lester Corporation?'

Bellis didn't move for a long moment and the eyes stayed with me. The smart bomb acquiring its target. 'I'm afraid I'm not at liberty to discuss the Lester Corporation or any other client, Mr Cole. You understand that, don't you?'

'I understand it, but I was hoping that you'd make an exception.'

The hard eyes relaxed and some of the Howdy Doody came back. Howdy Doody billing at a thousand dollars an hour. 'Do you suspect that this Mr D'Muere has something to do with Lewis Washington's death?'

'I don't know.'

'If you suspect someone of criminal activity, you should report it to the police.'

'Perhaps I will.' Elvis Cole makes his big threat.

Harold Bellis glanced at his watch and stood up. The watch was a Patek Philippe that wholesaled out at maybe fourteen thousand dollars. Maybe if you could blow fourteen grand on a watch and keep Hockney originals around for office decorations, you didn't think twice about giving eighty-five thousand to a total stranger with no credentials and a spotty past. Of course, you didn't get rich enough for the watch and the Hockneys by not thinking twice. Harold Bellis said, 'I'm sorry I couldn't be more help to you, Mr Cole, but I really have to see my client now.' He looked at my card again. 'May I keep this?'

'Sure. You can have a couple more, if you want. Pass'm out to your friends. I can use the work.'

Harold Bellis laughed politely and showed me to the door. The thin woman reappeared and led me back through the office and out to the lobby. I was hoping she'd walk me down to my car, but she didn't.

Outside, my car was still bracketed by the Rolls and the Mercedes, and gentlemen of indeterminate national origin were still going into Pierre's to buy three-hundred-dollar belts and twelve-hundred-dollar shoes. Slender women with shopping bags and tourists with cameras crowded the sidewalks, and foreign cars crept along the outside lanes, praying for a parking space. I had been inside maybe fifteen minutes and not much had changed, either with Beverly Hills or with what I knew, but I am nothing if not resourceful.

I fed quarters into the parking meter and waited. It was eleven twenty-five.

At sixteen minutes after noon, Harold Bellis came out of his building and walked north, probably off to a business lunch at a nearby restaurant. Eleven minutes later, his assistant, Martha, appeared out of the parking garage driving a late-model Honda Acura. She turned south.

I ran back across the street, rode the elevator up to Bellis's floor, and hurried up to the receptionist, giving her the Christ-my-day-is-going-to-hell smile. 'Hi. Martha said she'd leave my calendar with you.'

She gave confused. 'Excuse me?'

'When I was here this morning, I left my date book in Harry's office. I called and Martha said she'd leave it with you for me.'

The receptionist shook her head. 'I'm sorry, but she didn't.'

I gave miserable. 'Oh, man. I'm screwed. It's got all my appointments, and my account numbers. I guess it just slipped her mind. You think it'd be okay if I ran back there and checked?' I gave her expectant, and just enough of the little boy so that she'd know my fate in life rested squarely on her shoulders.

'Sure. You know the way?'

'I can find it.'

I went back past the assistants and the cubicles to Martha's office. It was open. I went in and closed the door, then looked over the files until I found the client index. It took maybe three minutes to find the client index and twenty seconds to find the Lester files.

The articles of incorporation of the Lester Corporation, a California corporation, were among the first documents bound in the Lester Corp files. The president of the Lester Corporation was listed as one Akeem D'Muere. D'Muere's address was care of The Law Offices of Harold Bellis, Attorney-at-Law. Sonofagun.

I flipped through the files and found records of the acquisitions of nine investment properties throughout the South Central Los Angeles area, as well as two properties in Los Feliz and an apartment building in Simi Valley. The purchases included two bars, a laundromat, and the pawnshop. The rest were residential. I guess the weasel-dust business pays.

The Premier Pawn Shop location was purchased nine months and two days prior to Charles Lewis Washington's death. There was a contract with a property management firm for six of the businesses, as well as receipts from contractors for maintenance and renovation work performed on seven of the businesses. Each property had a separate file. The Premier showed plumbing and electrical work, as well as a new heating and air conditioning unit, and there was also a receipt from something called Atlas Security Systems for the installation of an Autonomous Monitoring System, as well as a Perimeter Security Alarm. Similar systems had also been purchased for the two bars. I wasn't sure what an Autonomous Monitoring System was, but it sounded good. The cost of these things and their installation was $6,518.22, and there had been no mention of them in the police reports. Hmm.

I wrote down the phone number of Atlas Security Systems, then closed the file, and borrowed Martha's phone to call them. I told a guy named Mr Walters that I was a friend of Harold Bellis's, that I owned a convenience store in Laguna Niguel, and that I was thinking of installing a security system. I told him that Harold had recommended Atlas and something called an Autonomous Monitoring System, and I asked if he could explain it. Mr Walters could. He told me that the Autonomous Monitoring System was perfect for a convenience store or any other cash business, because it was an ideal way to keep an eye on employees who might steal from you. The AMS was a hidden video camera timed to go on and off during business hours, or whenever a motion sensor positioned to my specifications told it to. He gave me cost and service information, and then I thanked him and told him that I'd get in touch.

I hung up the phone, returned the files to their cabinets, left the door open as I had found it, then walked out past the receptionist and drove to my office.

As I drove, I thought about the video equipment.

No one shot at me on the way, but maybe they were saving that for later.

CHAPTER 16

When I got to my office at five minutes past one, there was a message on my machine from James Edward Washington, asking me to call. I did.

James Edward said, 'You know a taco stand called Raul's on Sixty-five and Broadway?'

'No.'

'Sixty-five and Broadway. I'm gonna be there in an hour with a guy who knows about what's going on. Ray came through.'

'I'll meet you there.'

I hung up, then called Joe Pike. He answered on the first ring. 'Pike.'

'I'm going to meet James Edward Washington at a place called Raul's on Sixty-five and Broadway in about one hour. He says he's got a guy who maybe knows something.'

'I'll be there.'

'There's more.' I told him about the Lester Corporation and Harold Bellis and the contract with Atlas Security. I told him about the video equipment.

Pike grunted. 'So Akeem D'Muere saw what happened to Charles Lewis.'

'It's possible.'

'And maybe it shows something different than the police report claims.'

'Yeah. But if that's the case, why doesn't Akeem use it to fry these guys? Why is he protecting them?'

Pike fell silent.

'Joe?'

'Watch your ass out there, Elvis. It's getting too hot for these guys to sit by. They're going to have to move.'

'Maybe that's how we finally crack this. Maybe we make it so hot that they've got to move, and when they move we'll see what they're doing.'

'Maybe. But maybe their idea of a move is to take us out.'

Nothing like a little inspiration.

Thirty-two minutes later I exited the freeway and turned north on Broadway past auto repair shops and take-out rib joints and liquor stores that had been looted in the riots and not yet rebuilt.

Raul's Taco was a cinderblock stand on the west side of Broadway between a service drive and an auto parts place that specialized in remanufactured transmissions. You ordered at a little screen window on one side of the stand, then you went around to the other side to wait for your food. There was a tiny fenced area by the pick-up window with a couple of picnic benches for your more elegant sit-down diners and a couple of little stand-up tables on the sidewalk for people in a rush. A large sign over the order window said WE HAVE SOUL-MAN TACOS. An hour before noon and the place was packed.

I drove up to Sixty-fourth, pulled a U-turn at the light, then swung back and parked at the curb in front of the transmission place. James Edward Washington and a young black guy maybe Washington's age were sitting across from each other at one of the picnic tables, eating tacos. The second guy was wearing a neon orange hat with the bill pointed backwards, heavy Ray Ban sunglasses, and a black Los Angeles Raiders windbreaker even though it was ninety degrees. Washington saw me and nodded toward the table. The other guy saw him nod and turned to watch me come over. He didn't look happy. Most of the other people in Raul's were watching me, too.

Guess they didn't get many white customers. Washington said, 'This is the guy Ray was talking about. Cool T, this is the detective.'

Cool T said, 'You say his name Elvis I thought he a brother.'

I said, 'I am. Amazing what a marcel and skin lightener will do, isn't it?'

Cool T shook his head and gave disgusted. 'And he think he funny, too.'

Cool T started to get up but Washington put a hand on his forearm and held him down. 'He's white, but he's trying to help about Lewis. That means he can be all the funny he wants.'

Cool T shrugged without looking at me. Aloof.

Washington took a taco wrapped in yellow paper out of the box and offered it to me. He said, 'This is a Soul-Man taco. These Mexicans grill up the meat and the peppers and put barbecue sauce on it. You like barbecue?'

'Sure.' I unwrapped the taco. The paper was soaked through with oil and barbecue sauce, but it smelled like a handful of heaven. The taco was two handmade corn tortillas deep-fried to hold their shape, and filled with meat and chili peppers and the barbecue sauce. The sauce was chunky with big rings of jalapeño and serrano peppers.

Cool T finished off the rest of his taco, then pointed out the peppers. 'It's pretty hot, you ain't used to it. They probably make one without the peppers, you ask.' He was showing a lot of teeth when he said it.

I took a bite, and then I took a second. It was delicious, but it wasn't very hot. I said, 'You think they'd give me more peppers?'

Cool T stopped showing the teeth and went sullen. Shown up by the white man.

Washington said, 'Cool T's been living on these streets

while I've been swabbing decks. He's seen what's going on.'

Cool T nodded.

'Okay. So what's Cool T know?' I finished my taco and eyed the box lustily. There were three more tacos in it. Washington made a little hand move that said help yourself. I did.

Cool T said, 'Those cops ain't cops no mo'. They just passin'.'

'What's that mean?'

'Mean they in business and they use the Eight-Deuce as what we call sales representatives.' He grinned when he said it.

I looked at Washington. 'Is this for real?'

Washington shrugged. 'That's what his girlfriend says.'

Cool T said, 'I friendly with this bitch used to live with a Gangster Boy.'

I said, 'Are you telling me that these officers are in the crack trade?'

Cool T nodded. 'They in the everything trade. Whatever the Eight-Deuce in, they in.' He selected another taco. 'Ain't been an Eight-Deuce home boy locked down in four or five months. Pigs take off the Rolling Sixties and the Eight-Trey Swans and all these other nigguhs, but not the Eight-Deuce. They look out for each other. They share the wealth.'

'The cops and the Eight-Deuce Gangster Boys.'

'Uh-hunh. They in business together.' He finished the taco and licked his fingers. 'Eight-Deuce point out the competition and the cops take it down. You wanna see it happen, I can put you onto something.'

'What?'

Cool T said. 'Nigguh been sellin' dope out a ice cream truck over by Witley Park. He at the park every Thursday and the park in Eight-Deuce turf and they tired of it. The cops going over there today to run him off.'

128

Washington said, 'I figured we could go over there and see what's what. I figure if it's our guys, maybe we can do something with it.'

I was liking Washington just fine. 'Okay.'

Cool T said, 'Not me. Anybody see me over there and something happen, I be meetin' up with Mr Drive-By.'

Cool T stood up. Washington held out his fist and Cool T brushed his own fist against it, back and top and sides, and then he walked away.

I looked at Washington. Well, well. 'You did okay.'

Washington nodded. Cool.

CHAPTER 17

When we walked out to the car, I saw Joe Pike parked at a fire hydrant a block and a half north. We made eye contact, and he shook his head. No one was following.

James Edward said, 'What're you looking at?'

'My partner.'

'You work with someone?' He was looking up Broadway.

'If you look for him like that, people will know someone's there.'

James Edward stopped looking and got into the car. I slid in after him. 'Use the mirror. Angle it so that you can see. He's in a red Jeep.'

James Edward did it. 'Why's he back there?'

'The men who killed your brother have been following me. He's there to follow the followers.'

James Edward readjusted the mirror and we pulled away. 'He any good?'

'Yes.'

'Are you?'

'I get lucky.'

James Edward settled back and crossed his arms. 'Luck is for chumps. Ray knows a couple of people and he asked them about you. He says you're a straight up dude. He says you get respect.'

'You can fool some of the people some of the time.'

James Edward shook his head and stared at the passing buildings. 'Bullshit. Any fool can buy a car, but you can't buy respect.'

I glanced over, but he was looking out at the streets.

James Edward Washington told me where to go and I went there and pretty soon we were on streets just like James Edward Washington's street, with neat single-family homes and American cars and preschool children jumping rope and riding Big Wheels. Older women sat on tiny porches and frowned because teenagers who should've been in school were sitting on the hood of a Bonneville listening to Ice Cube. The women didn't like the kids being on the Bonneville and they didn't like Ice Cube but they couldn't do anything about it. We drove, and after a while I knew we weren't just driving, we were taking a tour of James Edward Washington's life. He would say turn, and I would turn, and he would point with his chin and say something like *The girl I took to the prom used to live right there* or *Dude I knew named William Johnston grew up there and writes television now and makes four hundred thousand dollars every year and bought his mama a house in the San Gabriel Valley* or *My cousins live there. I was little, they'd come to my street and we'd trick-or-treat, and then I'd come back here with them and we'd do it all over again. The lady that lived right over there used to make caramel-dipped candy apples better'n anything you ever bought at the circus.*

We drove and he talked and I listened, and after a while I said, 'It has to be hard.'

He looked at me.

I said, 'There are a lot of good things here, but there are also bad things, and it's got to be hard growing up and trying not to let the bad things drag you down.'

He looked away from me. We rode for a little bit longer, and then he said, 'I guess I just want you to know that there's more to the people down here than a bunch of shiftless niggers sopping up welfare and killin' each other.'

'I knew that.'

'You think it, maybe, but you don't know it. You're down here right now cause a nigger got beaten to death. We're driving to a park where a nigger gonna be selling drugs and niggers gonna be buying. That's what you know. You see it on the news and you read it in the papers and that's all you know. I know there's people who work hard and pay taxes and read books and build model airplanes and dream about flying them and plant daisies and love each other as much as any people can love each other anywhere, and I want you to know that, too.'

'Okay.' He wasn't looking at me, and I wasn't looking at him. I guess we were embarrassed, the way men who don't know each other can get embarrassed. 'Thanks for telling me.'

James Edward Washington nodded.

'It's important.'

He nodded again. 'Turn here.'

At the end of the block was a playground with a basketball court and six goals, and, beyond the court, a softball diamond with a long shallow outfield. A few teenaged guys were on the court, but not many, and a guy in his early thirties was running wind sprints in the outfield, racing from second base to the far edge of the outfield, then walking back, then doing it all again. A row of mature elms stood sentry along the far perimeter of the outfield, then there was another street and more houses. A sky blue Sunny Day ice cream truck was parked at the curb in the shade of one of the elms and a tall guy in a Malcolm X hat was leaning against it with his arms crossed, watching the sprinter. He didn't look interested in selling ice cream.

James Edward Washington said, 'That's our guy.'

We turned away from the park, made the block, and came back to a side street that gave an unobstructed view of the basketball players and the outfield and the ice cream truck on the far street. I parked on the side street so we'd have an easy, eyes-forward view, and then I shut the engine. If the neighbors saw us sitting there, maybe they'd think we were scouting for the NBA.

Maybe eight or nine minutes later four guys in a white Bel Air turned onto the far street, slowed to a stop, and the guy with the X hat went over to them. One of the guys in the backseat of the Bel Air gave something to the X, and the X gave something to the guy in the Bel Air. Then the Bel Air drove away and the X went back to his leaning. A little bit later a kid on a bike rolled up the sidewalk, jumped the curb down to the street, and skidded to a stop. The kid and the X traded something, and the kid rode away. Washington said, 'Cool T better be giving it to us straight about those cops.'

I pointed at the X. 'He's here, isn't he?'

'He's here, but will the cops come, and if they come are they coming because they're cops or because they're working with the Eight-Deuce?'

'We'll find out.'

'Yes. I guess we will.' James Edward shifted in the seat, uncomfortable, but not because of the seat. 'They don't come and run this muthuhfuckuh off, maybe I'll do it myself.'

'Maybe I'll help you.'

Washington glanced at me and nodded.

A couple of minutes later Joe Pike came up along the sidewalk and squatted beside my window. I said, 'Joe Pike, this is James Edward Washington. James, this is my partner, Joe Pike.'

Pike canted his head to lock onto James Edward Washington and reached in through the window. You can't see his eyes behind the dark glasses, but it's always easy to tell where he's looking. His whole being sort of points in that direction, as if he were totally focused on you. James Edward took his hand, but stared at the tattoos. Most people do.

I told Pike about the X at the ice cream truck and what Cool T had said about Thurman's REACT team and their involvement with the Eight-Deuce Gangster Boys.

Pike nodded. 'Dees and his people are supposed to thump this guy?'

James Edward said, 'That's the word.'

Pike looked at the X. 'It's a long way across the playground to the ice cream truck. If Dees moves the action away from us, we've got too much ground to cover to catch up. We might lose them.'

I said, 'Why don't you set up on that side, and we'll stay here. If Dees moves that way, you've got them, and if he moves in this direction, we've got him.'

Pike stared behind us up the street, then twisted around and looked at the park. 'You feel it?'

'What?'

Pike shook his head. 'Doesn't feel right.'

He stepped away from the car and stood without moving for a time and then he walked away. I thought about what Joe had said. *They're going to have to make a move.*

James Edward watched Pike leave. 'He's sorta strange, huh?'

'You think?'

A few minutes later we saw Pike's Jeep pass the ice cream truck and turn away from the park. James Edward looked at me. 'You don't think he's strange?'

We moved deeper into the afternoon, and business was good for the man in the ice cream truck. Customers came by in cars and trucks and on motorcycles and bicycles and on foot. Some of the cars would slow as they passed and the X would stare and they would make the block a couple of times before they finally stopped and did their deal, but most folks drove up and stopped without hesitating. The X never hesitated, either. Any one of these people could've been undercover cops but no one seemed to take that into consideration. Maybe it didn't matter. Maybe business was so good and profits were so large that the threat of a bust was small relative to the potential gain. Or maybe the X just didn't care. Some people are like that.

Once, two young women pushing strollers came along the far sidewalk. The X made a big deal out of tipping his cap with a flourish and giving them the big smile. The women made a buy, too. The one who did the talking was pregnant. Washington rubbed his face with both hands and said, 'Oh, my Jesus.'

School let out. More players joined the basketball games. The guy running wind sprints stopped running, and the time crept past like a dying thing, heavy and slow and unable to rest.

James Edward twisted in the seat and said, 'How you stand this goddamn waiting?'

'You get used to it.'

'You used to be a cop?'

I shook my head. 'Nope. I was a security guard for a while, and then I apprenticed with a man named George Fieder. Before that I was in the Army.'

'How about that guy Pike?'

'Joe was a police officer. Before that, he was a Marine.'

James Edward nodded. Maybe thinking about it. 'You go to college?'

'I had a couple years, on and off. After the Army, it was tough to sit in a classroom. Maybe I'll go back one day.'

'If you went back, what would you study?'

I made a little shrug. 'Teacher, maybe.'

He smiled. 'Yeah. I could see you in a classroom.'

I spread my hands. 'What? You don't think there's a place for a thug in the fourth grade?'

He smiled, but then the smile faded. Across the park, a

girl who couldn't have been more than sixteen pulled her car beside the ice cream truck and bought a glassine packet. She had a pretty face and precisely cornrowed hair in a traditional African design. Washington watched the transaction, then put his forearms on his knees and said, 'Sitting here, seeing these brothers and sisters doing this, it hurts.'

'Yes, I guess it does.'

He shook his head. 'You aren't black. I see it, I see brothers and sisters turning their backs on the future. What's it to you?'

I thought about it. 'I don't see brothers and sisters. I don't see black issues. Maybe I should, but I don't. Maybe because I'm white, I can't. So I see what I can see. I see a pretty young girl on her way to being a crack whore. She'll get pregnant, and she'll have a crack baby, and there will be two lifetimes of pain. She'll want more and more rock, and she'll do whatever it takes to get it, and, over time, she'll contract AIDS. Her mother will hurt, and her baby will hurt, and she will hurt.' I stopped talking and I put my hands on the steering wheel and I held it for a time. 'Three lifetimes.'

Washington said, 'Unless someone saves her.'

I let go of the wheel. 'Yes, unless someone saves her. I see it the only way I can see it. I see it as people.'

Washington shifted in the bucket. 'I was gonna ask you why you do this, but I guess I know.'

I went back to watching the X.

James Edward Washington said, 'If I wanted to learn this private eye stuff, they got a school I could learn how to do it?'

James Edward Washington was looking at me with watchful, serious eyes. I said, 'You want to learn how to do this, maybe we can work something out.'

He nodded.

I nodded back at him, and then Floyd Riggens's sedan

turned onto the far street and picked up speed toward the ice cream truck.

I said, 'Camera in the glove box.'

Mark Thurman was in the front passenger seat and Pinkworth was in the backseat. The sedan suddenly punched into passing gear and the X jumped the chain-link fence and ran across the outfield toward the basketball court. He was pulling little plastic packs of something out of his pockets and dumping them as he ran.

James Edward opened the glove box and took out the little Canon Auto Focus I keep there. I said, 'You see how to work it?'

'Sure.'

'Use it.'

I started the Corvette and put it in gear in case the X led Riggens across the park toward us, but it didn't get that far. Riggens horsed the sedan over the curb and cut across the sidewalk at the far corner where there was no fence and aimed dead on at the running X and gunned it. The X tried to cut back, but when he did, Riggens swung the wheel hard over and pegged the brakes and then Riggens and Thurman and Pinkworth were out of the car. They had their guns out, and the X froze and put up his hands. Thurman stopped, but Riggens and Pinkworth didn't. They knocked the X down and kicked him in the ribs and the legs and the head. Riggens went down on one knee and used his pistol, slamming the X in the head while Pinkworth kicked him in the kidneys. Mark Thurman looked around as if he were frightened, but he didn't do anything to stop it. There were maybe a hundred people in the park, and everybody was looking, but they didn't do anything to stop it, either. Next to me, James Edward Washington snapped away with the little Canon.

Riggens and Pinkworth pulled the X to his feet, went through his pockets, then shoved him away. The X fell, and tried to get up, but neither his legs nor his arms were much use. His head was bleeding. Pinkworth said something sharp to Mark Thurman and Thurman walked back across the park, scooping up the little plastic envelopes. Riggens climbed the chain link and went into the ice cream truck and that's the last we saw of it because a burgundy metal-flake Volkswagen Beetle and a double-dip black Chevrolet Monte Carlo playing NWA so loud that it rocked the neighborhood pulled up fast next to us and three guys wearing ski masks got out, two from the backseat of the Monte Carlo and one from the passenger side of the Volkswagen. The guy from the Volkswagen was wearing a white undershirt maybe six sizes too small and baggy pants maybe forty sizes too big and was carrying what looked to be a Taurus 9mm semiautomatic pistol. The Taurus fit him just right. The first guy out of the Monte Carlo was tall and wearing a black duster with heavy Ray Ban Wayfarers under the ski mask and was carrying a sawed-off double-barrel 20-gauge. The second guy was short and had a lot of muscles stuffed into a green tee shirt that said LOUIS. He was holding an AK-47. All of the guns were pointed our way.

James Edward Washington made a hissing sound somewhere deep in his chest and the tall guy stooped over to point the double twenty through my window. He looked at me, then James Edward, and then he gestured with the double twenty. 'Get out the muthuhfuckin' car, nigger.'

James Edward got out of the car, and then the tall guy pointed the double twenty at me. 'You know what you gonna do?'

'Sure,' I said. 'Whatever you say.'

The tall guy smiled behind the ski mask. 'Tha's right. Keep doin' it, and maybe you see the sun set.'

CHAPTER 18

The guy with the Taurus brought James Edward Washington to the metal-flake Beetle and put him in the right front passenger seat. The Beetle's driver stayed where he was, and the guy with the Taurus got into the back behind Washington.

The guy in the long coat said, 'They gonna take off and you gonna follow them and we gonna follow you. You get outta line, they gonna shoot your nigger and I gonna shoot you. We hear each other on this?'

'Sure.'

'M'man Bone Dee gonna ride with you. He say it, you do it. We still hear each other?'

'Uh-huh.' While the tall guy told me, the shorter guy in the Louis Farrakhan tee shirt walked around and got into my car. When he walked he held the AK down along his leg, and when he got in, he sort of held the muzzle pointed at the floorboard. The AK was too long to point at me inside the car. The guy in the long coat went back to the Monte Carlo and climbed into the back. There were other guys in there, but the windows were heavily tinted and you couldn't see them clearly. If Pike was here, he might be able to see them, but Pike was probably on the other side of the park, still watching the cops. But maybe not.

Bone Dee said, 'You got a gun?'

'Left shoulder.'

Bone Dee reached across and came up with the Dan Wesson. He didn't look under my jacket when he did it and he didn't look at the Dan Wesson after he had it. He stared at me, and he kept staring even after he had the Dan Wesson.

I said, 'I always thought the AK was overrated, myself. Why don't you buy American and carry an M-16?'

More of the staring.

I said, 'You related to Sandra Dee?'

He said, 'Keep it up, we see whether this muthuh-fuckuh overrated or not.'

No sense of humor.

The Beetle started rolling and the guy in the shotgun seat of the Monte Carlo motioned me out. I tucked in behind the Bug and the Monte Carlo eased in behind me. I stayed close to the Beetle, and the Monte Carlo stayed close to me, too close for another car to slip between us. There was so much heavy-bass gangster rap coming out of the Monte Carlo, they shouldn't have bothered. No one would come within a half mile for fear of hearing loss.

We went west for a couple of blocks, then turned south, staying on the residential streets and avoiding the main thoroughfares. As we drove, Bone Dee looked through the glove box and under the seats and came up with the Canon. 'Thought you liked to buy American?'

'It was a gift.'

Bone Dee popped open the back, exposed the film, then smashed the lens on the AK's receiver and threw the camera and the exposed film out the window. So much for visual evidence.

The Bug drove slowly, barely making school zone speeds, and staying at the crown of the street, forcing oncoming cars to the side. Rolling in attack mode. Kids on their way home from school clutched their books tight to their chests and other kids slipped down driveways to get behind cars or between houses in case the shooting would start and women on porches with small children hurried them indoors. You could see the fear and the resignation, and I thought what a helluva way it must be to live like this. *Does South Central look like America to you?* A short, bony man in his seventies was standing shirtless in his front yard with a garden hose in one hand and a can of Pabst Blue Ribbon in the other. He glared at the guys in the Bug and then the guys in the Monte Carlo. He puffed out his skinny chest and raised the hose and the Pabst out from his sides, showing hard, letting them have him if they had the balls to take him and saying it didn't scare him one goddamn bit. Dissing them. Showing disrespect. An AK came out of the Volkswagen and pointed at him but the old man didn't back down. Hard, all right. We turned again and the AK disappeared. With all the people running and hiding, I began to think that running and hiding was a pretty good idea. I could wait until we were passing a cross street, then backfist Bone Dee, yank the wheel, and probably get away, but that wouldn't work too well for James Edward Washington. Not many places to hide inside a Volkswagen Beetle.

Two blocks shy of Martin Luther King Boulevard we turned into an alley past a '72 Dodge with no rear wheels and stopped at a long, low unpainted cinderblock building that probably used to be an auto repair shop. The alley ran behind a row of houses along to a train track that probably hadn't been used since World War II. Most of the railroad property was overgrown with dead grass, and undeveloped except for the cinderblock building. The houses all had chain-link fences, and many had nice vegetable gardens with tomato plants and okra and snap beans, and most of the fences were overgrown with running vines so the people who lived there wouldn't have to see what happened in the alley. Pit bulls stood at the back fences of two of the houses and watched us with small, hard eyes. Guess the pit bulls didn't mind seeing what happened. Maybe they even liked it.

The guy in the long coat got out of the Monte Carlo and

went to one of four metal garage doors built into the building and pushed it open. No locks. There were neither cars nor signs nor other evidence of human enterprise outside the building, but maybe inside was different. Maybe this was the Eight-Deuce clubhouse, and inside there would be pool tables and a soda fountain and clean-cut kids who looked like the Jackson family playing old Chubby Checker platters and dancing like the white man. Sure. Welcome to The Killing Zone.

When the door was open the Bug drove into the building.

Bone Dee said, 'Follow him.'

I followed. The Monte Carlo came in after me and then the guy in the long coat stepped through and pulled the door down. Nothing inside, either. The building was as empty and as uncluttered as a crypt.

When the door was down Bone Dee reached over, turned off the ignition, and took the keys. The guy in the long coat came over with the double-barreled twenty. There were no lights and no windows in the place, and the only illumination came from six industrial skylights built into the roof. No one had washed the skylights since they had been installed, so the light that came down was filtered and dirty and it was hard to see. One of the skylights was broken.

The guy in the coat made a little come-here finger gesture with his free hand and said, 'Get outta there, boy.'

I got out. Bone Dee got out with me.

The guy in the coat said, 'I like that old Corvette. You get dead, can I have it?'

'Sure.'

He ran his hand along the fender as if it were something soft, and would appreciate tenderness.

The doors on the Beetle opened and the two guys in there got out with James Edward Washington and pushed him toward me. The Monte Carlo opened up at the same time and three guys came out of there, two from the front and one from the back. The guy from the Monte Carlo's backseat was holding a Benelli combat shotgun and the two from the front were carrying AKs like Bone Dee. The guy who'd been in the backseat of the Beetle had put away the Taurus and come up with an old M-1 carbine. You count the double twenty and figure for handguns, and these guys were packing serious hurt. I spent fourteen months in Vietnam on five-man reconnaissance patrols, and we didn't carry this much stuff. Of course, we lost the war.

I said, 'Okay, are you guys going to give up now or do I have to kick some ass?'

Nobody laughed. James Edward Washington shifted his weight from foot to foot and looked as tight as a hand-me-down shirt. A fine sheen of sweat slicked his forehead and the skin beneath his eyes, and he watched the Monte Carlo like he expected something worse to get out. Something worse did.

A fourth guy slid out of the back of the Monte Carlo with the lethal grace of an African panther. He was maybe a half inch shorter than me, but with very wide shoulders and very narrow hips and light yellow skin, and he looked like he was moving in slow motion even though he wasn't. There was a tattoo on the left side of his neck that said *Blood Killer* and a scar on the left side of his face that started behind his eye, went back to his ear, then trailed down the course of his cheek to his jaw. Knife scar. He was wearing a white silk dress shirt buttoned to the neck and black silk triple-pleated pants and he looked, except for the scar, as if he had stepped out of a Melrose fashion ad in *Los Angeles Magazine*. Bone Dee handed him the Dan Wesson. The other three guys were watching me but were watching the fourth guy, too, like maybe he'd say jump and they'd race to see who could jump the highest. I said, 'You Akeem D'Muere?'

D'Muere nodded like it was nothing and looked at the Dan Wesson, opening the chamber, checking the loads, then closing the chamber. 'This ain't much gun. I got a nine holds sixteen shots.'

'It gets the job done.'

'I guess it does.' He hefted the Dan Wesson and lined up the sights on my left eye. 'What's your name?'

'Elvis Cole.'

'What you doin' here?'

'My buddy and I were looking for a guy named Clement Williams for stealing a 1978 Nissan Stanza.' Maybe a lie would help.

Akeem D'Muere cocked the Dan Wesson. 'Bullshit.' Nope. Guess a lie wasn't going to help.

I said, 'Why'd you force the Washington family to drop their wrongful-death suit against the LAPD?'

He decocked the Dan Wesson and lowered it. 'How much you know?'

I shook my head.

D'Muere said, 'We see.' He wiggled the Dan Wesson at Bone Dee and the other guy with an AK. 'Get on this fool.'

Bone Dee hit the backs of my knees with his AK and the other guy rode me down and knelt on my neck. Bone Dee knelt on my legs. The guy on my neck twisted my head around until I was looking up, then put the muzzle of his AK under my ear. It hurt.

Akeem D'Muere stood over me. 'It be easy to kill you, but easy ain't always smart. The people I know, they say you got friends at LAPD and you turnin' up dead maybe make'm mad, maybe make things even worse.'

Something moved across the skylights. Pike, maybe.

'Still, I can't let you keep runnin' around, you see? Things gettin' outta hand and they got to stop. *You* got to stop. You see that?'

'Sure.' It was hard to breathe with the guy on my back.

Akeem D'Muere shook his head. 'You say that, but it just talk, so I gotta show you how things are.' Akeem D'Muere went over to James Edward Washington, touched the Dan Wesson to James Edward's left temple, and pulled the trigger. The explosion hit me like a physical thing and the right side of James Edward Washington's face blew out and he collapsed to the concrete floor as if he were a mechanical man and someone had punched his off button. He fell straight down, and when his face hit the cement, a geyser of blood sprayed across the floor and splattered onto my cheeks.

I went as stiff and tight as a bowstring and pushed against the men on my back but I could not move them. James Edward Washington trembled and twitched and jerked on the floor as a red pool formed under his head. His body convulsed and something that looked like red tapioca came out of his mouth. The guy in the long coat who had opened and closed the big door went over to James Edward and squatted down for a closer look. He said, 'Look at this shit.'

The convulsing peaked, and then the body grew still.

Akeem D'Muere came back, squatted beside me, and opened the Dan Wesson's chamber. He shook out the remaining cartridges, then wiped down the Dan Wesson and dropped it next to me. He said, 'The fuckin' bitch next. She started this.'

I blinked hard five or six times, and then I focused on him. It was hard to focus and hard to hear him, and I tried to think of a way to shake off the men on my back and get to him before the AKs got to me.

Akeem D'Muere smiled like he knew what I was thinking, and like it didn't really worry him, like even if I tried, and even if I got out from under the men and past the AKs, he still wouldn't be worried. He looked over at the others. 'You got the keys?'

Bone Dee said, 'Yeah,' and held up my keys.

Akeem sort of jerked his head and Bone Dee went to the guy with the carbine and they went out of my field of view to my car.

Maybe thirty seconds later Bone Dee came back and Akeem D'Muere went over to James Edward Washington's body. He touched the body with his toe, then shook his head and looked at me. 'Don't matter none. This just another dead nigger.'

I tried to say something, but nothing came out.

Akeem D'Muere turned away. 'Let's get the fuck out of here.'

Bone Dee and the guy with the carbine got back into the Volkswagen and Akeem D'Muere and the guy with the Benelli riot gun went to the Monte Carlo. The guy on my shoulders stayed there and another guy with an AK went to the Monte Carlo and stood by the open passenger door, ready to cover me. The tall guy with the double twenty opened the big doors. When he did, something outside made a loud BANG and the tall guy was kicked back inside and Joe Pike came through fast, diving low and rolling toward the Volkswagen, then coming up and snapping off one shot at the guy on my shoulders and two shots through the Volkswagen's driver's-side window. The bangs were loud and would've been Pike's .357. The first bullet rolled the guy off my shoulders and the two in the Volkswagen pushed the driver over into the passenger side on top of Bone Dee. Pike yelled, 'Down.'

I stayed down.

The guy standing guard by the Monte Carlo dove into the open passenger door, and the big Benelli came out over the top of him and cut loose, putting most of its pellets into the Volkswagen. Pike popped two fast shots at the Monte Carlo, and then the Monte Carlo roared to life and fishtailed its right rear into the Volkswagen and then into the side of the garage door and then it was gone.

I ran forward and pulled Bone Dee out of the VW. The

driver was dead. Bone Dee screamed when I grabbed him and yelled that he'd been shot and I told him I didn't give a damn. I pushed him down on the cement and made sure he wasn't armed and then I went to James Edward Washington but James Edward Washington was dead. 'Jesus Christ.'

Pike said, 'You okay?'

I shook my head. I took a deep breath and let it out and then I began to shake.

Pike said, 'We're going to have company.' He put his Python down carefully, so as not to mar the finish. 'You hear them?'

'Yes.'

I think Pike heard them before me, but maybe not. The sirens came in from both sides of the alley and then people were yelling and two cops I'd never seen before leapfrogged through the door. They were in street clothes and were carrying shotguns, and one took up a position in the doorway and the other rolled in and came up behind the Volkswagen's left front fender, much as Pike had. They screamed POLICE when they made their advance and told us to put down our weapons. Habit. Our weapons were already down. I said, 'Guy by the Volkswagen is wounded. The other three are dead.'

A third cop appeared in the opposite side of the door with another shotgun. 'Keep your hands away from your body and get down on the ground. Do it *now*.' He had long hair tied back with a blue bandana.

Pike and I did what they said, but they came in hard anyway, like we knew they would, one of them going to Pike and one of them coming to me and the third going to Bone Dee. The one who went to Bone Dee was short. More cars pulled up outside, and you could hear the *whoop-whoop* of the paramedics on their way in.

The cop who came to me put his knee into my back and twisted my hands around behind me and fit me with cuffs. You get knees in your back twice at the same crime scene, and you know it's not shaping up as a good day. I said, 'My wallet's on the floorboard of the Corvette. My name is Elvis Cole. I'm a private investigator. I'm one of the good guys.'

The cop with the bandana said, 'Shut the fuck up.'

They cuffed Pike and they cuffed Bone Dee and then the short cop said, 'I got the keys,' and went to my Corvette. The cop with the bandana went with him. They moved with clarity and purpose.

The other cop picked up my wallet and looked through it. He said, 'Hey, the sonofabitch wasn't lying. He's got an investigator's license.'

The cop with the bandana said, 'Not for long.'

A couple of bluesuits came in and said, 'Everything cool?'

The cop with the bandana said, 'We'll see.'

The short cop fumbled with the keys, then opened the trunk and made one of the world's widest grins. You'd think he'd won Lotto. 'Bingo. Just where they said.' He reached into the trunk and pulled out a baggie of crack cocaine worth about eight thousand dollars and tossed it to the cop with the bandana. What Bone Dee and the guy with the carbine had been doing behind me.

I looked at Joe Pike and Pike's mouth twitched.

I said, 'It isn't mine.' I pointed at Bone Dee. 'It's his.'

The cop with the bandana said, 'Sure. That's what they all say.' Then he took out a little white card, told us we were under arrest, and read us our rights.

After that he brought us to jail.

CHAPTER 19

The cop with the bandana was named Micelli. He put Pike into a gray sedan and me into a black-and-white, and then they drove us to the Seventy-seventh. Micelli rode in the sedan.

The Seventy-seventh Division is a one-story red brick building just off Broadway with diagonal curbside parking out front and a ten-foot chain-link fence around the sides and back. The officers who work the Double-seven park their personal cars inside the fence and hope for the best. Concertina wire runs along the top of the fence to keep out the bad guys, but you leave personal items in your car at your own risk. Your car sort of sits there at your own risk, too. The bad guys have been known to steal the patrol cars.

We turned through a wide chain-link gate and rolled around the back side of the building past the maintenance garage and about two dozen parked black-and-whites and up to an entry they have for uniformed officers and prospective felons. Micelli got out first and spoke with a couple of uniformed cops, then disappeared into the building. The uniforms brought us inside past the evidence lockers and went through our pockets and took our wallets and our watches and our personal belongings. They did me first, calling off the items to an overweight property sergeant who noted every item on a large manila envelope, and then they did Pike. When they did Pike, they pulled off the hip holster for his .357, the ankle holster for his .380, an eight-inch Buck hunting knife, four speed-loaders for the .357, and two extra .380 magazines. The overweight sergeant said, 'Jesus Christ, you expecting a goddamned war?'

The uniform who did Pike grinned. 'Look who it is.'

The sergeant opened Pike's wallet, then blinked at Pike. 'Jesus Christ. You're him.'

The uniformed cop took off Pike's sunglasses and handed them to the sergeant. Pike squinted at the suddenly bright light, and I saw for the first time in months how Pike's eyes were a deep liquid blue. My friend Ellen Lang says that there is a lot of hurt in the blue, but I have never been able to see it. Maybe he just hides it better with me. Maybe she sees his eyes more often than I.

Micelli came back as they were finishing and I said, 'Play this one smart, Micelli. There's a detective sergeant in North Hollywood named Poitras who'll vouch for us, and an assistant DA named Morris who'll back Poitras up. Give'm a call and let's get this straight.'

Micelli signed the property forms. 'You got connections, that what you telling me?'

'I'm telling you these guys know us, and they'll know we've been set up.'

Micelli grinned at the property sergeant. 'You ever hear that before, Sarge? You ever hear a guy we're bringing in say he was set up?'

The sergeant shook his head. 'No way. I've never heard that before.'

I said, 'For Christ's sake, Micelli, check me out. It's a goddamned phone call.'

Micelli finished signing the forms and glanced over at me. 'Listen up, pogue. I don't care if you've been hamboning the goddamned mayor. You're mine until I say otherwise.' He gave the clipboard to the property sergeant, and then he told the uniforms to bring us to interrogation. He walked away.

Pike said, 'Cops.'

The uniforms brought us through a heavy metal door and into a long sterile hall that held all the charm of a urinal in a men's room. There were little rooms on either side of the hall, and they put Pike into the first room and me into the second. The rooms sported the latest in interrogation-room technology with pus-yellow walls and water-stained acoustical ceilings and heavy-duty sound-proofing so passing liberals couldn't hear the rubber hoses being worked. There was a small hardwood table in the center of the floor with a single straight-backed metal chair on either side of it. Someone had used a broken pencil to cut a message into the wall. *In interrogation, no one can hear you scream.* Cop, probably. Detainees weren't allowed pencils.

They kept me waiting for maybe an hour, then Micelli and a cop in a gray suit came in. The new cop was in his late forties and looked to be a detective lieutenant, probably working out of homicide. Micelli took the chair across the table from me and the guy in the suit leaned against the wall. Micelli said, 'This conversation is being recorded. My name is Detective Micelli, and this is Lieutenant Stilwell.' You see? 'I'm going to ask you questions, and your answers will be used in court. You don't have to answer these questions, and if you want a lawyer, but can't afford one, we can arrange for a public defender. You want someone?'

'No.'

Micelli nodded. 'Okay.'

'Did you call Poitras?'

Micelli leaned forward. 'No one's calling anyone until we get through this.'

Stilwell said, 'How do you know Lou Poitras?'

Micelli waved his hand. 'That doesn't mean shit. What's it matter?'

'I want to know.'

I told him about me and Poitras.

When I finished, Stilwell said, 'Okay, but what were you doing down here?'

'I got a tip that a REACT cop named Eric Dees is involved with a gangbanger named Akeem D'Muere and I'm trying to find out how.'

Micelli grinned. Stilwell said, 'You got proof?'

'A guy named Cool T gave me the tip. He was a friend of James Edward Washington. Washington is one of the dead guys.'

Micelli said, 'That's fuckin' convenient.'

'Not for Washington.'

Micelli said, 'Yeah, well, we got a little tip, too. We got tipped that an asshole fitting your description and driving your car was down here trying to move a little Mexican brown to the natives. We got told that the deal was going down in an abandoned building off the tracks, and we went over there, and guess what?'

'Who gave you the tip, Micelli? Dees? One of the REACT guys?'

Micelli licked the corner of his mouth and didn't say anything.

I said, 'Check it out. Twenty minutes ago I saw Akeem D'Muere put a gun to James Edward Washington's head and pull the trigger. I'm working for a woman named Jennifer Sheridan. Akeem D'Muere has a mad on for her, and he said that she's next.'

Stilwell crossed his arms. 'Two of the dead men found in the garage were named Wilson Lee Hayes and Derek La Verne Dupree. Both of these guys had a history of trafficking in narcotics. Maybe you were down here to meet them and the deal went bad. Maybe you and your buddy Pike tried to rip those guys off.'

I spread my hands.

Micelli said, 'You own a 1966 Corvette?' He gave me the license number.

'Yeah.'

'How come there was a half kilo of crack in the trunk?'

'Akeem D'Muere's people put it there.'

'They dumped eight thousand dollars' worth of dope, just to set you up?'

'I guess it was important to them.'

'Eight-Deuce Gangster Boys buy and sell dope, they don't give it away. No profit in it.'

'Maybe it wasn't theirs. Maybe Dees gave it to them. Maybe it came from the LAPD evidence room.'

Micelli leaned forward across the table and gave me hard. 'You're holding out for nothing. Your buddy's already come clean.'

'Pike?'

Micelli nodded. 'Yeah. He gave it to us. He said you guys found a connection for the dope. He said you thought you could turn the trick with the Eight-Deuce for a little extra cash. He said that after you set the deal you got the idea that you could just rip these guys off, then you'd have the cash and the dope. Maybe sell it three or four times. Really screw the niggers.'

I gave them the laugh. 'You guys are something Micelli.'

Stilwell said, 'If you don't like our take on it, how about yours?'

I gave it to them. I told them about Mark Thurman and Eric Dees and Charles Lewis Washington. I described how I had been followed, and how Pike and I had boxed Riggens and Pinkworth at the Farmer's Market. I told them about Dees warning me off. I told them about the meeting with Cool T, and Cool T putting us onto the park, and the Eight-Deuce Gangster Boys lying in wait for us. Micelli squirmed around while I said it, like maybe he was bored with the nonsense, but Stilwell listened without moving. When I ran out of gas, Stilwell fingered his tie and said, 'So you're saying that Dees set you up to get you out of the way.'

'Yeah.'

'Why doesn't he just bump you?'

'Maybe he knows that if I get bumped, guys like Joe Pike and Lou Poitras will stay with it, and he doesn't want that. He wants to buy time so he can regain control of things.'

'But if he gets you jugged, he's got to know you're going to talk. He's got to know we're going to call him in and ask him about it.'

I said, 'He knows I'm going to be sitting here with a guy like Micelli. He knows I can't prove anything and all it looks like is that I'm trying to dodge the charge. If I'm alive, he's still got control. If I'm dead, guys like Pike and Poitras are a couple of loose cannons.'

Micelli made a big deal out of throwing up his hands. 'He's wasting our time with this crap. I got tickets to the Dodgers tonight. I want to get there before the stretch.'

I said, 'Listen to me, Stilwell. D'Muere said he's going for the girl. Even if you guys don't buy my end of it, send a car around to her apartment. What's that cost you?'

Stilwell stared at me another couple of seconds. Then he pushed away from the wall. 'Finish up, Paul.' Then he left.

Micelli and I stayed in the interrogation room for another hour. I would go through my story and then Micelli would ask me who was my connection and how much was I going to get for the dope, as if I had said one story but he had heard another. Then he would have me go through my story again. The room was bugged and there were probably a couple of guys listening in. They would be taking notes and a tape recorder would be recording everything I said. They'd be looking for discrepancies and Micelli would be waiting for my body language to change. He'd keep trying out scenarios until I seemed comfortable with one, even if it was one I denied. Then he'd know he struck pay dirt. Of course, since I was telling the truth, he wasn't going to get the body language when and where he wanted it. He probably wasn't too concerned about that, though. Time was on his side. Maybe I shouldn't have passed on the lawyer.

After about the sixth time through, the door opened and Stilwell came back, only this time Eric Dees was with him. Micelli said, 'You been listening to this stuff?'

Dees grinned. 'Yeah. He's pretty good at this.'

Stilwell said, 'You arrest the guy in the park?'

Dees nodded. 'Sure. He's down in cell four.'

'Cole said you ripped off his dope.'

Dees smiled wider. 'Gathered it for evidence, duly logged and checked in.'

I said, 'Come off it, Stilwell. He knew I was going to be in here. He knew I was going to be talking.'

Stilwell stayed with Dees. 'You got anything going with these gangbangers?'

Dees spread his hands. 'Trying to bust'm. Cole's been nosing around and I tried to warn him off and maybe that's when he got the idea for the dope deal. I don't know. I don't want to talk about an ongoing investigation in front of a suspected felon.'

Stilwell said, 'Sure.'

Dees said, 'I've got to go wrap it up with my guys. You need anything else?'

'That's it, Eric. Thanks.'

Dees left without looking at me.

I said, 'Jesus Christ, Stilwell, what do you expect him to say?'

'Just about what he said.'

'Then what are you going to do about it?'

Stilwell grabbed my upper arm and lifted. 'Book you on three murder counts and a dope. I think you're guilty as sin.'

CHAPTER 20

They took me out into the detectives' squad room and began the booking process. Dees wasn't around, and after Micelli spoke to a couple of uniforms, he and Stilwell left.

The processing cops had already begun with Pike and, as I watched, they used paraffin on his hands and took his picture and fingerprinted him and asked him questions so that they could fill out their forms. He nodded once and I nodded back. It was strange to see him without the glasses. He seemed more vulnerable without them. Less inviolate. Maybe that's why he wears them.

They led Pike away through a hall toward the jail and then they started with me. A uniform cop named Mertz led me from station to station, first using the paraffin, then getting my prints, and then taking my picture. I crossed my eyes when they took the picture and the cop who worked the camera said, 'No good, Mertz. He crossed his goddamned eyes.'

Mertz picked up a baton and tapped it against his thigh. 'Okay, smart ass. Cross'm again and I'll smack you so hard they'll stay crossed.'

They took the picture again but this time I didn't cross them.

When Mertz was filling out my personal history form, I said, 'When do I get a bail hearing?'

'Arraignment's tomorrow. One of the detectives ran over to the court to get a bail deviation so we could bind you over.'

'Jesus Christ. Why?'

'You see the crowding down there? You're lucky they'll arraign you by next Monday.'

When the processing was finished, Mertz turned me over to an older uniform with a head like a chayote squash and told him to take me to felony. The older uniform led me back along a hall to a row of four-by-eight-foot cages. Each cage had a seatless toilet and a sink and a couple of narrow bunks, and it smelled of disinfectant and urine and sweat, sort of like a poorly kept public men's room. 'No place like home.'

The older uniform nodded. Maybe to him it was home.

There were two black guys in the first cage, both of them sitting in the shadows of the lower bunk. They had been talking softly when we approached, but they stopped when we passed and watched us with yellow eyes. Once you were in the cells, there was no way to see who was in the next cell, and no way to reach through the bars and twist your arm around to touch someone in the next cell, even if someone in the next cell was reaching out to touch you. I said, 'Which one's mine?'

The uniform stopped at the second cell, opened the gate, and took off my handcuffs. 'The presidential suite, of course.'

I stepped in. A Hispanic guy in his early thirties was lying on the lower bunk with his face to the wall. He rolled over and squinted at me, and then he rolled back. The uniform closed the gate and locked it and said, 'You wanna make a call?'

'Yeah.'

He walked back down the hall and out the heavy door and was gone. One of the black guys in the cell next to me said something and the other laughed. Someone in one of the cells on the other side of me coughed. I could hear voices, but they sounded muted and far away. I said, 'Joe.'

Pike's voice came back. 'Fourth cell.'

Someone yelled, 'I'm trying to sleep, goddamn it. Shut the fuck up.' It was a big voice, loud and deep, and sounded as if it had come from a big man. It also sounded about as far away as Joe Pike.

I said, 'D'Muere said he's going for Jennifer Sheridan.'

Joe said, 'Dees wouldn't go for that.'

'Dees may not know. D'Muere wasn't talking like a guy who was worried about what Eric Dees thought.'

The big voice yelled, 'Goddamn it, I said shut up. I don't want to hear about your goddamn –' There was a sharp meat-on-meat sound and the voice stopped. Joe continued, 'Maybe he isn't. Maybe things aren't the way we were told.'

'You mean, maybe they aren't partners.'

Pike said, 'Maybe Dees is an employee. Maybe D'Muere is the power, and Eric Dees is just trying to control him. Maybe putting us in here is part of that.'

'Only maybe while we're in, Jennifer Sheridan gets offed.'

Pike said nothing.

The heavy door opened and the cop with a squash for a head came back pushing a phone that was bolted to a kind of a tripod thing on heavy rollers. The cop pushed it down to my cell and parked it close enough for me to reach the buttons. 'You can make as many calls as you want, but it won't take long distance, okay?'

'Sure.'

He went out and left the door ajar because of the phone cable.

I called Marty Beale's direct line and a male voice answered. It wasn't Marty, and it wasn't Jennifer Sheridan. 'Watkins, Okum, & Beale. Mr Beale's office.'

'Jennifer Sheridan, please.'

'She didn't come in today. May I take a message?'

'I'm a friend, and it's important that I speak with her. Do you know where I can reach her?'

'I'm sorry, sir. I'm an office temp, and I didn't get here until this afternoon.'

'Do you know why she didn't come in?'

'I'm sorry, sir.'

I hung up and called Jennifer Sheridan's apartment. On the third ring, the phone machine answered. After it beeped, I said, 'It's Elvis. If you're there, pick up.'

No one picked up.

I called Lou Poitras. A woman's voice answered, 'Detectives.'

'Lou Poitras, please.'

'He's out. You want to leave a message?'

'How about Charlie Griggs?'

'Hold on.' I heard her ask somebody in the background about Griggs. She came back on the line. 'He's with Poitras. You want to leave a message or not?'

I hung up and leaned against the bars. 'She didn't go to work and she's not at home.'

Pike said, 'Could mean anything.'

'Sure.' Mr Optimism.

'We could help her.'

'In here?'

Pike said, 'No. Not in here.'

'Joe.' I knew what he was saying.

'Wait.'

The cop with the squash head came back for the phone, and forty minutes after that the heavy door opened again and in came the squash with a Hispanic cop sporting a flattop crew cut. The squash said, 'You guys are going to be bused over to County. On your feet.'

You could hear the men in the cells coming off their bunks.

The squash went down the row, unlocking the doors and telling the prisoners to step out into the hall. When the squash got down to Pike's cell, he said, 'What in hell happened to you?'

160

The big voice said, 'Fell.'

Pike was three people behind me.

They lined us up and led us down another corridor past the booking area. The young Hispanic cop brought up the rear.

We went down another short hall and then out into a kind of outdoor alcove. Two uniformed cops were walking into the maintenance building to our right and a third uniformed cop was coming in from the parking lot to our left. A large blue bus that said SHERIFF on the side was parked maybe sixty feet away. The deputy sheriff who drove the thing was talking to a guy in the maintenance building. The cop coming in from the parking lot walked past us and went inside through the same door that we had just come out of. The deputy sheriff yelled, 'Hey, Volpe,' and went into the maintenance building. Pike said, 'Now,' then stepped out of the line and launched a roundhouse kick into the side of the Hispanic cop's head. The Hispanic cop went down. The squash heard it and turned and I hit him two fast straight rights low on the jaw, and he went down, too. The Hispanic guy who had shared my cell said, 'The fuck you guys doing?' He looked surprised.

The black guys with the yellow eyes held on to each other and smiled. The big guy who'd been with Pike said, 'Fuckin' A,' and ran to the right past the maintenance building and toward the front gate. Two other guys ran after him. Pike and I went to the left through the parking lot, keeping low and moving toward the street. We made the fence just as men began shouting. The fence ran back along the side of the building past a trash dumpster and maybe half a dozen fifty-five-gallon oil drums and a motorcycle that looked like somebody's personal property. We followed the fence back toward the oil drums, and pretty soon we were on the side of the building. The shouts got louder and there were the sounds of men running, but all of the noise seemed behind us.

We went up onto an oil drum, chinned ourselves to the roof, then jumped back across the concertina wire to the street. A couple of kids on mountain bikes watched us with big eyes.

We walked toward the houses just as an alarm buzzer went off at the police station. An older man rocking on a porch stood and looked at us. 'What's going on?'

I told him they were running tests.

We stayed on the street until he couldn't see us, and then we cut between two houses and started to run.

Somewhere behind us, there came the sound of sirens.

CHAPTER 21

We went over fences and through vegetable gardens and between houses. We checked each street for police, then crossed steadily and with purpose as if two white guys on foot were an everyday thing in South Central Los Angeles. Twice we had to pull back between houses for passing patrol units, and once we surprised an elderly woman coming out of her home with a basket of wet laundry. I gave her my best Dan Aykroyd. 'Gas company. We've had reports of a leak.' The Aykroyd works every time.

We moved from her yard to the next, and worked our way north.

More black-and-whites roared past, and sirens that started far away drew close. The cops knew that anybody who made it through the gates would be on foot, so they'd concentrate their people within a close radius. More and more cops would flood into the surrounding streets, and pretty soon there would be helicopters. Pike said, 'We need wheels.'

'They impounded my car. You think they got the Jeep?'

'I was on the next street over. They didn't know about it.'

'That makes it, what, ten or twelve blocks from here? Might as well be in Fresno.'

Pike said, 'If we have limits, they are self-imposed.' Always count on Pike for something like that.

Two black-and-whites sped east on Florence under the freeway. After they passed, we trotted west into an Arco station that had one of those little Minimart places. A couple of cars sat at the pumps, and a Hostess delivery van sat at the Minimart. A young black guy in his early twenties got out of the van with a box of baked goods and went into the Minimart. Pike said, 'Wheels.'

'Maybe he'll give us a ride.'

Pike frowned.

The delivery guy came out of the Minimart, threw his box into the van, and climbed in after it. I went up to his window and said, 'Excuse me. We need a lift about ten blocks west of here. Think you could help?'

The delivery guy said, 'Hey, sure. No problem.'

Only in L.A.

Maybe ten minutes later he dropped us off at Joe Pike's Cherokee. Joe keeps a spare key duct-taped to the inside of the front fender. He found it, unlocked the cab, and we climbed inside. Joe dug under the dash and came out with a plastic bag containing five hundred dollars in cash, a driver's license that said his name was Fred C. Larson, a Visa card in the same name, and a Walther TPH .22-caliber pocket gun. *Be prepared.*

I said, 'Fred?'

Pike headed toward the freeway. 'They'll cover our houses and our businesses.'

'We don't go home. We try for Jennifer Sheridan. We've got to get her off the street before D'Muere finds her.'

'Where does she live?'

I told him. Pike drove quickly, and neither of us spoke during the ride.

We parked in front of her building maybe forty minutes later and pressed her call button, but no one answered. We pressed more buttons until someone finally buzzed open the glass door and we went up to the third floor.

We were knocking on her door when a woman with two small children came out of the apartment across the hall. The woman was maybe in her forties and heavy across the hips. She made a *tsking* sound when she saw us and said, 'I'd appreciate it if you ask her not to make so much noise tonight. All the hammering woke up Teddi.'

I looked at her. 'What hammering?'

She pulled the door shut and locked it. The two children ran down the hall. I guess one of them was Teddi. 'Well, the knocking. It was so loud it woke Teddi and Teddi woke me and I had to look. It was after two.' She squinted at Pike. 'Was it you?'

Pike shook his head.

I said, 'Someone was hammering at her door after two in the morning?'

The woman nodded, but now she wasn't interested in talking. Her children had disappeared around a corner and she wanted to go after them. 'Yes, and someone got quite loud, too. It was very inconsiderate.'

'More than one voice?' I was thinking D'Muere.

'I don't believe so.' She glanced at Pike again. 'Well, I thought it was him but I guess not. Her boyfriend. That big guy. I think he's a police officer.'

'Mark Thurman?'

'I don't know his name. We just see him in the hall.'

'He was here at two this morning?'

She nodded. 'Making a terrible racket. Then they left together.' Now she frowned at me and looked at my hair.

I said, 'What?'

She gave embarrassed, and then she hurried away down the hall. 'I've got to find those damn kids.'

I looked at Pike. He said, 'You've got something in your hair.'

I touched my hair and felt something crusty. My fingers came away speckled red. James Edward Washington's blood. 'If she's with Thurman, she's running. If she's running, that means she's safe.'

'Until she gets found.'

'Yeah.'

Thirty minutes later we checked into a motel Pike knew two blocks from the beach in Santa Monica. It was called the Rising Star Motel. Fred C. Larson signed the register.

The room was simple, but functional, with two double beds and a bath and cheap wall paneling that had been scarred by years of transient use. There was a little round table and two chairs by the window, and a TV bolted to a dresser. The bolts looked thick and heavy enough to pin down a Saturn Five.

Pike left after a couple of minutes, and I went into the bathroom and inspected myself.

I went out to the ice machine, brought back a bucket of ice, then peeled off my shirt, put it in the sink, covered it with the ice, and ran in cold water. I wanted to call Mrs Washington and tell her about James Edward, but I didn't. James Edward Washington's blood was on my shirt and in my hair. How could I tell her about that? When the shirt was soaking, I took off the rest of my clothes, went into the shower, and let the water beat into me. The water was hot. I used the little motel soap and a washcloth, and I scrubbed hard at my face and my neck and my hands and my hair, and then at the rest of me. I washed my hair twice. The police had let me wash off, but that had been with Handi Wipes and paper towels and Borax soap. There's only so much you can do with a Handi Wipe. I scrubbed until my skin was pink and my scalp stung with the hot water, and then I got out to see about the shirt. I rubbed the fabric as hard as I had rubbed my skin, but it was too late. The bloodstains were set, and would always be there. How could I tell Ida Leigh Washington about that?

Twenty minutes later there was a double rap at the door and Joe Pike let himself in. He was carrying an olive green Marine Corps duffel and a large grocery bag and he was wearing new sunglasses. The sunglasses would've been the first thing he bought. He put the grocery bag on the little round table and the duffel bag on the bed. He looked at me and nodded. 'Better.'

'You went by the gun shop?'

He took waist holsters and handguns from the duffel. 'Called one of the guys and had him pick up some things. We met at the market.'

'Have the cops been by your shop?'

Pike nodded. 'They've got an undercover van parked down the block. It'll be the same at your place, too.'

Great.

Pike unwrapped the holsters and inspected them, and then tossed one to me. Clip holsters. We could snap them to our waistbands and wear our shirts out over them for that Miami thug look. Pike handed me a Smith & Wesson .38. He counted four hundred dollars out of a plain white envelope, handed half to me. 'There's food in the bags.'

He'd bought soap and deodorant and toothbrushes and paste and razors and the things you need to keep yourself up. He'd also bought a six-pack of cold Thai beer. I put the toiletries in the bathroom, and then we ate. While we ate I called my office to check for messages, but there were none. I called my home next and there were two messages from Jennifer Sheridan. In the first message she identified herself and asked if I was there and, when I didn't answer, she hung up. In the second, she again asked if I was there, but this time when I didn't answer she said that she would call back later tonight. She said that it was very important that she speak with me. She was speaking softly and she didn't sound happy.

Pike watched me listen. 'Jennifer?'

'She's going to call later tonight.'

Pike stared at me.

'I've got to be there, Joe.'

Pike's mouth twitched, and he stood up, ready to go. 'If it were easy, it wouldn't be fun.'

CHAPTER 22

We cruised the Mulholland Snake from Cahuenga Pass to Laurel Canyon, and then back again. It was after ten, and the traffic was light and getting lighter, mostly affluent stragglers who'd put in extra hours at the office or in the bar and were only now cresting the mountain in their effort toward home.

When we saw that there were no police stationed at either end of Woodrow Wilson Drive, Pike shut the lights and pulled over. 'You want me to take you in closer?' The turnoff to my house was maybe a mile in along Woodrow Wilson.

'Nope. Too easy to get boxed if we meet a black-and-white coming the other way.'

Pike nodded. 'I know. Just thought I'd offer.'

'There's a turnout about a mile and a half east that the kids use as a parking place, on the valley side overlooking Universal Studios. Wait there. If the police come I'll work my way downslope, then come back around onto Mulholland and meet you there.'

'If you don't get caught.'

Some support, huh?

I slipped out of the Jeep, then trotted off Mulholland and onto Woodrow Wilson Drive, taking it easy and slipping into bushes or shadows or behind parked cars whenever headlights showed around a curve. Woodrow Wilson Drive is narrow and winding and affects sort of a rural quality, even in the midst of high-density housing and fourteen million people. There are trees and coyotes and sometimes even deer, and, though there are many homes in the area, the houses are built for privacy and are often hidden from view. Frank Zappa lives there. So does Ringo Starr. Smaller streets branch off of Woodrow Wilson, and, like mine, lead to areas often more private, and even more rustic. If the police were waiting for me, or came while I was there, it would be easy to work my way downslope, then loop around and work back to Mulholland. Of course, it's always easy if you don't get caught.

I passed three joggers and, twice, couples walking dogs, once a man and woman with an Akita, and once two men with a black Lab. I nodded at them and they nodded back. Elvis Cole, the Friendly Felon, out for an evening's stroll.

I left Woodrow Wilson and turned up my road and moved into the trees. The mountain shoulders up there, and the road follows the shoulder into a little canyon. I crept through the scrub oak until the road curved around to my house, and then I saw the plain unmarked sedan sitting in the shadows beneath a willow tree, maybe sixty yards past my front door. I kept the trunk of an oak between myself and the car and I waited. Maybe eight minutes later someone on the passenger's side moved, then the driver moved, and then they were still again. Shadows within shadows. If there were cops outside the house, there might be cops inside the house. The smart thing to do would be to leave and forget about being in my living room when Jennifer Sheridan called. Of course, if I wasn't there when she called, maybe she'd never call again. For all I knew, Akeem D'Muere was closing in on her at this very moment and her last call would be a call for help and I wouldn't be there to answer it because I'd be off doing the smart thing. Whatever that was.

Across the canyon, headlights moved on mountain roads and someone somewhere laughed and it carried on the night breeze. A woman. I thought about it some more and then I moved down the slope toward my house. Sometimes there is no smart move.

I worked through the trees and the brush until I was beneath my house, and then I climbed up to the deck. There were no police posted along the back and, as best I could tell, none within the house. Of course, I wouldn't know that for sure until I went in, would I?

I checked to see if the two cops were still in their sedan, and then I went back downslope and found the spare key I keep beneath the deck. I moved back across the slope to the far side of the house, climbed up onto the deck, and let myself in through the glass doors.

The house was still and dark and undisturbed. No cops were lying in wait, and the SWAT team didn't rappel down from my loft. If the police had been here, they had come and gone without breaking the door and without abusing my possessions.

The message light on my machine was blinking. I played it back, worried that it was Jennifer and that I had missed her call, but it was Lou Poitras. He called me an asshole, and then he hung up. You've got to love Lou.

I went into the kitchen, opened a Falstaff, and drank some. The moon was waxing three-quarters, and blue light spilled through the glass steeples at the back of my A-frame to flood the living room. I didn't need the light. Behind me the cat door clacked and the cat walked into the kitchen. He went to his food bowl.

I said, 'It's been a pretty crummy day. The least you could do is say hello.'

He stared at his bowl.

I took out his dry food and fed him. I watched as he ate, and then I took down a larger bowl and put it on the floor and emptied the box into it. I didn't know when I would get back, so I figured that this would have to do. I turned on the kitchen tap just enough to drip. He could hop up and drink.

I went to each door to make sure it was locked, then found a nylon overnight bag and packed it with toiletry items and three changes of clothes. The police had my wallet and all the things in it, but I had spare American Express cards and Visa cards in my dresser, along with gas cards and three hundred dollars in cash. I packed that, too.

When I was done I called Charlie Bauman, a lawyer I know who has an office in Santa Monica. I called him at home. Charlie answered on the fourth ring and said, 'Hey, Elvis, how's it going, buddy?' There was music somewhere behind him and he sounded glad to hear from me.

I said, 'I'm sitting on the floor in my living room, in the dark, and I'm wanted on three murder counts and a dope charge.'

Charlie said, 'Shit, are you out of your nut?' He didn't sound so happy to hear from me anymore.

I told him about it. When I got to the arrest and the questioning, he stopped me.

'You should've called me. Never give up your right to an attorney. That was bush.'

'I'm calling you now, Charlie.'

'Yeah, yeah. *After* you fuck up.'

I gave him the rest of it. When I finished, he didn't say anything for a while.

'Charlie?'

'You assaulted a police officer, and you escaped?'

'Pike and I. Yeah.'

'Shit.'

I didn't say anything.

Charlie said, 'Okay. You've got to come in. Come to my place, and we'll go in together. I'm sure we can pull bail, even after this.'

'No.'

'What do you mean, no?'

'I can't come in yet, Charlie. There's something I've got to do.'

Charlie went ballistic. 'Are you *fucked*?'

I hung up.

The house was quiet with a stillness that went beyond the auditory or the visual. Outside, a police helicopter tracked across the horizon, overflying Hollywood. Closer, cars wound their way along mountain roads. The phone rang, but I did not answer it. The machine caught it, and Charlie said, 'Okay, so you're not going to go in. Shit, pick up, willya?'

I picked up.

He made a sigh. 'All right. I'll talk to the DA. I'll start trying to work things out.'

'Sure.'

'Shit, don't get killed.' He hung up. What a way to say good-bye.

I went back to the aloneness of my house and wondered if in fact Jennifer Sheridan was going to call. Maybe I was just wasting my time, and risking my freedom.

The cat came out of the kitchen and watched me for a while, the way cats will, but then he tired of it and left. I thought that, were I a cat, it might be nice to go with him. Creep through a little grass, stalk a few field mice, maybe hang with a couple of nice lady cats. I guess cats grow weary of human pursuits. So do humans.

Thirty-six minutes later gravel crunched outside my front door and a light played through the entry windows. The cops from the sedan, come to take a look-see.

Footsteps moved to the carport and a second light tracked along the opposite side of the house. I scrambled behind the couch, and tried to wedge myself under it. The footsteps came out onto the deck, and now both lights raked over the couch and the living room and the stairs that lead up to my loft. There was maybe eight feet and a couple of dust bunnies between me and the two cops. I held my breath. The lights worked over the couch again and then the footsteps went away. My, my. Nothing like an adrenaline jolt to help you wile away the hours.

Seventy-two minutes after the cops had come to call, the phone rang again, and this time it was Jennifer Sheridan. When I picked up, she said, 'Thank God you're there.'

'Where are you?' Her voice was low, as if maybe she were calling without Mark knowing. Or maybe because she was just tired.

'I'm with Mark.'

'Where with Mark?'

'I made a mistake getting you involved in this. You have to stop, now. You have to leave us alone.'

'It's too late to leave you alone, Jennifer.' I told her about the Eight-Deuce Gangster Boys. I told her about Eric Dees working through the Eight-Deuce to set me up and I told her about James Edward Washington getting his brains blown out. I said, 'They're killing people. That means Mark is involved. They set us up with the Eight-Deuce and Akeem D'Muere killed James Edward Washington and that's the same as if they had ordered him killed. They're accessories before the fact, and if you're a part of it now, then you're an accessory after the fact. Do you understand that?'

She was breathing hard, but she didn't sound frantic. She sounded resolved. 'We can't come back, yet. We have to stay away.'

'Because of Mark?'

'It's not like what you think. Eric is going to work everything out. We only have to be up here a little while.' Up here.

I said, 'Eric isn't going to work it out, Jennifer. D'Muere is out of control. You need to come in. Tell me where you are.'

'I can't do that. I'm calling to ask you to stop. I want you to leave us alone.'

'I can't do that. It's larger than you now, Jennifer. There's James Edward.'

Jennifer Sheridan hung up.

I stood in the dark with the phone in my hand, and then I replaced the receiver and reset the answering machine. I made sure all of the windows were locked and the alarm was armed and the faucet still dripped for the cat, and then I picked up the overnight bag, let myself out, and moved back down the slope to the trees.

It took just under an hour to work my way back to Mulholland and to the turnout where Joe Pike was waiting. It was a broad, flat area looking out on the valley. Pike's Jeep was there. So were a Toyota Celica and a Chevy van. Music came from the van.

I slipped into the passenger side of the Jeep and Pike looked at me. The smell of coffee was strong. 'She call?'

'Yes. She wouldn't tell me where she is.'

'You think she's in danger?'

'I think they're all in danger. I'm just not sure who they're in danger from.'

Pike's mouth twitched. 'It's often like that, isn't it?'

'Yes. Often.' I stared at the lights of the San Fernando Valley and listened to the music from the van. It sounded Spanish. I said, 'If we can't find her, then we have to stop Akeem. That means we go back to the source.'

Pike nodded. 'The guy who set us up.'

'Cool T. Cool T might know.'

Pike shook his head. 'What a name.'

Pike started the Jeep and we drove back down into the city and to the motel, and the next day we went for Cool T.

CHAPTER 23

Joe Pike and I left the motel for Ray Depente's place at five minutes after eight the next morning. We drove to Ray's much as you would drive anywhere. SWAT wasn't waiting on the roof, and the police hadn't cordoned off the area, and a squadron of black-and-whites with screaming sirens didn't give chase. We were just two guys in a Jeep. Wanted for murder, maybe, but there you are.

We stopped at a Denny's for breakfast, and while we were eating, two uniformed cops came in and sat in the smoking section. Pike and I paid, and walked out past them, but they never looked our way. Detective material.

At seven minutes before nine, we pulled into the little parking lot next to Ray Depente's, and went inside.

Ray Depente was sitting at his desk in the little glass cubicle, talking on the phone and leaning back with his feet up. The older woman who managed the office was behind him, peering into a file cabinet. When we stepped out of the door, Ray saw us and put down his feet and stood up. He mumbled something into the phone, then hung up and came around the desk and out onto the floor. The cops would've been here. They would've talked to him.

I said, 'Hi, Ray. This is a buddy of mine. Joe Pike.'

Ray stopped just outside of striking range and looked over Joe Pike and then squinted back at me. You could see him braining out what he'd have to do and how he'd have to do it to neutralize us. Pike slid two steps to the side, giving himself room if Ray made the move. There weren't many people in the gym. A young Asian guy sporting a black belt worked three women and a man through an intermediate *kata*, and a young Hispanic guy practiced roundkicks on a heavy bag in the far corner. Some of his leg moves were so fast you couldn't follow them.

Ray said, 'You've got no business here. Leave now, before I call the police.'

'I didn't kill James Edward, Ray. Akeem D'Muere set me up for the bust and D'Muere pulled the trigger.'

'Ain't the way the police tell it.' Ray took a half step back and turned so that his shoulders were angled to the plane of attack. 'Why don't we give'm a call, let everybody sit down and talk about it.' He made a little head move toward his office.

Pike said, 'That won't happen.'

Ray shifted again, adjusted his angle more toward Joe. 'Maybe not, but you never know.' Behind him, the class grunted and worked through their *kata*, and the heavy bag snapped with deep coughing *whumps*. 'I won't tell you again to leave, then we'll see what happens.' The woman in the little office closed the file and looked out at us and then came around the desk to stand in the door as if she could somehow read the tension.

I said, 'You don't know me, but you know James Edward. You think he was digging for a deal?'

Ray Depente canted his head like he'd been trying not to think of that, and his eyes flicked from me to Pike, then back. There was a physical quality to time, as if it were suddenly still, and moving through it was like moving through something dense and unyielding. 'Maybe you used him for a fool. Maybe you thought you could come down here and rip off the brothers, but it didn't work out that way. The police said you escaped. An innocent man don't escape.'

'Bullshit. James Edward and I came here to find out what happened at the Premier Pawn Shop. James Edward is dead because the cops involved didn't want us to find out, and neither does Akeem. Your man Cool T set us up.'

'I know you're lying. Cool T's righteous.'

'He set us up. He told us when and where to be, and the Eight-Deuce were there waiting for us.'

Ray was fighting it. You could see him starting to think that maybe I was being square. He wet his lips. 'Why in the hell did you come back here?'

'Because Akeem wants to kill a woman named Jennifer Sheridan, and I can't let that happen.'

'I don't know anything about it.'

'You don't, but maybe Cool T does, or knows somebody who does.'

Behind us, the Hispanic kid launched a flurry of kicks at the heavy bag, then collapsed to the mat, sweat falling like rain from the dark cloud of his hair. Ray Depente abruptly straightened from his fighting stance. 'I've got a class due in forty-five minutes.'

'This won't take long.'

'All right. Let's talk about it. If what you say makes sense, I'll see what I can do.'

Ray led us back across the wide parquet floor to the little cubicle and said, 'Miriam, I need maybe a few minutes alone with these gentlemen. Would you excuse us, please?' Miriam moved out of the door when she saw us coming and stood beside her desk. She peered at me and at Pike with obvious distaste. 'Who's going to answer the phones?'

'I will, Miriam. I remember how they work.'

'That fella from NBC is supposed to call.' She didn't like this at all.

'I can handle it, Miriam. Thank you.'

She *humphed* and bustled out, and then he closed the door, and went behind his desk. He took the phone off the hook.

A couple of hard chairs sat against a wall that was

mostly pictures and mementos of Ray Depente's Marine Corps years. I took one of the chairs, but Pike stayed on his feet, looking at the pictures. Ray in fatigues showing gunnery-sergeant stripes. An older Ray showing master sergeant. An 8×10 of Ray Depente screaming at a platoon of recruits. Another of him smiling and shaking hands with President Reagan. Ray in dress blues with enough ribbons on his chest to make him walk sideways. Pike shook his head at the pictures, and said, 'Jarhead.'

Ray Depente's eyes flashed. 'You got a problem with that?'

Pike's mouth twitched. 'I went through Pendleton.'

Depente's eyes softened and he settled back, maybe looking at Pike with a little more respect. *There are two basic types of individuals: Marines, and everybody else.* He gave a thin, tight smile. 'Yeah. You got the look, all right.' He crossed his arms and looked at me. 'Okay, we're here and I'm listening.'

I told him about Eric Dees and the REACT team, and that these guys were now apparently involved with the Eight-Deuce Gangster Boys. I told him about the meeting at Raul's Taco, and what Cool T had told us. 'Cool T said that the REACT cops were in business with the Eight-Deuce. He told us that the Eight-Deuce would hip the REACT cops to the competition, and the cops would bust the dealers. He knew we were looking for a connection, and that's what he gave us. He told us that the REACT cops were going to step on a dope dealer in the park. The cops showed up, but so did the Eight-Deuce. They knew that we were there, and they were looking for us.'

Ray shook his head. 'I believe what you say, but I know Cool T to be a right brother. If he told you this, it's because he believed it.'

I spread my hands.

Ray gave me certain. 'Bet your life on it.'

Pike said, 'James Edward did.'

Ray's jaw flexed and he shifted in the chair. 'Yeah. I guess he did.' He fixed the sharp eyes on me again. 'Least, that's what you say.'

I said, 'Cool T said that the Eight-Deuce are working for the REACT cops, but it's not tracking out like that. These cops are acting like they're scared of Akeem, and they're trying to handle him, but they don't have the horsepower. That puts a woman I know in jeopardy. She's hiding with one of the officers involved, and if she's hiding, it's because the cops don't think they can control Akeem. I need to find out how this thing fits together. If I find out how it fits, maybe I can find her, or maybe I can stop Akeem.'

'And you think Cool T's the way.'

'Yes.'

Ray rubbed at the hard ridges above his eyes and looked out at the students on his mat. A couple of men in their forties had come in and were watching the class spar. Two of the women were sparring, and the remaining woman and man were doing the same. They danced forward and back, punching and kicking and blocking, but none of the punches and kicks landed. They weren't supposed to land. Ray shook his head. 'My goddamned Christ, first Charles Lewis, and now James Edward. How long you figure Akeem D'Muere and these officers been lying down together?'

'Since Charles Lewis.' I told him about the video equipment. I told him how, after Charles Lewis, the REACT team stopped arresting members of the Eight-Deuce Gangster Boys, and that they hadn't arrested any since.

'You figure those officers wrongfully killed that boy, and Akeem got it on tape, and he's holding it over them.'

'I'm not sure, but that's what I think.'

Ray Depente picked up his phone and punched a

number. He stared at me while it rang, and kept his eyes on me when he spoke. 'This is Ray. Cool T over there?'

I crossed my arms and tilted back the chair and watched Ray Depente watch me.

He made seven calls, and when Ray Depente found what he was looking for, he put down the phone, stood up, and said, 'I know where he is. Let's go find out what the fuck is going on.'

CHAPTER 24

The three of us took Pike's Jeep, and drove south on Hoover to a row of low industrial buildings on the west side of the street. A two-way alley ran from the street between the buildings to a little truck yard in the rear. Ten-wheel trucks like they use for local deliveries moved in and out of the alley, but a couple of eighteen-wheelers were parked at the curb. Guess the big trucks wouldn't fit through the little alley.

The eighteen-wheelers had their sides open, and men with hand trucks moved between the trucks and one of the warehouses, going into the eighteen-wheelers empty and coming out full like ants raiding a pantry. Ray said, 'Park across the street. Cool T got him a temp job unloading those things. If he's here, we'll see him.'

Pike drove past, made a U-turn, and parked so that we had a clear view of the action.

Maybe ten minutes later Cool T came out of the warehouse with an empty hand truck. I nodded. 'That's him.'

Cool T still wore the neon orange cap turned backwards, but the sunglasses were gone, and he had a little yellow Sony Walkman clipped to his belt and a set of headphones in place over the cap. His lips were moving, singing along with something on the Sony. He pushed the hand truck up a long metal ramp and disappeared into the near truck, but a couple of minutes later he reappeared with maybe eight cases of power steering fluid and went back down the ramp and into the warehouse. I said, 'Let's go.'

We trotted across Hoover, then around the side of the warehouse and up a little flight of stairs onto the loading platform. Freestanding metal industrial shelves towered maybe fifteen feet high, jammed with crates of shock absorbers and air filters and transmission fluid. Guys with loaded hand trucks were coming in through a big door on the side and working their way down the long aisles between the shelves. Once they got inside, everybody seemed to be going in different directions, but I guess they knew what they were doing. The crates already stacked on the shelves looked neat and orderly.

A bald guy maybe in his late fifties was sitting at a little desk, digging through receiving forms with a rat-tail file, and shouting at the men with the hand trucks. He looked over when he saw us and said, 'I got all the muscle I need. Come back tomorrow.'

Ray said, 'Myron Diggs is expecting us.'

Pike said, 'Myron.'

Ray looked at Joe. 'You think Cool T is his Christian name?'

The guy at the desk said, 'Oh. Well, if Myron is expecting guests, who am I to object?' Everybody's a comedian. Everybody's got an act they want to sell. 'I hire a guy to do a full day's work. He don't want to work, he can find himself another goddamn job. That's all I got to say about it.' A peach, this guy.

Ray said, 'It won't take long.'

The bald guy didn't look satisfied. 'Yeah, right. It never takes long.' He made a gesture toward the back quarter of the warehouse. 'Try over around E-16. He's doin' auto parts.'

We moved past the bald guy and into the aisles and back toward E-16. The warehouse covered maybe twelve thousand square feet, and most of it was mazed with shelves and aisles that had little letters and numbers on them just like the sections in a parking garage. When we found the *E*s, Pike said, 'Better if we split up.'

'Okay.'

Ray and Joe Pike turned off at the first intersection, and I continued back to the third. I had gone maybe six aisles when I found Cool T wrestling the eight cases of power steering fluid off of his hand truck. I said, 'Hey, Cool T. Let's take a walk.'

Cool T made a noise when he saw me, and then he looked nervous and pulled off the headset. 'What you doin' here?' He began backing away. 'I don't wanna be seen with you, man. Lot of these guys are gangbangers.'

Joe and Ray came into the aisle behind him, cutting him off. When he saw Ray he frowned. 'Ray, what you doin' here?' He looked back at me. 'What the fuck goin' on?'

Ray said, 'We've got to talk, Cool.'

Cool T was waving us away. 'You tryin' to get my ass killed? This muthuhfuckuh after the Eight-Deuce. They see I with him, they'll be treatin' me to Mr Drive-By.' He was looking down the other aisles, seeing who was there. 'You know better'n this, Ray. James Edward know better than this.' He tried to push past me.

I grabbed his arm. 'James Edward died yesterday.'

It stopped him the way a heavy caliber rifle bullet will stop you. It brought him up short and his breath caught and his eyelids fluttered and he sort of blinked at me. 'Fuck you sayin'?'

'We went over to the park, like you said. We saw the ice cream guy selling dope, and then the cops came, but the Eight-Deuce came, too. They knew we were there, Cool. They were gunning for us.'

'Bullshit.'

'They took us to a little place by the railroad tracks. Akeem D'Muere put a Dan Wesson thirty-eight-caliber revolver to James Edward's temple and blew his brains out.'

Cool T's mouth opened and closed and his eyes made little jerky moves. 'That's a fuckin' lie.'

I said, 'You fed us a bullshit story to get us there so they could set us up for a phony dope bust. It was a setup.'

'You a muthuhfuckin' liar.' Cool T lunged at me and threw a straight right hand. I stepped to the outside and hooked a left up and inside under his ribs. He stumbled sideways and when he tried to come back at me Ray Depente tied him up and twisted his arms behind his back. 'That's enough, boy.'

Cool T's eyes were red and he struggled against Ray, but a Sherman tank could probably struggle against Ray and it wouldn't do any good. Cool T said, 'He fuckin' lyin'. I didn't set'm up. I love James Edward like a goddamned brother.' The red eyes began to leak.

Ray Depente looked at me. 'He didn't know. He wasn't part of it.'

'No. I guess he wasn't.'

Ray Depente turned Cool T loose, and Cool T wiped at the wet around his eyes and smeared it over his cheeks. He shook his head. 'James Edward dead because of me.'

'You didn't know.'

'This shit ain't happenin'.'

I said, 'It's happening.'

'They feedin' me stuff to set you up, that means they know I with you. They know I was askin' about them, and that means they'll be comin' for me. They'll kill me just like they killed James Edward.'

There didn't seem to be a whole lot to say to that.

He shook his head. 'I can't believe the goddamned bitch lied to me. I got all that stuff from a woman I diddle. She run around with some of those niggers in the Eight-Deuce. She get rock from some of those niggers.'

I said, 'We need to talk to her, Cool T.'

Cool T looked at Joe. 'Who this guy?'

'This is Joe Pike. He's with me.'

Cool T nodded. 'Then he gonna die, too.'

Pike's mouth twitched.

I said, 'Akeem wants to kill a woman named Jennifer Sheridan. I've got to find out what Akeem knows and doesn't know, and if he has a line on the woman. Do you see?'

'Okay.'

'Maybe the girl who set us up, maybe she knows.'

Cool T put his hands together and pressed them against his mouth like he was praying. He looked tall and gaunt, and the sort of loose-jointed energy that he'd had only a few minutes ago seemed gone, as if he had pulled himself inward and, in the pulling, had made himself hard and fierce. He let his hands drop to his sides. 'She a sister named Alma Reeves.'

'You know where to find her?'

'I know.' He turned back to the hand truck and wrestled it from under the stack of boxes and rolled it to the side of the aisle and left it neatly against the wall. 'I take you over there.'

'What about your job?'

'Fuck the job. This for James Edward.'

CHAPTER 25

Alma Reeves lived in a small stucco bungalow with a nice flagstone walk and a single car in the drive and a little picket fence that needed painting. We cruised the block once so that we could check out the house and the street. I said, 'Does she live alone?'

Cool T was sitting behind me, next to Ray Depente. 'She live with her mama and sister. The sister got a pretty good job with State Farm, so she won't be around, but the mama be there. She old.'

'Okay.'

Across the street and two houses down, three teenaged guys in cutoff baggies and gold chains and backwards baseball caps sat on a low brick wall, laughing about something. Pike said, 'What about the three guys on the wall?'

'The one in the middle Eight-Deuce. The other two are wanna-bes.'

Pike didn't like it. 'No good. They see us go in, it'll be bad for the family.'

Cool T said, 'Fuck'm.'

Pike looked at him.

Cool T said, 'These niggers used to me. I here all the time.'

Ray said, 'Don't use that word again.'

Cool T gave hands. 'What?'

Ray put hard eyes on him. 'I'm looking where you're looking, and I don't see any. I'm looking in this car, and I don't see any in here, either.'

The hard eyes got heavy and Cool T looked away.

Ray said, 'I just want to get that straight.'

Cool T nodded.

I cleared my throat. 'Oh, boys.'

They both looked at me. Pike looked at me, too.

'Sorry. That didn't come out right.'

Pike shook his head and turned away. You can't take me anywhere. I said, 'If Joe and I go in through the front, it won't take a rocket scientist for those guys to figure out who we are. We can let Cool T out here like we're dropping him off, then we'll park on the next street over and come in through the backyard.' I looked at Cool T. 'Will she let you in?'

'I get in.'

Pike stopped at the drive and Cool T got out, and then Pike kept going. One of the guys on the low wall pointed at Cool T and Cool T pointed back, and then we turned the corner. Pike turned right, then right again, and we counted houses until we were in front of a tiny saltbox that would butt against the back of Alma Reeves's place. Joe said, 'Here,' and pulled to the curb.

Ray said, 'Let me get out first and go up to the house. Folks inside see a couple of white men sneaking up the drive, they'll call the police for sure.'

Ray got out and walked up the drive to the front door and knocked. After a little bit, Ray shook his head and motioned us forward. Nobody home.

We went up the drive and through a neatly kept backyard and over a low chain-link fence and onto Alma Reeves's property. Cool T was standing in the back door, waiting for us and holding by her left forearm a young woman who couldn't have been more than seventeen. She looked scared.

We trotted past two rows of nicely set tomato plants and across their yard and up three cement steps and into a small yellowed kitchen with a picture of Jesus on the wall. A heavy woman with gray hair was leaning against the doorjamb between the kitchen and the dining room, saying, 'Y'all stop that and get out of here. Y'all get out of here, now.'

Cool T pulled the door closed after us. He locked it. The heavy woman's voice got higher, and she said, 'Cool T! Cool, what you doin', boy? I'm talking to you, Myron.'

Ray Depente said, 'It's all right, Mama. Nothing bad is gonna happen here.'

Cool T jerked Alma Reeves's arm. ''Less it has to.'

I said, 'Cool.'

'Goddamn it. She the reason James Edward dead.' He shook her arm again. 'Fuckin' bitch, set me up like I'm some kinda chump, lie to me like that so a brother gets killed.' Cool T raised his hand and Alma fell back against the refrigerator with a whimper and Pike stepped in and caught Cool T's arm.

'No.'

The heavy woman said, 'Alma, what is he talking about? Alma, you talk to me!' Nobody was looking at the heavy woman.

Cool T glared at Pike, but then he let go of the girl and stepped back. When he let go, she stumbled back and fell. Cool T was so angry that he was trembling. He was so angry that his eyes were rimmed red again, and filled with tears, but the tears weren't because she had lied to him. 'Goddamn it, this outrageous shit has been goin' on too long down here, brother on brother. This shit got to stop.'

Alma Reeves was shouting. 'He *made* me, Cool. He said you was asking and he told me what to say. I didn't know he was gonna *kill* anyone. I swear to *Jesus* I didn't know.'

Alma Reeves was sitting on the floor, looking up at us, and I wondered how frightening it must be for these two women to have four men push into their home and act in this manner. I squatted down by her. 'How did Akeem know that Cool was working with us?'

She jerked away from me. 'I can't be talkin' about all this. Don't you understand anything? I be talkin' about this and it gets back, I'm dead for sure.'

The heavy woman was pulling at her hair. 'What do you mean, dead? Alma, what have you gotten yourself messed with?'

Alma looked at her mother. Then she closed her eyes.

I said, 'Ray, why don't you take Mrs Reeves into the living room.'

Ray took the heavy woman away. She begged us not to do anything to her baby. She said it over and over as Ray pulled her away, and hearing it made me feel small and foul and ashamed of myself. I said, 'Look at me, Alma.'

She didn't move.

I said, 'Akeem doesn't know that we're here. No one but the people in this room knows that we're here, and no one else is going to know. Do you understand that?'

She opened her eyes.

'No one saw us come in, and no one will see us go out. We are going to move against Akeem. If you help us, no one will know. If you don't help us, I'll make sure Akeem believes that you turned on him. Do you see?' Small and foul and mean.

She said, 'Oh, you muthuhfuckuh.'

I nodded.

Alma Reeves said, 'I got what you call a little dependency problem.'

Cool T said, 'She went along with Akeem for the rock. She a crack 'ho.'

She flared at him. 'I ain't no 'ho. Don't you call me that.'

I said, 'Cool.'

He said, 'She say she want to quit, so I got her in a program, but she didn't stay. That's why she diddle around with trash like the Eight-Deuce. 'Ho'ing for the rock.'

Alma Reeves was the kind of unhealthy thin that doesn't come from dieting. Who needs protein and vitamin B when you can suck on a crack bong? Ray came back in the room. I said, 'What did Akeem tell you to say to Cool T?'

'That the cops was gonna lean on a brother be sellin' rock at the park. He say I was supposed to tell Cool, then call him and tell him right away.'

'Alma, this is important. Did Akeem say anything about a girl named Jennifer Sheridan?'

She shook her head. 'I don't know.'

'It's very important, Alma. He's already killed James Edward, and I think he wants to kill her.'

'I don't know. I'm not over there that much. I don't know.'

Pike said, 'Where does Akeem live?'

'He in a place just off Main over here.' She made a little hand wave toward the east. 'Used to be a rock house.' She told us where it was and what it looked like.

Ray said, 'Shit. That means it's built like a fort. There'll be reinforced walls and steel on the doors and windows.'

Cool T laughed. 'What you fools thinkin' about doin', stormin' the 'hood like at Normandy?' He laughed louder.

I said, 'Reconnoiter. We go, we watch, we learn whatever we can learn, and we maybe try to pick up Akeem when he's alone. If someone comes, we follow them. Whatever we can do.'

Cool T said, 'What about Alma?'

We looked at her. 'I didn't know Akeem was gonna kill that boy. I swear I didn't. Why I wanna tell Akeem now I told you?'

Cool T said, 'Crack. Crack 'ho do anything for the rock.'

Alma screamed, 'I can't help it. Don't you call me that.'

Cool T went to the little dinette and pulled out a chair. 'Maybe I'll just set a spell.' He gave me sleepy eyes, eyes that were tired maybe from seeing too many brothers killed by other brothers. James Edward Washington eyes. 'Make sure she don't call up old Akeem.'

Ray said, 'Thanks, Cool.'

I looked back at Alma, and then I found a notepad and a Bic pen on one of the counters. I wrote down a name and a phone number. 'You want to get into a program and try to get off this stuff?'

She stared at me.

I dropped the pad into her lap. 'There's a woman I know named Carol Hillegas. She runs a halfway house in Hollywood. If you want to get into a program, give her a call.' I looked at Cool T. 'If she wants to go, call Carol and take her over there. It won't cost anything.'

Alma Reeves stared down at the pad.

Cool T got up from his chair, came over, and took the notepad out of her lap. 'Crack 'ho ain't gonna do nothin' to help herself. Maybe I'll give a call for her.'

We went out as we came, through the backyard and over the little chain-link and out the rear neighbor's drive to Pike's Jeep. Ray Depente gave directions and we made the short drive to Akeem D'Muere's.

D'Muere's house was maybe five houses from an intersection, and we could see it well. It was a small cinderblock with an ill-kept front lawn and a couple of overgrown roses that looked like they needed water and heavy steel grates over the windows. Rock house. When we edged to a stop at the intersection, Floyd Riggens came out of the house, punched a black guy who was maybe nineteen years old, and knocked him down.

Then Warren Pinkworth was running out of the house and pulling Riggens away, and Eric Dees was coming out of the house, too.

I said, 'Well, well.'

Pike's mouth twitched.

More of the Gangster Boys came out of the house and Pinkworth shook Riggens like he was an idiot. Riggens did a lot of finger jabbing toward the kid, but he didn't try to get back into it. He walked out to the street and got into a sedan. Akeem D'Muere came out after Dees, and the two of them argued, but they probably weren't arguing about Riggens.

Pike said, 'If these guys are willing to risk being seen here, whatever they've got going must be falling apart.'

Ray Depente twisted in his seat. 'What are we going to do?'

'Watch.'

Ray didn't like that. 'There the motherfuckers are, right there. Shouldn't we call the police? They can see for themselves.'

'See what, Ray?' I looked at him. 'Dees is conducting an investigation. He's questioning Akeem D'Muere and other members of the Eight-Deuce Gangster Boys for information they might have as to my whereabouts, or the drug deal James Edward and I were trying to put together.'

Pike said, 'Uh-huh. And these guys might know. Two of them were found dead at the scene. Probably been a parade of cops through here.'

Ray's jaw worked and his eyes were wide.

I said, 'Can you get back from here okay, Ray?'

He looked at me.

'We have to find Jennifer Sheridan, and Dees knows where she is. Dees would've told Thurman to hide her, and he's worried, so he'll make contact. We're going to follow him when he leaves. Do you see?'

Ray Depente didn't move.

Akeem D'Muere said something sharp to Eric Dees, then went back into his house. Dees stood for a moment like he wanted to do something, but then he walked out to the street. Pinkworth and Riggens were out there, sitting in Riggens's sedan. There was another car behind them, but that was probably Dees's.

I said, 'Ray.'

Ray stared past me at the crack house, and then he nodded, maybe more to himself than to me. He said, 'Tell me that this sonofabitch is going to pay for James Edward.'

'He'll pay. I promise.'

Ray Depente turned heat-seeker eyes my way. 'Bet your ass he will.'

Ray Depente got out of the Jeep and walked back the way we had come.

Pike shook his head. 'Hate to have that sonofabitch mad at me.'

'Uh-hunh.'

Eric Dees finished speaking to Pinkworth and Riggens, then climbed into his own car. Pinkworth drove away first, and when Dees drove away, Pike and I followed.

CHAPTER 26

It didn't take long.

Eric Dees went west toward LAX, then climbed onto the San Diego Freeway and headed north, up through Los Angeles and the Sepulveda Pass and into the San Fernando Valley.

He left the freeway at Roscoe, turned west again toward Van Nuys Airport, then pulled into the parking lot of a Tommy's hamburger stand where Mark Thurman was sitting at a window table, waiting for him. Jennifer Sheridan wasn't around.

We snapped a turn into a Nissan dealership next to the Tommy's just as Mark Thurman left his window table and came out to meet Eric Dees. Pike eased the Jeep toward them along one of the aisles of new Nissans, and parked behind a row of vans. We got out of the Jeep and moved up between two of the vans and watched.

Dees got out of the car, and Thurman hugged him, and Dees hugged him back, slapping Mark Thurman's shoulder the way you do when you're moved to see someone that you haven't seen in a while and they are someone you care about. Cars moved in and out of the lot, and Hispanic guys who looked like they did yard work and women who looked like they worked in offices came out of or went into the Tommy's, and looked at Dees and Thurman as they did, but Thurman and Dees seemed not to notice, nor to care. Dees put out his hand and Thurman gripped it tight, as if he were using it to anchor himself.

Thurman seemed tired and drawn, but then, so did Eric

Dees. They looked nervous, and they looked glad to see each other, and they didn't look like homicidal co-conspirators rendezvousing to foil justice and commit evil. I wasn't sure what they should look like, but they didn't look like that. Pike said, 'What?'

I shook my head. 'I don't know. It's not the sort of meeting I expected.'

Pike nodded and maybe his mouth twitched.

A balding salesman in a bright blue Miles Vandeveer sport coat smiled his way over and said, 'That's an outstanding little van you're looking at there, gentlemen. You wanna trade in this old clunker, I'll give you a fair deal.' He slapped the side of Pike's Jeep. Hard.

Pike's head swiveled toward the salesman. 'Clunker.'

I stepped in front of him. 'We're just looking, thanks. If we have any questions, I'll come get you.'

The salesman gestured at the van. 'Great new five-year, fifty-thousand-mile warranty with these vehicles.' He looked back at the Jeep, and this time slapped the hood. 'Be a big step up from a maintenance hog like this old bitch.'

I said, 'Oh, man.'

Pike leaned toward the salesman and said, 'Look at me.'

The salesman looked.

Pike said, 'Touch the Jeep once more, and I will hurt you.'

The salesman's smile faltered, then failed. He swallowed hard. 'Yes, well. I'll be in the showroom if you gentlemen have any questions.'

I said, 'That will be fine.'

He made a last stab at the smile, couldn't quite manage it, and walked backwards until he bumped into a green Stanza. When he hit the Stanza, the impact turned him around, and the fast walk became a sort of skipping hop, as if he had to go to the bathroom. Then he ducked into the showroom and peered out at us through the glass. A saleswoman with red hair came up beside him, and he started with the big gestures, filling her in.

I said, 'Great, Joe. Nothing like a little restraint. What if he calls the cops?'

Pike gave sullen. 'Clunker.'

Thurman and Dees went into Tommy's and bought a couple of Cokes and returned to Thurman's window table. Eric Dees did most of the talking. Thurman nodded a lot, and occasionally said something, but mostly he just sipped at his drink. Thurman looked scared. He looked like Eric Dees was telling him things that were maybe hard to understand, but necessary to hear. At one point, Thurman got agitated and spread his hands, gesturing broadly, but Dees reached across the table and gripped his shoulder to explain something, and after a while Mark Thurman calmed.

The meeting didn't last long. Ten minutes later they came back into the parking lot and went to Eric Dees's sedan. Dees put his hand on Thurman's shoulder again, and said something else, and this time Mark Thurman smiled. Bucking up. Hanging tough. With Eric Dees telling him everything would be fine if he just hung in a little while longer. You could see it on his face. The pep talk by the old man. Then they shook hands and Eric Dees got into his sedan and drove away. Pike said, 'Now what?'

'We stay with Thurman.'

Mark Thurman crossed the parking lot to his blue Mustang even before Eric Dees had pulled away. He tossed his cup into a big cement trash container, climbed into the Mustang, and pulled out onto Roscoe heading east. Pike and I trotted back to the Jeep and roared through the car dealership and out into traffic after him. The salesman in the blue sport coat watched us go, then made a big deal out of saying something to the saleswoman who'd come up beside him. I think he gave us the finger.

We followed Thurman up onto the 405 and climbed north through the valley past Mission Hills and the Simi Freeway interchange and the San Fernando Reservoir. I kept waiting for him to exit, and maybe head west toward his apartment, but he didn't. We continued north into the Newhall Pass and the Santa Susana Mountains until the 405 became the Golden State, and when we came to the Antelope Valley Freeway just before Santa Clarita, Mark Thurman exited and followed it east, up through the San Gabriels. I said, 'Thurman's from Lancaster.'

Pike glanced at me.

'Mark Thurman is going home.'

The landscape became parched and barren and more vertical than not. Pockets of condominiums clung to the mountains, and fields of low-cost housing spread across creek beds, and huge billboards proclaimed YOU COULD BE HOME NOW IF YOU LIVED HERE. Ten years ago, only rattlesnakes and sagebrush lived here.

Thurman followed the freeway through the mountains past quarries and rock formations and drop sites for dead bodies, and then we were out of the mountains and descending into the broad flat plain of Antelope Valley. The valley up there is high desert, and the communities there grew up around top-secret military projects and government funding. Chuck Yeager broke the sound barrier up there. Edwards Air Force Base is there, with its shuttle landings and Stealth fighters, and, beyond that, the Mojave Desert spreads out to the north and east, a hot dry desolate plain that is ideal for crashing top-secret government hardware. In the foothills of the San Gabriels there is water and fruit orchards, and, in the winter, there is even snow. But the valley is different. In the valley, there is only scrub brush and heat and cactus, and secret things that no one is supposed to know.

Maybe six miles after we descended out of the San Gabriels, Mark Thurman left the highway and turned into a flat middle-class housing tract with stucco houses and azalea bushes and two-car garages so filled with the clutter of life that at least one of the family's cars had to stay in the drive. We turned in after him, and Pike shook his head. 'No traffic and no movement. We follow him in there, he'll make us.'

'Then let him go.'

We let Mark Thurman draw ahead and turn and disappear from sight.

We pulled to the side of the street and waited, and maybe five minutes later we started again. We made the same turn that Mark Thurman made, and then we drove slowly, crisscrossing the subdivision streets, and looking for his blue Mustang.

Two streets over, we found it, parked in the open garage of a pleasant two-story house with a neatly kept lawn and a fig tree in the front yard.

We parked in the drive behind the Mustang, walked up to the front door, and rang the bell. Footsteps came toward the door, the door opened, and Mark Thurman looked out at us. I said, 'Hi, Mark.'

Mark Thurman tried to shove the door shut. He was big, and strong, but he started the move too late and we had the angle.

The door crashed open, and Joe Pike went in first and I went in after him. Thurman threw a fast straight right, but it was high over Joe Pike's left shoulder. Pike hit Mark Thurman three times in maybe four-tenths of a second. Once in the neck and twice in the solar plexus.

Mark Thurman made a choking sound, then sat down and grabbed at his throat.

Somewhere deeper in the house a voice called, 'Who is it, Mark?'

I called back. 'Mark lost his voice, Jennifer. Better come out here and give him a hand.'

CHAPTER 27

Jennifer Sheridan came out of a door off the back of the entry and saw Mark Thurman on the floor. When she saw Thurman she ran to him, yelling, 'What did you do to him?'

Pike said, 'Hit him.'

We pulled Thurman to his feet and helped him into the living room. He tried to push away from us, but there wasn't a lot of *umphf* in it. I said, 'Take it easy. We've got the gun.'

Jennifer gave confused. 'What gun?'

Pike showed her Mark's revolver, then stuck it in his belt. 'Is anyone else here?'

Jennifer followed us into the living room, hovering around Mark Thurman as we put him into a green Naugahyde Ez-E-Boy. 'No. The house belongs to Mark's aunt, and she's away. That's why we're using it.'

Pike grunted approval, then pulled the drapes so that no one could see in from the street.

Jennifer Sheridan touched Mark Thurman's face with her fingertips. His face was already starting to puff. 'I'd better get some ice.'

He tried to push her away. 'Goddamn it, why'd you tell them?'

She stepped back. 'I didn't.'

I said, 'I'm a detective, Mark. I did a little detective work and found you.' I told him about watching Akeem D'Muere's, and about picking up Dees and following him to Tommy's.

Thurman tried to act like it was no big deal. 'So what? That doesn't prove anything.' He looked at Jennifer. 'Jesus Christ, Jen, this guy is a wanted fugitive.'

She said, 'No, Mark. He wants to help us. He got into trouble trying to help.'

Mark yelled, 'Don't tell this guy anything.' Panicked. 'He's just making guesses. He doesn't know anything.' He tried to push up from the chair, but Joe Pike shoved him down.

I said, 'I know that the Premier Pawn Shop is owned by Akeem D'Muere. I know that eleven weeks before Charles Lewis Washington died, D'Muere hired a security contractor called Atlas Security to install a hidden surveillance camera at the Premier.' When I said it, his face dropped maybe a quarter of an inch. He tried not to show it, but there it was. 'The camera was there when you guys pulled the sting. It would've recorded what happened.' I felt like Perry Mason, laying out my summation for the court. Did that make Jennifer Della Street? Was Pike Paul Drake? 'Akeem D'Muere has a tape of what happened that night, and because he has the tape he has you.'

Jennifer moved behind him and put her hand on his back. 'It's killing him.'

'For Christ's sake, Jennifer, be quiet.' He was looking scared.

Jennifer said, 'That's why it went so bad for us. They made him swear to keep quiet and he did, but he just isn't like that.'

Mark said, 'Eric's taking care of it. Don't admit anything. What if he's wired?'

Jennifer Sheridan pulled at him, trying to make him see, trying to make him come to his senses. 'He's not wired and Eric's getting you into trouble.' She turned from him and looked at me. 'He thinks he's protecting them. He wasn't part of all that. He's not like the others.'

'Nothing happened, goddamn it.' Thurman pointed at me. 'I'm telling you that nothing happened.'

'Damn it, Mark,' she shouted. 'Stop protecting them. *Stop lying for them.*'

I said, 'Leave him.'

They looked at me as if I'd fired a shot into the floor.

I said, 'He doesn't love you, Jennifer. He's willing to take you down with him, just because he isn't strong enough to stand up to the guys he works with.'

Mark Thurman boiled up out of the chair like an angry bull and hit me with his shoulder, driving me back across the living room. Jennifer Sheridan shrieked and yelled, 'Mark,' but then Pike was next to her, wrapping her in his arms.

I stayed high on Thurman's shoulders and let him carry me across the room and into the wall. He was angry and scared and probably not thinking too well, but he was also large and strong. We hit the wall and he backed away to throw a punch, and when he did I spun left and kicked him on the right side of his face and then I slipped to the side, and kicked him behind the left knee. He went down. I could've kicked him on the outside of his knee and broken the ligaments, but I didn't want to do that. I said, 'Don't be stupid, Mark. You're not helping you and you're not helping Jennifer.'

He shoved his way up and this time he sort of crabbed in sideways, like he wanted to box. He feinted with his left and threw a straight right and when he did, I pushed it past and snapped a side kick to his head that made him stumble back and drop his hands. I kicked him twice more, and punched him hard once in the solar plexus, and he went down. I'd hit him hard enough to keep him there.

I squatted beside him and said, 'You're going to listen to this.'

He shook his head. Like a five-year-old. His nose was

swelling and there was a smear of blood along his lower lip.

I said, 'Eric Dees and Akeem D'Muere conspired to set me up for this dope bust. In the course of that action, Akeem D'Muere murdered James Edward Washington. That makes Dees a co-conspirator to murder.'

Thurman was breathing hard. Sucking deep breaths and letting them out.

'You tried to keep all of this from Jennifer, but Jennifer hired me, and you finally brought her in. You told Jennifer about Charles Lewis Washington and Akeem D'Muere, and that means you've implicated her. You're a cop. You know what that means.'

Mark Thurman looked at her.

'She's become an accessory after the fact to murder. She can be charged, and she can be tried. Do you see that? Do you see what you've done to her?'

Jennifer Sheridan frowned. 'Mark?'

I said, 'Who are you going to protect, boy? Eric Dees, or Jennifer?'

Mark Thurman raised his hands as if he were about to say something, but the something didn't come and he lowered them. He looked from me to Jennifer Sheridan, and then back to me. He said, 'It was Floyd.'

You'd know it was Floyd. It'd have to be.

'I'm not even sure what happened. Floyd was hitting him, and then Pinkworth was hitting him, and he just died.' Jennifer Sheridan knelt down beside him and put her hand on his arm.

I said, 'You told yourselves it was an accident. Everybody's thinking Rodney King, and you decide to cover up.'

He nodded. 'Only a couple of days later, here comes the tape. Just like Rodney. Only this time the bad guys had the tape, and not the good guys. Akeem had the tape.'

There was quiet in the small house.

Jennifer Sheridan said, 'He went along because he didn't know what else to do. You can see that, can't you?'

I didn't answer.

'He didn't do it for himself. Don't you see that?'

I looked at Pike and Pike looked at me.

Mark Thurman said, 'What are you going to do?'

I shook my head. 'I don't know.'

He said, 'It was just an accident.' I looked at him and he wasn't a cop anymore. He was a big handsome kid who looked confused and scared, and more than a little bit lost. He said, 'I dream about it every night, and I just don't know. It got out of hand, and we didn't know what to do. Even Floyd was surprised. Floyd didn't expect to kill him. It just happened.' He tried to think of another way to say it. His mouth opened and closed a couple of more times. His brow knotted. Then he just shook his head.

'So you decided to protect each other.'

'You think I'm proud of this? You think I don't see that poor guy? Jesus God, I don't know what to do.' He was shaking his head. Jennifer Sheridan looked like she wanted to hold him and take care of him and make it all better even though she knew it was wrong. Maybe that's what love is.

I said, 'How many copies of the tape are there?'

'We got one. I don't know how many D'Muere has. Maybe a million.'

'Who has the copy you saw?'

'Eric.' Jennifer Sheridan put out her hand and Mark Thurman took it. Jennifer smiled, and Mark Thurman smiled back at her. They looked relieved, as if by finally sharing this the weight was becoming bearable. Mark said, 'I know where he hides it.'

I took a deep breath and then I let it out. I felt tired and my back hurt where the muscles lace over the shoulder blades. Tension, I guess. Stress.

Jennifer Sheridan said, 'Will you help him?'

I looked at Jennifer Sheridan looking at me and I nodded. 'Okay,' I said. 'I want to see the tape.'

CHAPTER 28

Jennifer Sheridan helped Mark Thurman to the couch and sat next to him. He could've made it on his own this time, but he let her help.

I said, 'Has everyone on the REACT team seen the tape?'

'Yeah.'

'Has anyone else?'

He shook his head. 'Not on our side. Who would we show it to?'

Pike went to the window and looked out the curtain. He said, 'Eric would have a plan. Akeem pops up with the tape, says do what I want or I burn you, Eric isn't going to just roll over.'

Thurman nodded. 'Eric said we should play along until we could find something to make Akeem back off.'

'Like what?'

'We started running intelligence on him and doing twenty-four-hour surveillance. We even went out and bought these video cameras. We figured if we got him doing a capital offense on tape, we could trade him. You burn us, we burn you, like that.'

Pike moved to the other side of the window and looked out the curtain from that side. 'Dorks.'

Thurman gave him hard. 'Hey, what would you do?'

Pike didn't bother to look at him. 'I wouldn't be where you are. I wouldn've killed Charles Lewis Washington, and then lied about it. I would've done the right thing.'

Jennifer Sheridan frowned. 'You don't need to be so harsh.'

I said, 'A man died, Jennifer. It doesn't get much harsher than that.'

She put her hand on Mark Thurman's thigh.

I said, 'Okay. So you were looking for something to press Akeem. Did you get anything?'

'Not yet.'

'So the five of you went along with him, committing crimes.'

'That's right.' Thurman made a tiny nod, the kind where your head barely moves, and he wouldn't look at me.

'And Eric figured you guys would keep on like that until you found something to use against Akeem?'

'Yeah.'

'Committing crimes.'

'Yeah.' He stared at the floor and looked even more ashamed. He was a guy with a lot to be ashamed of.

Jennifer said, 'Why do you have to keep asking him about these things? He feels bad enough.'

I said, 'I have to ask him because I don't know the answers. I have to know what he's done so that I'll know how to help him or even if I can help him. Do you see?'

She saw, but she didn't like it. 'I thought you said that you'd help.'

'I'm deciding. Maybe I'll help him, but maybe I won't. Maybe I can't.'

She liked that even less. I looked back at Thurman, and then I stood up. 'Where does Dees keep the tape?'

'He's got it hidden in his garage.'

'You know where?'

'Yeah. If he hasn't moved it.'

'Let's go see.'

We took Thurman's Mustang, and Thurman drove. Joe Pike stayed with Jennifer Sheridan.

Forty-two minutes later we left the freeway in Glendale and turned onto a pleasant residential street lined with mature trees and sidewalks and the sort of modest middle-class houses that more suggested Indiana or Iowa than Southern California. Mark Thurman said, 'Are you sure about this?'

'I'm sure. Which one?'

Thurman pointed out a white frame Cape Cod with a tiny front yard and a couple of nice magnolia trees and lots of surrounding shrubbery. The drive ran along the left side of the house to the garage. Like the rest of the houses on Dees's street, it was prewar, and the garage was detached. Someone had bolted a basketball goal above the garage door, and the net was yellowed and frayed. It had been there a long time. Thurman said, 'We can't just ask him, you know.'

'We're not going to ask him. We're going to steal it.'

Thurman nodded and frowned, like he knew I was going to say that. 'What if it's not there?'

'If it's not there, we'll find out where it is, and then we'll figure a way to get it from there.' A 1984 Nissan 4×4 sport truck sat in the drive beneath the basketball goal. One of those heavy roll bars with a row of lights across the top was mounted in the bed behind the cab, and the suspension was jacked up about eight inches too high so the little truck could sport oversized knobby tires. 'Who belongs to the truck?'

'Eric Junior. I guess he's home from school.'

'How about Mrs Dees? Would she be home?'

Thurman cruised past the house without my having to tell him. 'She works at Glendale General. She's a nurse, but I don't know if she works today, or when she gets home, or any of that.'

'Okay.'

'Would the kid recognize you?'

'Yeah, I think so. I've been here a few times, but not many.'

'How about the neighbors?'

He shook his head. 'No.'

We K-turned in someone's drive, went back, and parked one house away on the driveway side. I said, 'I'm going to see what the boy's up to. You're going to wait for my signal, then go into the garage and get the tape.'

Thurman looked nervous. 'Jesus Christ, it's broad daylight.'

'During the day, we look like we belong. At night, we look like crooks. You're a cop.'

'Well. Sure.'

'Give me the keys.'

He looked at me, then he took out the keys and gave them over. I put them in my pocket, then got out of the car and went up the Deeses' sidewalk to the front door. I pretended to ring the bell, though I didn't, and then I pretended to knock, though I didn't do that, either. If the neighbors were watching, it would look good for them.

I stood at the door and listened, and heard voices deep in the house, but they were the kind of voices that come from a television, and not from real people. The front door was under an overhang, and there was a long brick veranda that ran along the front of the house under the overhang, and a couple of large frame windows. The windows were open to let in the light. I went to the near window and looked in and tried to see the boy and the television, but I couldn't. The way the hall and the entry were laid out from the living room, it was a good bet that the boy and the TV were on the side of the house opposite from the garage. I went back to the edge of the porch and motioned to Thurman. He got out and went down the drive to the garage, and he didn't look happy about it. I stood by the front windows and watched. If the boy came through the house, I could always knock on the door for real and pretend like I was selling aluminum siding. If Mrs Dees drove up, I could pretend I was a real estate agent, and make a big deal out of listing her house, and maybe keep her away from the garage until Thurman made his getaway. If Eric Dees drove up, maybe I could run like hell before he shot me to death. There are always options.

It didn't take Mark Thurman long.

Less than three minutes later he came back along the driveway, and made a short quiet whistle to get my attention. When I looked, he held up an ordinary TDK half-inch VHS cassette. I walked away from the front door and got back into the Mustang maybe ten seconds after Mark Thurman.

He sat behind the wheel in the keyless Mustang with both hands on the cassette. He held it tightly. 'Now what?'

We went to the motel.

The sky had turned a deep violet by the time we got into Santa Monica, and the air was cooling nicely. The room had a VCR hooked to the TV, and that's where we'd screen the tape.

Thurman said, 'Is this where you've been holed up?'

'Yeah.' Like we were outlaws.

When we got into the room, Thurman looked around and saw the four left over Thai beers. They were warm. 'Say, could I have one of those?'

'Sure.'

'You?' He held out a bottle.

'No.'

I turned on the TV. Nightly News with Peter Jennings came on, and I loaded the cassette. Peter Jennings vanished in a flash of static, and a grainy high-angle shot of the interior of the Premier Pawn Shop filled the screen. Black and white. A muscular black guy maybe in his late twenties sat in a swivel chair behind the counter, watching a tiny TV. He wore a white Arrow shirt with the sleeves rolled up, and his hair was cut close with a couple of racing stripes carved above each ear. Charles Lewis Washington. There was no one else in the shop.

As I watched, Mark Thurman came up behind me and drank deep on the beer. He shifted his weight from foot to foot, not fast like he had to pee, but enough to show he wasn't comfortable. He said, 'There's a lot of this kind of stuff at first.'

'Okay.'

'We could maybe fast forward it.'

'Let's just watch.'

He went to the machine and turned it off. 'Look, this isn't easy.'

'I know.'

'You don't have to treat me like a piece of shit.'

I stared at him for maybe ten seconds. 'It doesn't matter if I like you or not, and it doesn't matter how I treat you or not. Whatever it is that I'm doing, I'm doing for Jennifer. Not for you.'

Mark Thurman stared at me for another couple of seconds, then he said, 'Can I have another of those beers?'

I turned on the VCR and watched the rest of the tape. Mark Thurman went into the bathroom and drank.

CHAPTER 29

The image was sort of overexposed and blurry, and not nearly as nice as your basic home video. From the angle the camera must've been maybe nine or ten feet up, and was mounted so that it framed the length of the shop.

The tape ran without incident for another couple of minutes before Floyd Riggens and Warren Pinkworth entered from the bottom of the frame. There was no sound. Charles Lewis got out of his chair and went to the counter, and the three of them spoke for a few minutes. Then Pinkworth took two cardboard boxes out of his pocket and put them on the counter. Each box was about the size of a bar of soap, but they weren't Ivory. Washington opened the top box and shook out twenty rounds of what looked to be 5.56mm rifle cartridges. Same kind of stuff you pop in an M-16. He examined the bullets, and then he put them back into the box and pushed both boxes toward Pinkworth. The three of them talked some more, and Riggens left the frame. In a couple of minutes he came back, only now Pete Garcia was with him, carrying a pretty good-sized pasteboard box. It looked heavy. Garcia put the larger box on the counter and Charles Lewis looked inside. Whatever was there, you couldn't see it, but it was probably more of the little cardboard ammo boxes. Washington nodded as if he were agreeing to something, and when he did Riggens and Garcia and Pinkworth were all screaming and pulling out badges and guns. Charles Lewis Washington jumped back so far that he fell over the swivel chair. Riggens went over the counter after him. Riggens raised his pistol twice and brought it down twice, and then he jerked Washington to his feet and moved to hit him again. Washington covered up and pulled away. The narrow aisle behind the counter opened into the shop, and Washington, still holding his arms over his head, stumbled from behind the counter and into Pete Garcia. Maybe you could say it looked like he was attacking Garcia, but it didn't look like that to me. It looked like Washington was trying to get away from Riggens. Garcia hit Washington on the upper back and the arms four times, and then pushed him down. Pinkworth was pointing his gun in a two-handed combat stance, and shouting, and he stomped at Washington's head and back. Riggens came from behind the counter and waded in beside Pinkworth. Garcia was pointing his gun at Washington's head. Washington seemed to reach for him and Garcia kicked at his arm. At the bottom of the screen, Mark Thurman ran in wearing a tee shirt that said POLICE on the front and back. He stopped beside Garcia and aimed his gun, also in the two-handed combat stance. Charles Lewis Washington pushed up to his knees and held out his right arm like maybe he was begging Riggens and Pinkworth to stop. They didn't. Washington rolled into sort of a ball, but Riggens continued to hit him. Thurman started forward, then stopped and said something to Garcia, but Garcia made a hand move telling him to stay back. Thurman lowered his gun and stepped back. He looked confused. Eric Dees ran in then, also wearing a POLICE tee shirt, and stopped midway between Garcia and Pinkworth to assess the situation. Garcia shouted and pointed at Washington, and Dees pulled Pinkworth back. He tried to train his gun on Washington, but Riggens kept getting in the way. Washington was on his stomach now, trying to crawl under a shelf. The white Arrow shirt was streaked with blood. He was moving slowly, the way you might if you were stunned and unable to think clearly.

Thurman raised his gun, then lowered it. He looked like he wanted to move forward, maybe do something, but he didn't. Washington again raised his hand as if begging Riggens to stop. Riggens hit his hand. Dees grabbed Riggens's arm and pulled him back, but Washington started crawling away again. I guess if I was hurt bad, and confused, I'd try to crawl away, too. Riggens pointed at him and shouted, and went back to hitting him, and this time he was swinging for the head. Pinkworth moved in and swung for the legs, but he needn't have bothered. Charles Lewis Washington had already stopped moving. Dees pulled Riggens off again and Garcia moved in, gun first as if he thought maybe Washington was faking it and might suddenly jump up and mow them all down. He checked Washington's neck for a pulse, then shook his head. Garcia holstered his gun and said something to Dees, and now he checked Washington's wrist, but he didn't find a pulse there, either. Eric Dees came over and checked for himself. Mark Thurman holstered his gun, leaned against the counter, and threw up. Eric Dees went to him, said something, and then went back to the body. Mark Thurman moved out of the frame.

I let the tape play for another thirty seconds or so, and then I turned it off.

Mark Thurman said, 'Let it play and it shows us figuring out what to do. You can see Floyd planting a gun so we could say he was armed.'

I looked over at him. Thurman was in the bathroom door. I said, 'I've seen enough for now.'

'Yep.' He killed the rest of the beer. 'When I came into it everybody was screaming. I thought maybe the guy had a gun or something. It wasn't like I was scared, I just didn't know what to do.' He went to the little round motel table and took another beer. Twenty-five years old, looking for a friend, and there were no friends around. 'What could I have done?'

'You could have stopped them.'

He pulled at the warm beer and nodded. 'Yes. I'd say that's pretty clear. But I didn't, did I?'

'No. That's something you'll have to live with. You had an opportunity to behave well, but you behaved poorly. Had you behaved well, Charles Lewis Washington might still be alive.'

He sucked down the rest of the beer and you could tell that he was living with that, too.

I said, 'You're going to have to give up Dees and the other guys.'

'I can't do that.' There was one beer left. He went for it.

'You don't have a choice, Mark.'

'The hell I don't.' Angry now. Walled in by circumstances and goddamned tired of it. 'Jesus Christ, I feel bad enough. Now you want me to be a traitor? You want me to sell out my friends?'

'I want you to do what you should've done when it began. I want you to do the right thing.'

He raised his hands like he didn't want to hear it and he turned away.

I took two fast steps toward him, grabbed the back of his shirt, and shoved him across the little table. He said, 'Hey,' and dropped the beer.

I said, 'Charles Lewis Washington was living with a woman named Shalene. They had a baby named Marcus. Now that baby is going to grow up without a father. Do you understand that?'

'Let me up.' He grabbed my wrists, trying to pry my hands off and push up off the table, but I wouldn't let him.

'He had a brother named James Edward and a mother and a grandfather.' The muscles across my back and the tops of my shoulders felt tight and knotted. I dug my fingers into his face and neck and pressed. 'You have been part of something bad. It's unfair, and it's ugly, and you didn't know what you were supposed to do, but now you do, and you have to be man enough to stand up. If you don't, Ida Leigh Washington will have lost two sons for nothing and I will not allow that.'

He wasn't trying to pry me off anymore. He still gripped my wrists, but it was more as if he were holding on than pushing away.

I let go of him and stepped back, but he stayed on the table. He covered his face with his hands and then he sobbed. The sobs grew louder, and his body jerked, and he said things that I could not understand. I think he said that he was sorry.

I went into the bathroom, wet a towel, and brought it out to him. I helped him to sit up and gave him the towel, but it didn't do much good. He sat in one of the cheap motel chairs, bent over with his face in his hands, crying.

Finally, I held him close.

He would hurt for a long time, though not as long as Ida Leigh Washington. Still, he would hurt, and maybe this was his way of getting used to it.

CHAPTER 30

At twelve minutes after seven the next morning, I phoned Lou Poitras at home. Thurman didn't want to listen, so he went outside and stood in the parking lot. Crime is certainly glamorous, isn't it?

Poitras's middle daughter, Lauren, answered and asked who I was. I told her Maxwell Smart. She said, 'Nyuh-uh. You're Elvis Cole.' She's nine, and we'd known each other maybe seven years.

'If you knew who I was, why'd you ask?'

'Mommy told me always ask.' These kids.

'Lemme speak to your daddy.'

'Daddy was talking about you last night. He said you were an asshole.' She giggled when she said it. These kids are something, aren't they?

'Let me speak to him.'

The phone got put down and you could hear her running away, yelling for Lou and yelling that it was me. Lou Poitras came on maybe twenty seconds later, and said, 'Where you calling from?' His voice was tight in a way I hadn't heard it before.

'Why, Lou? You going to have me arrested?'

'Maybe I should. You screwed up bad, Hound Dog.'

'If not me, who? If not now, when?'

'Stop with the goddamn jokes. This isn't funny.' There was a kind of fabric sound that made me think he was moving with the phone, maybe getting away from his family.

I said, 'I need to see you, and I need to be certain that I'm not going to be taken into custody when I do.'

'You gonna turn yourself in?'

'No. I'm going to talk to you about cutting a deal that involves myself and Joe Pike and an LAPD officer, and I need someone to take it up the line to the DA.'

His voice went harder, and low, like maybe he didn't want his wife or kids to hear. 'Are you telling me that an LAPD officer is involved in this?'

'I've got visual proof that Charles Lewis Washington was unarmed when he was beaten to death five months ago. I've also got eyewitness proof that since that time, Eric Dees and his REACT team have been participating with the Eight-Deuce Gangster Boys in an ongoing series of misdemeanor and felony crimes.'

Lou Poitras didn't say anything for maybe forty seconds. Behind him, I heard his wife yelling for the kids to quit dogging it and get ready for school. Lou said, 'You're sure?'

'Sure enough to call you. Sure enough to think I can get the deal.' Nobody a good cop wants to bust more than a bad cop.

Poitras said, 'What kind of visual proof?'

'Videotape from a black-and-white surveillance camera.'

'There wasn't a tape in the Washington thing.'

'It was a hidden camera.'

'And this tape shows the incident?'

'Yes.'

'In its entirety?'

'Yes.'

'Can I see it?'

'You going to come alone?'

'You know better than that.' Giving me pissed. Giving me Had Enough. 'There's a video repair place called Hal's on Riverside just east of Laurel in Studio City. The guy owns it knows me. It's early, but he'll open up to let us use a unit. Can you meet me there in forty minutes?'

'Sure.' Most of the traffic would be coming this way.

Lou Poitras hung up without saying good-bye.

I put the cassette into a plastic Hughes Market bag, locked the room, and went out to the parking lot. Thurman was waiting in his car.

Thirty-five minutes later we pulled off the freeway in Studio City and found Hal's Video in a shopping center on the south side of the street. Lou Poitras's car was in the parking lot, along with a couple of other cars that looked abandoned and not much else. Eight A.M. is early for a shopping center. We parked next to Poitras's car, but Thurman made no move to get out. He looked uneasy. 'You mind if I stay out here?'

'Up to you.'

He nodded to himself and seemed to relax. 'Better if I stay.' It was going to be hard, all right.

I took the plastic bag with the videocassette and went into Hal's. It was a little place, with a showroom for cheap VCRs and video cameras made by companies you'd never heard of and signs that said AUTHORIZED REPAIR. Lou Poitras was standing in the showroom with a Styrofoam cup of coffee, talking to a short overweight guy with maybe four hairs on his head. Hal. Hal looked sleepy, but Lou didn't.

I said, 'Hi, Lou.'

Poitras said, 'This is the guy.' Some greeting, huh?

Hal led us into the back room where he had a VCR hooked to a little Hitachi television on a workbench. The Hitachi had been turned on. Its screen was a bright, motionless blue. Waiting for the tape. 'Everything's set up. You want me to get it going?'

Poitras shook his head. 'Nah. Go have breakfast or something. I'll lock up when we leave.'

'Forget breakfast. I'm gonna go home and go back to sleep.'

Hal left, and when we heard the front door close, Lou said, 'Okay. Let's see it.'

I put the tape in the VCR and pressed PLAY and Charles Lewis Washington appeared in the swivel chair behind the counter at the Premier Pawn Shop. I fast-forwarded the tape until Riggens and Pinkworth entered, and then I let it resume normal play. I said, 'You know those guys?'

Poitras said, 'No. They the officers?'

'There were five guys in Eric Dees's REACT team. Dees, Garcia, Thurman, Riggens, and Pinkworth. That's Riggens. That's Pinkworth.'

'Is there sound?'

'Unh-unh.'

A couple of minutes later Riggens left and came back with Garcia and the case of bullets. I said, 'That's Pete Garcia.'

Poitras's face was flat and implacable as a stretch of highway. He knew where we were going, and he didn't like it.

Charles Lewis Washington nodded to conclude the deal, and the three onscreen officers produced their guns and badges. Riggens went over the counter, and the beating began. I said, 'You see Washington go for a gun, Lou?'

Poitras kept his eyes on the screen. 'They're behind the counter part of the time. You can't see behind the counter.'

Washington came from behind the counter, and Garcia whacked him into Pinkworth. Riggens and Pinkworth beat him as he held up his hand and begged them to stop. If he had a gun behind the counter, he didn't have one now. Thurman entered the picture. 'That's Mark Thurman.'

Poitras nodded.

'Here comes Dees.'

'I know Dees.'

'I don't see the gun, Lou. I don't see any aggressive or threatening behavior.'

'I can see that, Hound Dog.' His voice was soft and hoarse, and the planes of his jaw and temples flexed and jumped and he had grown pale. I quit while I was ahead.

Pete Garcia checked Charles Lewis Washington for a pulse and shook his head, no, there was none.

I pressed the fast-forward again and we watched the men moving and talking at high speed, like in a cartoon. Riggens left the shop, then came back with a paper bag. He took a gun out of the bag. He put it in Charles Lewis Washington's hand. I said, 'There's the gun, Lou.'

Lou Poitras reached out and touched the off button, and the merciful blue reappeared. 'How'd you get this?'

'Mark Thurman and I stole it from Eric Dees's garage.'

'How'd Dees get it?'

'A gangbanger in South Central named Akeem D'Muere has the original. He's using it to blackmail Dees and the REACT team into supporting his drug trade.' I told him how Akeem D'Muere owned the Premier Pawn Shop, how he had had a surveillance camera installed, and how he had forced the Washington family to drop their suit against the city to protect Dees's team.

Poitras said, 'Okay. What's all this got to do with you and the charges against you?'

I gave him the rest of it, from the time Jennifer Sheridan hired me to James Edward Washington and Ray Depente and Cool T, and being set up by Eric Dees and the Eight-Deuce Gangster Boys so it would look like I was trying to pull down a drug deal. Poitras said, 'That's shit. Why set you up? Why not just kill you?'

'Akeem's a killer, but Dees isn't. He got into this mess trying to cover up for his people because of what happened to Charles Lewis Washington, and he's been looking for a way to get out. He's trying to control

Akeem. He doesn't want to make it worse. He just wants to survive it.'

Poitras's face split with a feral grimace. 'What a great guy.'

'Yep.'

'So what's the deal?'

'All charges against Joe and myself are dropped, and the city has to do right by the Washington family.'

Poitras shook his head, and the grimace came back. 'You and Pike we can handle, but when you start talking a wrongful-death suit, you're talking the mayor's office and the city council. You know what that's like. They're gonna ask how much. They're going to try to weasel.'

'Weaseling isn't in the deal. They have to negotiate in good faith. No weaseling, no disrespect.'

Lou said, 'Jesus Christ, they're lawyers. Weaseling is all they know how to do.'

'If the Washingtons sue, they'll win big. The city can fight them and drag it out, but they'll still win and the city will look bad because of the fight. So will the department. Do it my way, and no one has to know about the deal. The department can claim they uncovered the tape as a result of an internal investigation, and use going public as proof that the police can be trusted to wash their own dirty laundry. The city makes a big deal out of apologizing to the Washingtons, and everybody ends up looking like a hero. Jesus Christ, Lou, those people have lost two sons.'

Poitras gave a shrug. 'I don't think they'll go for it, but I'll try. What else?'

I said, 'Thurman skates and stays on the job.'

Poitras's face went as flat as a stone wall. 'Every one of these officers is taking the hard fall. Every one of them will do time.'

'Not Thurman. You can fine him, you can demote him, whatever you want, but he stays on the job.'

Poitras's eyes sort of flickered and his sport coat pulled across his shoulders as his muscles swelled. A fine ribbon-work of veins appeared on his forehead. I have known Lou Poitras for almost ten years, and I couldn't recall having seen him so angry. 'These guys shit on the badge, Hound Dog. I don't want guys like this in my department.'

'Thurman's young, Lou. He didn't have a hand in it. You saw.'

'He's sworn to protect. That means you protect even from other officers. He just stood there.'

'He froze. His team is like his family. Dees is like a father. He wants a second chance.'

'Fuck him.'

'You get four out of five, Lou. That's the way it works.'

Lou Poitras's jaw danced and rippled and he looked at the tape in the VCR, maybe thinking he should just take the tape, but maybe not, maybe thinking he should just arrest my ass. But maybe not. He let out a deep, hissing breath and his jacket smoothed as the heavy muscles in his shoulders and chest relaxed. Making peace with it. He said, 'Okay. Maybe we can make it fly. I'll have to run it up the line. It'd help if I had the tape.'

'Sorry, Lou. It's all I've got.'

He nodded and put his hands in his pockets. Wouldn't have to shake hands with me, his hands in his pockets. 'You going to be around?'

'No place in particular. We escaped fugitives lead nomadic lives.'

'Yeah. I guess you do.' He thought about it, then said, 'Call me at one o'clock. If I'm not in the office, Griggs will be there. I should know by then.'

'Okay, Lou. Thanks.' I took the tape from the VCR and we went out to the showroom toward the door. You could look out the glass there. You could see the cars, and who was in the cars. Poitras said, 'Is that Thurman?'

'Yeah.'

He stared at Thurman with empty eyes. He wet his lips and he stared.

I went to the door, but Lou Poitras didn't go with me. I guess there weren't many escaped felons he'd let walk away.

I stopped in the door and looked back at him. 'Tell me the truth, Lou. When you heard about the charges, did you doubt me?'

Lou Poitras shook his head. 'Nope. Neither did Griggs.'

'Thanks, Lou.'

When I turned away, he said, 'Try not to get stopped for a traffic violation. Our orders are shoot to kill.'

Ha ha. That Lou. Some kidder, huh?

CHAPTER 31

Thurman said, 'How'd it go?' He didn't look at me when he asked.

'We'll know by one o'clock.'

'I want to call Jennifer.'

'Okay. You hungry?'

'Not especially.'

'I am. We've got to kill time and not get caught until one. We'll grab something to eat. You can call Jennifer. We'll move around.'

'Fine.'

We drove over the hill into Hollywood. I drove, and Thurman sat in the passenger seat. Neither of us said very much or looked at the other, but there wasn't any tension in the car. There was more an awkwardness.

We followed Laurel Canyon down out of the hills, then turned east on Hollywood Boulevard. As we drove, Thurman's eyes raked the sidewalks and the side streets and the alleys, just like they had done when he was riding a black-and-white here, just like they had done when he saved the nine-year-old girl from the nut on the bus. He said, 'Hollywood was my first duty assignment when I left the academy.'

'Yeah.'

'My first partner was a guy named Diaz. He had twelve years on the job and he used to laugh a lot. He used to say, Jesus Christ, why you wanna do this for a living? A good-looking white guy like you, why don't you get a real job?'

I looked over at him.

Thurman laughed at the memory. 'I said I wasn't born on Krypton like Clark Kent and I wasn't good enough to be Batman like Bruce Wayne, so this was the next best thing. You get to wear a uniform and drive around in a fast car and put the bad guys behind bars. Diaz got a kick out of that. He started calling me Clark Kent.' Thurman fell silent and crossed his arms and stared ahead into Hollywood. Maybe remembering Diaz. Maybe remembering other things. 'You think they'll let me stay on the department?'

'We'll see.'

'Yeah.' We rode like that for a while, and then he said, 'I know you're not doing it for me, but I appreciate what you're doing in this.'

'They haven't gone for it yet, Thurman. A lot could go wrong.'

We went to Musso & Frank Grill for breakfast and used the pay phone there to call Lancaster. Mark Thurman spoke to Jennifer Sheridan and I spoke to Joe Pike. I said, 'It's happening fast. We should know by one o'clock.'

'You want us to come down?'

'No. If it goes right, we'll call you, and then we'll come up. Once we turn over the tape, they'll move on Akeem and the Eight-Deuce. I don't want Jennifer down until those guys are off the street.'

'Sounds good.'

We took our time with breakfast and didn't leave Musso's until the waiters and the busboys were giving us the glare treatment. When we left, we walked down Hollywood Boulevard to Vine, and then back again, looking at the people and the second-rate shops and trying to kill time. We passed the place where Thurman had gone onto the bus to save the nine-year-old girl. He didn't bring it up.

We picked up the car and drove east to Griffith Park where you can rent horses and ride along trails or in carefully controlled riding pens. The park was crowded, and most of the trail riders were families and kids, but most of the pen riders were serious young women with tight riding pants and heavy leather riding boots and their hair up in buns. We bought diet Cokes and watched them ride.

At eleven minutes before one that afternoon, we pulled into the parking lot at Griffith Observatory at the top of the Hollywood Hills and went into the observatory's great hall to use their pay phone. I figured it was a pretty safe place from which to make the call. You don't find a lot of cops browsing through the meteorite display or admiring the Chesley Bonestell paintings.

At exactly one o'clock by the observatory's time, I called Lou Poitras at his office. Charlie Griggs answered. Mark Thurman stood next to me, watching people come in and go out of the hall. Griggs said, 'North Hollywood detectives. Griggs.'

'This is Richard Kimball. I've been falsely accused. A guy with one arm did it.'

Griggs said, 'Let's see you smart off like that when they put you in the gas chamber.' Always a riot, Griggs.

'Is Lou there, or do I have to deal with the B team?'

Griggs put me on hold and maybe six seconds later Poitras picked up. 'I brought in Baishe, and we talked to a woman named Murphy at the DA.' Baishe was Poitras's lieutenant. He didn't much like me. 'Murphy brought in someone from the chief's office and someone else from the mayor's office, and we got together on this. Everybody's pretty anxious to see the tape.'

'What about Thurman?' When I said his name, Thurman looked at me.

'They'd like to have him, but they're willing to give him up to get the other guys. They don't like it much.'

'They don't have to like it, they just have to guarantee it. Does he stay on the job?'

'Yeah.'

'Do I have their word?'

'Yes.'

When Poitras said yes, I nodded at Thurman and he closed his eyes and sighed as if the results had just come back negative. I said, 'Are they going to deal square with the Washington family?'

'Shit, this comes out, the Washingtons are going to own City Hall.'

'Are they going to deal square?'

'Yes. That came from the DA's person and the mayor's person.'

'Okay. What's the next step?'

'They want Thurman to come in with the tape. They've made a lot of promises with nothing to go on except my word, and they don't like that. It all hinges on the tape. As soon as they see the tape, they'll move on Dees and those other assholes, and they'll move on Akeem D'Muere and anyone wearing Eight-Deuce colors. Everybody comes in.'

'Okay.'

'We can do it whenever you say. Sooner is better than later.'

I looked at Thurman. We would have to call Jennifer and Pike, and then we'd have to go get them and come down. It was eight minutes after one. 'How about your office at six?'

'Make it Baishe's office. Let him feel like he's in charge.'

'Done.'

I hung up the phone and told Mark Thurman the way it was going to be. I said, 'We have to call Lancaster.'

Thurman said, 'Let's not. I want to be the one to tell Jennifer. I want to see her face when I tell her that it's over.'

'I told her we'd call.'

'I don't care. I want to get flowers. Do you think we

228

could stop for flowers? She likes daisies.' He was like a cork that had been pulled down very far into deep water and suddenly released. He was racing higher and higher, and the higher he got the faster he moved. The sadness and the shame were momentarily forgotten and he was grinning like a kid who'd just won first prize in one of those contests they're always having in the backs of comic books.

I said, 'Sure. We can get daisies.' I guess I was grinning, too.

He said, 'Oh, boy.' Oh, boy.

We took the four-mile drive down out of Griffith Observatory and stopped at a flower shop in Hollywood for the daisies and then we hopped on the freeway and went north toward Lancaster and the house where Mark Thurman and Jennifer Sheridan had been hiding. It didn't take very long at all.

The neighborhood was alive with kids on skateboards and men and women working on their lawns and teenagers washing cars and the varied stuff of a Saturday afternoon. Joe Pike's Jeep was in front of the house where we had left it, and the drapes were still closed. We pulled into the drive and parked and Thurman got out first. He said, 'I want to go in first.' He held the flowers like a sixteen-year-old going to his first prom.

I followed him up the walk and stood beside him when he rang the bell once, then unlocked the door, and went in yelling for Jennifer Sheridan. He needn't have bothered.

Pete Garcia was sitting on the couch and Floyd Riggens was sitting in the green Ez-E-Boy. Riggens had his legs crossed and a cold Pabst in his right hand. He made a nasty grin when we walked in and said, 'Jennifer's not here, asshole. We've got her, and we want the goddamned tape.'

CHAPTER 32

No one said anything for maybe three seconds, and in that time you could feel the silence in the house, and the emptiness. There was me and Thurman and Riggens and Garcia, but no one else. I knew without looking. No one else. Garcia seemed nervous.

Thurman squinted, like maybe he hadn't heard right. 'Jennifer?' Loud.

Riggens said, 'You think I'm kidding?'

Thurman yelled toward the back of the house, then went to the foot of the stairs. 'Jennifer?' Getting frantic.

Riggens grinned. 'He thinks I'm kidding, Pete.'

I said, 'What did you do with her, Riggens?'

'Put her someplace safe until we get this straight. There's the copy of the tape, there's the copy of Jennifer. You see where we're going with this?'

'Where's Pike?'

Garcia said, 'Fuck him.' When Garcia moved, he seemed to jerk, and when he wasn't moving he rubbed his palms on his thighs like they were wet.

'What happened to Pike?' Maybe something in my voice.

Riggens made a little shrug, but he'd heard it, too. 'Who the fuck knows. They separated in town and we got her. He's not so much. He wasn't so goddamn much.'

Thurman came back from the stairs, his eyes nervous and his face flushed. 'She's gone.'

Riggens said, 'What did I say?'

'You bastard.' Thurman threw the flowers at Riggens

and started for him, but Riggens lifted his left hand and showed a 9-mil Browning. His face went cold as an ax blade. 'You wanna fuck with me? You want to see how far it'll push?'

Thurman stopped. He didn't look like a kid going to the prom anymore. He looked like an oversized street cop with a serious mad on. He looked dangerous.

I said, 'Mark.'

Riggens straight-armed the Browning and told Thurman to back up, but Mark Thurman didn't move.

I said, 'Mark.'

Garcia's eyes flicked from Thurman to me and then to Riggens. Beads of sweat had risen on Garcia's forehead and he wiped his palms again. I didn't like that.

I stepped close behind Thurman, then eased him back.

Riggens said, 'You sold us out, you fuck.'

Mark Thurman said, 'If she's hurt, I'll kill you, Floyd.' He looked at Garcia. 'I'll kill every one of you.'

Floyd nodded. 'You shoulda thought about that before you decided to sell us out, you prick.' He gestured again with the Browning. 'Where's the tape?'

I said, 'What tape?'

Pete Garcia said, 'Oh, fuck this.' He jerked up from the couch so quickly that Mark Thurman stepped back.

Garcia said, 'Just shoot the sonofabitch, Floyd. Jesus Christ.'

I said, 'Oh, that tape.'

Riggens shifted the muzzle from Thurman to me. 'Come on. You guys give us the tape, and we'll give you the girl. That's the way it's going to work.'

I shook my head. 'Too late, Riggens. We gave it to IAD.'

Garcia said, 'Then the broad's dead.' He shouted it, as if what little control he had over himself was going.

Mark Thurman said, 'That's not true. We still have it.'

I looked at him.

Thurman said, 'It's in the car. Floorboard behind the

driver's side.' He looked at me. 'I'm not going to risk Jennifer.'

Riggens said, 'Go see, Pete.'

Garcia went outside and came back maybe two minutes later with the tape. 'Got it.'

Riggens cocked his head toward a large-screen Zenith in the corner. 'Check it out.'

Garcia took the tape to the VCR and fumbled with the controls. His hands were shaking so badly that it took him a couple of tries to get the cassette into the machine. I didn't like all the shaking. Garcia wasn't the nervous type, but he was nervous today. I thought about why he might be nervous, and I didn't like that, either.

When the Zenith filled with Charles Lewis Washington and the Premier Pawn Shop, Riggens said, 'Fine. Eric's waiting. We'll take your car.'

The four of us went out to Mark Thurman's Mustang. Floyd Riggens asked if Thurman knew how to get to something called the Space Age Drive-In, and Thurman said that he did. Riggens told Thurman to drive and me to ride in the shotgun seat. Riggens and Garcia sat in back.

We worked our way out of the subdivision and onto the Sierra Highway, driving up through the center of town. It took maybe ten minutes to cross through Lancaster, and pretty soon we were away from the traffic and the traffic lights and into an area that the local cognoscenti probably called the outskirts of town. Not as many houses out here. Less irrigated lawn, more natural desert.

Maybe a quarter mile past a Tastee-Freez, Floyd Riggens said, 'There it is.'

The high sail of the Space Age Drive-In Movie Theater's screen grew up out of the desert maybe two hundred yards from the highway behind a marquee that said CL SED. It was surrounded by barren flatland and overgrown scrub brush and yucca trees. A narrow tarmac road branched off the highway and ran up past the marquee and a little outbuilding where people had once bought tickets to giant-ant movies, and disappeared along a high fence beside the movie screen that had probably been built so that people couldn't park on the side of the road and watch the movies for free.

Riggens said, 'Turn in just like you were going to the movies.'

We turned up the little road and followed it up past the marquee and the ticket booth and toward the entrance between the screen and the fences. The fences shouldered off of the movie screen and seemed to encircle the perimeter of the drive-in. A chain-link gate had been forced out of the way.

The Space Age Drive-In looked like it had been closed for maybe a dozen years. The tarmac road was potholed and buckled, and the outbuilding had been boarded over, and the fences had wilted and were missing boards. A long time ago someone had painted a cowboy in a space suit riding an X-15 on the back of the screen, tipping his Stetson toward the highway, but like the fences and the ticket booth and the marquee, he hadn't been maintained and he looked dusty and faded. Much of his face had peeled.

We went through the gate and passed into a large open field of crushed rock and gravel with a series of berms like swells on a calm sea. Metal poles set in cement sprouted maybe every thirty feet along the berms, speaker stands for the parked cars. The speakers had long since been cut away. A small cinderblock building sat in the center of the field with two cars parked in front of it. Concession stand. Eric Dees's green sedan and its blue stable mate were parked in front of the stand. The concession stand's door had been forced open.

Riggens said, 'Let's join the party.'

Pinkworth came out of the stand as we rolled up and said, 'They have it?' He was holding a shotgun.

Riggens grinned. 'Sure.'

Garcia got out with the tape and went into the concession stand without saying anything. More of the nervous, I guess.

Pinkworth and Riggens told us to get out of the car, and then the four of us went inside through an open pair of glass double doors. There were large windows on either side of the doors, but they, like the doors, were so heavy with dust that it was like looking through a glass of milk.

The concession stand was long and wide with a counter on one side and a little metal railing on the other. A sort of kitchen area was behind the counter, and a couple of single-sex bathrooms were behind the railing. I guess the railing was there to help customers line up. The kitchen equipment and metalwork had long since been stripped out, but tattered plastic signs for Pepsi and popcorn and Mars candy bars still spotted the walls. There was graffiti on some of the signs, probably from neighborhood kids breaking in and using the place as a clubhouse. Pete Garcia and Eric Dees were standing together by another pair of glass double doors at the back of the stand. Garcia looked angry and maybe even scared. Jennifer Sheridan was sitting on the floor outside the women's bathroom. When Jennifer and Mark saw each other, she stood and he ran to her, and they hugged. They stood together and held hands and she smiled. It was an uneasy smile, but even with all of this, she smiled. Love.

Eric Dees took the tape from Pete Garcia, then grinned at me. 'Sonofabitch if you didn't cause some trouble.'

I said, 'How'd you figure it, Dees?'

'You put in eighteen years on the job, you make a few friends.' As he spoke he put the tape on the floor, then stepped on it. He took a can of Ronson lighter fluid out of his pocket, squirted the fluid on the cassette, then lit it. Once it was going, he used more of the fluid. 'They heard the talk, and they let me know there's an investigation going down. They said there's something about a tape, so I check and find out the tape is gone.' The fire was going pretty good, so he put away the fluid and came over and stood close to Mark Thurman. 'You fucked up bad, Mark. You should've just let it sit.'

Mark Thurman said, 'Jesus Christ, Eric, we were wrong.' The smell of the burning plastic was strong.

Riggens said, 'Hey, we went through that. We agreed. *You* agreed. You gave your word.'

Thurman shook his head. 'It was wrong. We did the bad thing together, and then we covered it up together. We should've stood up together, Floyd. Doesn't that bother you?'

'Going to fuckin' jail bothers me more!' Riggens was yelling. 'Losing the job and the pension and getting raked through the papers bothers me a helluva lot more!'

Garcia was pacing near the doors, glancing out like he expected something.

Dees said, 'You think I like this? You think I want it?' He looked at the fire. It was already dying away. 'You should've trusted me, Mark. I was going to work it out. I'm *still* going to work it out.'

Riggens said, 'Fuckin' A.'

I said, 'How, Dees? You going to bring Charles Lewis Washington back to life?'

Riggens screamed, 'Fuck you. With no tape, no one can prove anything. So maybe you showed it. Big fuckin' deal. Without the tape it's just hearsay, and we can ride that out.'

I nodded. 'Unless there's a copy.'

Garcia stopped the pacing and looked at me. Pinkworth shifted behind Eric Dees and Riggens sort of let his mouth open. Dees said, 'I'm willing to bet that you haven't made a copy. I figure you take the tape, you're thinking about cutting a deal, why do you need a dupe? You got a dupe, why make a big deal out of holding out? You'd just say, okay, here's the tape. You see?' Garcia was looking from Dees to me, Dees to me.

I spread my hands. 'But it's still a bet. You bet, sometimes you lose.'

Dees nodded. 'Yeah, but probably not this time.'

Guess you didn't earn command of a REACT team if you weren't smart. Of course, if you were smart, you didn't get yourself into a fix like this, either.

Mark Thurman said, 'Okay, the tape is gone and you're going to work things out. Let us out of here.'

Dees shook his head. 'Not yet.'

Jennifer said, 'You said if you got the tape back, you'd let us go. You said that.'

'I know.'

The crunching sound of tires over gravel came from outside, and Akeem D'Muere's jet black Monte Carlo eased between the fences and came toward the concession stand. Garcia said, 'He's here.' Pinkworth and Riggens went to the doors.

Eric Dees took out his 9mm Beretta service gun and Mark Thurman said, 'What the hell is D'Muere doing here, Eric?'

Floyd Riggens turned back from the doors. 'Akeem's pissed off about all the trouble. He wants to make sure it don't happen again.'

Jennifer said, 'What does that mean?'

I met Eric Dees's eyes. 'It means that Akeem wants to kill us, and Eric said okay.'

CHAPTER 33

Eric Dees said, 'Floyd. Pink. Get on them.'

Riggens drew his gun and Pinkworth worked the slide on his pump gun. Pete Garcia looked like he was about to pee in his pants. Jennifer Sheridan said, 'Oh, shit.'

Thurman shouted, 'Are you nuts? Have you lost your fuckin' mind?'

I took two steps forward, putting myself closer to Riggens and Pinkworth. 'You can't live it out, Dees. We come up dead, they're going to know. They'll backtrack the case and put it in bed with you.'

Dees nodded, but he nodded the way you nod when you're not really thinking about it. 'We'll see.'

Thurman said, '*Dees*.'

Eric Dees went outside and walked toward the Monte Carlo. The front passenger door opened and two black guys slid out with sawed-off Mossberg shotguns. They said something to Dees and the three of them came toward the concession stand.

Thurman yelled, 'Jesus Christ, Riggens. Pete.'

Pete Garcia said, 'Shut up. Just shut up.'

Pike moved across the cloudy glass at the back side of the concession stand. Everyone was looking toward the front, at Eric Dees with the hitters, so nobody saw him but me.

Eric Dees and the two Eight-Deuce hitters came in through the double doors, Dees squinting from the bright desert sun and the hitters stone-faced behind heavy-framed Wayfarer sunglasses. The hitters held their shotguns loosely, right hands on the pistol grips, left hands cradling the slides. Nothing like being comfortable with your work.

I said, 'Think it through, Dees. It's falling apart around you.'

Dees made a little gesture at Pinkworth and Riggens. 'Pink, you and Riggens take off.' He glanced at Garcia. 'Come on, Pete. We're outta here.'

Thurman shook his head, giving incredulous, still not believing that this could be happening. 'You're just giving us to these guys?'

Riggens said, 'Yeah.'

Riggens and Pinkworth holstered their guns and went to the door. Garcia wiped his hands on his thighs and hopped around some more, but he didn't move to leave. 'I can't believe we're doing this, Eric. We can't go along with this.'

Riggens stopped. Pinkworth was already outside, but he stopped, too, when he realized that Riggens wasn't with him.

Garcia looked at Dees, then Riggens. 'We can't do this. This is fuckin' nuts.'

Riggens went red in the face. 'What'd you say?'

Pinkworth came back and stood in the door.

Riggens screamed, 'You losing your fuckin' nut? We got a lot at stake here.'

Garcia screamed back at him. 'We know these people. This is fuckin' conspiracy. Fuckin' cold-blooded murder.'

The taller of the two hitters said, 'Shit.' He racked the slide on his shotgun.

Dees said, 'It's too late to back out, Pete. This is the only chance we have. You know that. Come on. All you have to do is let it happen.'

Pete Garcia said, 'No, Eric,' and reached under his shirt for his gun. When he did, the tall hitter lifted his shotgun and the shotgun went off with a sound that was as sharp and loud as a seismic shock. Pete Garcia was kicked back into the counter and then Joe Pike stepped into the glass doors at the back of the shack and fired his shotgun twice. The milky glass erupted inward and the tall hitter flipped backwards. Dees and Riggens came out with their pieces and fired at Pike, but Pike wasn't there anymore. The short hitter ran under their fire toward the broken doors, boomed his shotgun into the remaining glass, then looked out. 'Muthuhfuckuh gone.'

Something scuffed on the roof, and the short hitter let off another volley through the ceiling.

Warren Pinkworth ran for the blue sedan. Beyond him, the Monte Carlo kicked up a cloud of rocks and sand and fishtailed across the berms. Eric Dees dove out through the double doors and shot at something on the roof, but whatever he shot at he didn't hit. He said, 'Shit.'

I pushed Jennifer Sheridan down, and when I did, Mark Thurman went for Floyd Riggens. I yelled, 'No,' and Floyd Riggens shot him. Thurman spun to the left and sat down and Jennifer Sheridan screamed. She clawed past me, baring her teeth as if she'd like to tear out Riggens's throat.

I pushed her down again, then came up with the tall hitter's shotgun just as the short hitter turned and fired two times. Both of his shots went wide to the right. I shot him in the face, and then I fired out through the double doors at the Monte Carlo and hit it, but then it was behind the fence and away and Floyd Riggens was shooting at me. I dove behind the little wall that shielded the entrance to the bathrooms.

There were more gunshots outside, and then Eric Dees was in the double doors, yelling, 'Floyd, get your ass out here!' Outside, Pinkworth climbed into the blue sedan and ground it to life.

Riggens fired twice more at me, then went for the

doors. Riggens's eyes were wide and red and he looked like he was crying, but I wasn't sure why. He stopped over Mark Thurman. Mark Thurman looked up at him, and Riggens said, 'This is all your fault.' Then he raised his gun to fire. Jennifer Sheridan picked up Pete Garcia's pistol and shot Floyd Riggens in the chest. The bullet kicked him back, but he kept his feet. He opened his mouth and looked down at himself and then he looked at Jennifer Sheridan and fell.

Outside, Warren Pinkworth put the blue sedan in gear and sped away. Eric Dees shouted, 'You fuck,' fired two times at me, then dove behind the counter. Everything went still and quiet and stayed that way.

Pete Garcia rolled onto his side and moaned.

Jennifer Sheridan dropped Garcia's gun, then grabbed Mark Thurman by the shirt and dragged him toward the rest rooms. He had to outweigh her by a hundred pounds, but she kicked off her shoes for better traction and made a sort of groaning sound and did what she had to do. The floor was gritty with shattered glass, but she seemed not to notice.

Gravel crunched outside the concession stand, and Joe Pike took a position behind the broken double doors.

I said, 'That's it, Dees. It fell apart. It's over.'

Eric Dees moved behind the counter.

Pike looked in through the broken doors and I pointed at the counter. 'Dees.'

Eric Dees moved behind the counter again.

Pike said, 'Don't be stupid, Eric. Let's go home standing up.'

Dees said, 'What else have I got, Joe?'

Eric Dees charged around the near end of the counter, firing as he came, and when he did, Joe Pike and I fired back.

Dees went down hard, and I ran forward and kicked his pistol away, and then it was over. Dees was on his back, blinking at the ceiling and clutching at his chest. Most of the pellets had taken him there. A dozen feet away, Pete Garcia said, 'Oh, God,' but he didn't say it to anyone in the room.

Pike came up beside me and looked down. 'Hey, Eric.'

Eric Dees said, 'Joe.'

Pike said, 'There a radio in the unit?'

'Yeah.'

'I'll try to raise an ambulance.'

Pike went out to the green sedan.

Dees opened and closed his mouth and blinked up at the ceiling again. He said, 'How's Pete? Is Pete okay?'

I checked Pete Garcia and Floyd Riggens, and then I went to Mark Thurman. Jennifer Sheridan said, 'He's bleeding.'

The bullet had caught him low on the left side. She had ripped away part of her blouse and was using it to press on the wound. There was plenty of blood. Her hands were covered with it.

'Let me see.'

She pulled away the little compress and a steady rhythmic surge of blood pulsed from his abdomen. Artery.

He said, 'I gotta stand up.'

She said, 'You've got to stay down. You're bleeding, Mark. I think it's an artery.'

'I want to get up.' He pushed her off and flopped around and finally I helped him stand. When he was up he pushed me off and tried to walk. It was more of a sideways lurch, but he did okay.

Jennifer said, 'Damn it, Mark, *please*. We have to wait for the ambulance.'

Mark Thurman stumbled sideways. I caught him and helped him stay up. He said, 'You gotta help me.' He had lost a lot of blood.

Jennifer Sheridan said, 'Make him lie down.'

'He's okay.'

I helped Mark Thurman lurch across the concession stand to Eric Dees. Mark Thurman dug a slim billfold out of his back pocket, opened it, and held it out. It was his LAPD badge. He said, 'Do you see this?'

'What in hell are you doing?' Little bubbles of blood came out of Dees's nose when he said it and I wasn't sure if he was seeing the badge or not.

Mark Thurman breathed hard and sort of wobbled to the side but he kept his feet. His shirt and his pants were wet with his own blood. He said, 'I'm doing something that I should've done a long time ago, you sonofabitch. I am an LAPD officer, and I am placing you under arrest. You are under arrest for murder, and conspiracy to commit murder, and because you're a lousy goddamned officer.' Then Mark Thurman fainted.

Eric Dees was dead by the time the ambulance arrived.

CHAPTER 34

Jennifer Sheridan rode in the back of the ambulance when they brought Mark Thurman and Pete Garcia to the Lancaster City Hospital. Pike and I followed behind in Mark Thurman's Mustang.

The Lancaster cops assumed that something bad had gone down between a group of gangbangers and a group of LAPD officers, and neither Joe nor I told them different. The Lancaster police, as might be expected, assumed that the police officers on the scene had been there as the representatives of Truth and Justice. We didn't tell them different about that, either. Joe Pike got one of the Lancaster cops to give him a lift back to his Jeep.

The emergency room staff tried to keep Jennifer Sheridan out of the ER, but Mark Thurman woke up enough to say that he wanted her with him, and they relented. I went with him, too. Because of the nature of the bleeding, the ER staff prepared to take Mark Thurman into the operating room. One of the doctors grumbled about having no X rays, but I guess nobody wanted to wait. Pete Garcia was already on the table, and it didn't look good for him.

Jennifer and I stood beside Mark in a green tile hallway and waited for the orderlies to wheel him into the OR. Jennifer held his hand. Mark Thurman smiled at her, then his eyes moved to me. It was a sleepy smile. They had pumped him full of Demerol. 'What do you think will happen now?'

I made a little shrug. 'It'll come out. No way to keep it in.'

Mark looked lost and maybe a little fretful. 'The tape's gone. There's no more proof of what happened that night. They catch Pinkworth, all he's going to do is deny everything. Akeem D'Muere isn't going to offer anything.'

'There's Garcia.'

Mark Thurman sighed. 'If he makes it.'

'There's me and there's Pike.'

'Yeah. But that's just words. You weren't there that night.'

'No. But we'll offer what we can. If no one believes, then there it is.'

A nurse came and told Mark that it would be just a minute more.

I said, 'What do you want to do, Mark?'

He looked at Jennifer, and she nodded, and then he looked at me. 'I don't care about the tape. I want to go forward. I want to tell them what happened to Charles Lewis Washington. Can you set that up?'

I patted his shoulder and the orderlies came and took him away.

Jennifer Sheridan and I went into the little waiting room they have there and I bought her a cup of coffee. Then I went to the pay phone and called Lou Poitras. It was eighteen minutes after six, and he wasn't happy to hear from me. 'You're late. I got half a dozen people sitting here waiting for you and your boy Thurman. You getting cold feet?'

'The tape's gone, Lou. Dees burned it.'

Lou Poitras put me on hold. A couple of minutes later he picked up again. 'I had to change phones. I didn't want those people to see me have an aneurism.'

'Dees is dead. So is Riggens. Garcia and Thurman are under the knife now, and Pinkworth ran. I'd guess he'll go home. He'll think about it for an hour, then call in with a story.'

Lou Poitras said, 'Jesus Christ.'

'Thurman wants to come in, Lou. Tape or no tape. He wants to make a statement about what happened in the pawnshop, and what's been happening since, and he's willing to testify.'

Lou Poitras made a soft sound, but said nothing for several seconds. 'There's no deal without the tape, Hound Dog. None of these people will make a promise on verbal testimony. If he comes forward, he takes his chances.'

'He knows that. He wants to step forward anyway. If Garcia makes it, he'll probably be willing to corroborate.'

'That would help.'

'But even if Garcia doesn't, Thurman comes forward.'

'I understand.' There was maybe just a little bit more respect in Lou Poitras's voice than there had been. 'We're going to have to bring you in. Tell me where you are.'

I told him.

When I hung up, Joe Pike was sitting beside Jennifer Sheridan. He was holding her hand. I sat on the other side of her and took her free hand. She didn't look happy. She said, 'I can't believe I killed a man. I just shot him.'

'Yes.'

'A man I've known and talked to. Before they were divorced, the four of us had dinner once. We ate at the Sizzler.' She was staring at a point in the middle space, somewhere very far from here.

I said, 'You shot a man who was going to murder Mark Thurman. If you hadn't shot him, Mark would be dead. Do you see that?'

She nodded.

'It's what you have, and you must use it. You're going to hurt. You're going to miss sleep, and you're going to feel guilty, and it's going to get worse before it gets better, but you can survive it. You helped Mark survive, and now he will help you. He is alive because of you. When you hear him breathe, when you see him smile, it is because of you. Tell yourself that and know that it's true. Tell it to yourself as often as you need. If you forget, call me and I will tell you.'

She leaned her head against my shoulder and we sat like that. A few minutes later I told them about the call to Lou Poitras and the way it was going to be.

When I finished, Jennifer Sheridan said, 'I don't want to leave Mark.'

I rubbed her hand. Joe still had the other. 'You'll be fine. They're going to want to talk to you, and to Mark, but probably not until later. Joe and I will go now.'

She looked down at our hands, then up again. 'What will I say?'

'The truth.'

'Will they put him in jail?'

'I don't know. I don't think so, but I don't know. A lot of people out there are going to want his head.'

She nodded again, and this time smiled sort of sadly. 'He just wanted to be a police officer.'

'Yes. But now he'll have to move on, and so will you.'

'It's going to be such a big change. What will he do?'

'Something.'

'Well, we still have each other. We can make it.'

'Yes,' I said. 'If you want to make it, you can.'

She smiled again, and this time the smile didn't seem so sad. 'Thanks for sticking it out with me.'

'Jennifer, you're worth it.'

Twenty-two minutes later a couple of California Highway Patrol cops in khaki uniforms came into the waiting room. The shorter of the two said, 'Who's Cole?'

'Me.' I stood, and Pike stood with me. Jennifer got up with Pike and took my hand.

The same cop said, 'We're supposed to take you down to L.A. Is this guy Pike?'

Pike said, 'Yeah.'

'Okay. The both of you.'

The taller guy began to dig out his cuffs, but the shorter guy waved them away. 'We don't need that.'

Jennifer's grip on my hand tightened. I gave her the smile and squeezed her hand back and said, 'Everything's going to be fine.' Mr Confidence.

The high desert sky was turning a nice purple when the state cops loaded us into a black-and-white highway cruiser and blasted off down the Antelope Valley Freeway. Less than an hour later, the sky was dark when we pulled into the parking lot of the Seventy-seventh Division in South Central Los Angeles. I thought they'd take us to Parker Center, but there you go. Criminals always return to the scene of the crime. Even if we have to be taken.

They were expecting us. The Seventy-seventh's halls and squad rooms were jammed with cops and reporters and lawyers and handcuffed young black men who looked like they were Eight-Deuce gangbangers. A couple of them I recognized. I didn't see Akeem D'Muere, but Harold Bellis was talking to the homicide lieutenant, Stilwell. Stilwell looked bored, but Bellis looked confident. He also looked like he had just been called away from dinner. L'Orangerie, no doubt. *Des Oeufs de Poule au Beluga*, no doubt. The appetizer alone would've cost more than Stilwell's take-home for the day.

Stilwell saw me, went to a closed door that said WATCH COMMANDER, then opened the door and stuck in his head. Lou Poitras came out with two women and four men. The squad room was so crowded that if any more people came out of the office, they'd have to kick out the bad guys to make room for the good guys. One of the women was a prosecutor in the DA's office named Murphy, and one of the men was a uniformed captain who was probably the watch commander. I didn't recognize the others.

A guy in a wrinkled pinstripe with no tie said, 'Is this Cole?' He said it like he was in charge.

Lou Poitras pointed at me, then Pike. 'Cole. Pike.'

The pinstripe said, 'Let's go through it. I want to wrap this up.'

The pinstripe was a guy named Garvey from the chief's office and the other woman was a muck-a-muck named Greenberg from the city council. Of the two other guys, one was named Fallon, also from the DA's, and the other was from the mayor's office. The guy from the mayor was named Haywood. Fallon and Haywood took Joe Pike into an office down the hall, and Greenberg went with them. Garvey and everybody else took me into the watch commander's office. When we were settled, Murphy said, 'You're not under arrest at this time, Mr Cole, but we reserve the right to prosecute you for anything that you might admit to or say during this interview.'

Lou Poitras said, 'Jesus Christ, Murphy.'

Garvey made a take-it-easy gesture. 'At ease, Sergeant.'

Murphy said, 'Who's your attorney?'

'Charlie Bauman.'

She nodded. 'I know Charlie. I'd advise you to call him.'

I took her advice. An uncharacteristically smart move.

Everyone left for coffee while I called Charlie, told him where I was, and told him that I wouldn't say anything until he arrived. When I was done, I opened the door and saw Lou Poitras standing in the squad room with his boss from North Hollywood, a lieutenant named Baishe. Baishe has always looked shriveled and tight to me, sort of like a daddy longlegs, and he's never liked me much, but when I opened the door, he was jabbing the street cop Micelli in the chest and telling him that he'd acted like a goddamned bush-league asshole. Micelli said he didn't have to take this shit from some North Hollywood dick and jabbed back, and when he did Lou Poitras slapped his hand to the side and told him to step away. Poitras was maybe five inches taller than Micelli and eighty pounds heavier, and he looked like he was itching to use it. Micelli told Poitras to fuck himself, but he stepped away. Stilwell was over by a couple of uniforms, staying out of it. I said, 'Christ, Baishe, were you defending me?'

When Baishe saw me grinning, he scowled and said, 'Hell, no. I always knew you'd fuck up big time. I'm just surprised it took you this long.' A man with friends is the wealthiest man in the world.

Poitras told me to wait in the office, then asked if I wanted a cup of coffee. I told him that I did and waited in the open doorway for him to bring it. While I was waiting two Hispanic cops brought in Akeem D'Muere. His hands were cuffed, but he walked tall and defiantly, as if he were in some way larger than life, as if he were above all this and impervious to it and amused by it. Harold Bellis went to him, immediately complaining to the officers about the handcuffs. No one jumped to take them off. Stilwell went over to the uniforms, and they led D'Muere and Bellis toward the interrogation rooms. When they led D'Muere past, he saw me. I made my hand into a gun, pointed it at him, and dropped the hammer. He smiled. Amused.

Charlie Bauman came in maybe ten minutes later.

Murphy from the DA and Garvey from the chief saw him before I did, and then Charlie came to me. 'You say anything yet?'

'I learned my lesson last time.'

'Okay. These guys wanna have a powwow, so lemme see what I can work out.'

He went back to them, and pretty soon they were joined by Greenberg and Haywood. When Charlie came back, he said, 'They want a freebie, and I'm willing to give it to them, but it's up to you. You run through what you know and answer their questions, but it'll be off the record. If they decide to prosecute, they can't use your statements against you. Do you agree?'

'Yes.'

We went back into the watch commander's office, and I went through everything from the beginning, just as I had when I'd gone through it with Stilwell and Micelli, only this time there was more of it to tell. Everyone looked interested except the watch commander, who spent a lot of time saying things like, 'I've known Eric Dees for ten goddamned years. He's a fine officer,' or, 'Talk is cheap, but where's the goddamned evidence?' He said stuff like that until Murphy told him to shut up or leave the room.

I told them how Mark Thurman and I had stolen the tape from Eric Dees's garage, and described what I had seen on the tape and how I had tried to make the deal through Poitras. Poitras confirmed it. Then I told them what had happened at the Space Age Drive-In and what had happened to the tape. Murphy said, 'And the tape is destroyed?'

'Yeah. Dees burned it.'

The watch commander said, 'Ha.' As if that proved something.

Murphy ignored him and looked at Garvey. He shrugged. 'Might be possible to recover some of it. Won't know until we look.' Garvey picked up the phone and punched numbers. 'Where is it?'

I told him.

He repeated it into the phone.

We spent a total of three hours and fourteen minutes on it, and then Murphy said, 'Why don't you kick back for a while. We've got to talk with Pike, and then we've got to see where we stand.'

'Sure.' Mr Kick Back. That's me.

They let me stay in the commander's office. They left the door open and told me to help myself to coffee or the bathroom, but not to leave the building. Charlie Bauman

250

went with them. The squad room had sort of settled down, with most of the reporters and lawyers gone, and most of the Gangster Boys in holding cells or interrogation rooms. It was closing on midnight, and from somewhere along one of the halls I could hear Jay Leno.

Maybe forty minutes later Charlie Bauman and the others came back. The people from the DA and the mayor and the city council stopped in the hall to talk, and Charlie and Pike came over to me. Charlie looked tired. 'There's a lot of little stuff, but they're not going to press on the Washington thing. They believe you didn't do it.'

'What about Lancaster?'

Charlie said, 'Man, Lancaster is nothing compared to this other stuff. They need to talk to Thurman, and they need him to testify, but as long as he backs up what you said, you guys can walk.'

'He will.'

'Then you're done. Go home and get some sleep.'

Lou Poitras broke away from the group and came over and offered his hand. 'Well, you've squeaked through another one, Hound Dog.'

I nodded. ''Tis better to be lucky than good.'

He looked at Joe Pike, and Pike looked back, but neither man offered a hand. 'How're you doing, Joe?'

Pike said, 'Fine. Thank you. And you?'

'Good.'

They stared at each other some more, and then Lou cleared his throat and turned away. Awkward.

Joe Pike and Lou Poitras have hated each other for almost twelve years, and in all of that time, this was the first that they had spoken civilly to each other. Crime makes for strange bedfellows.

Joe and I were walking out with Charlie Bauman when Harold Bellis and Akeem D'Muere came out of the interrogation hall. I thought maybe they were leading D'Muere to booking, but then I realized that no one was leading him and that they were heading for the exit. D'Muere saw me looking at him and made his hand into a pistol and dropped the hammer. He didn't smile. Then he and Bellis were gone. I looked at Murphy and Fallon and the big shots from the city. 'How come that sonofabitch is walking out?'

Murphy said, 'We can't file.' Her jaw was knotted and her mouth was a razor's slash.

Maybe I hadn't heard them right. 'He murdered James Edward Washington. You've got my statement.'

Fallon said, 'We can't use it.' He didn't seem any happier than Murphy.

I looked at Pike. 'Did I suddenly lose my grip on reality?'

Two uniforms came through with a young black kid in cuffs. The kid was smiling. Murphy watched him pass, her face set, and then she said, 'That young man says that he did it.' The kid was maybe fourteen.

'He didn't do it. I was there. I saw it. D'Muere pulled the trigger.'

'Three other young men admitted to being present and also said the kid did it. They pulled him out of a lineup.'

Pike said, 'Come on, Murphy. D'Muere found a kid to play chump. The boy does juvie time and comes home a hero.'

Murphy's hard jaw softened and she suddenly looked like a woman who wanted to go home, take off her shoes, and drink three or four glasses of some nice chardonnay. 'You know it and I know it, but that young man still says he did it and three eyewitnesses say he did it, too. We can't file against D'Muere, Elvis. That's just the way this one's going to work out.' She didn't wait for me or Pike or anyone else to speak. She and Fallon left, walking heavily as if the weight of the city were on them. Greenberg followed after them.

'But he murdered James Edward Washington.' I didn't know what else to say.

Garvey said, 'Go home, Cole. You've done a lot, and you've done it well, but there's nothing more to be done.'

CHAPTER 35

The watch commander authorized the release of my car and the personal possessions that had been taken from us at the time of our original arrests. He could have ordered a staff uniform to do it, but he did it himself, and we were out of there faster because of it. I guess that was his way of showing respect.

It was seventeen minutes before two that morning when we walked out of the Seventy-seventh, got into my car, and legally drove off the police grounds and onto the city's streets. We climbed onto the freeway, then worked our way north through the system toward Lancaster. There weren't many cars out, and the driving was easy.

Pike's Jeep was where he had left it, on a little circular drive outside the hospital. I parked behind it, and then we went inside to the waiting room and asked the nurses about Mark Thurman.

A nurse maybe in her early forties with a deep tan and a light network of sun lines checked his chart. 'Mr Thurman came through the surgery well.' She looked up at us, first Pike, then me. 'Are you the gentlemen who brought him in?'

'Yes.'

She nodded and went back to the chart. 'It looks like a bullet nicked a branch of the external iliac artery in his left side. No damage to any of the organs, though, so he's going to be fine.' She closed the chart as she said it.

Pike said, 'Is Jennifer Sheridan still here?'

A black nurse who'd been sitting with a young Chinese

orderly said, 'A couple Lancaster police officers came for her. That was at about eleven-thirty. She said to tell you that she would be fine. Mr Thurman was out of surgery by then, and she knew he was okay.'

Pike said, 'What about the other officer? Garcia?'

The two nurses stopped smiling, and the black nurse said, 'Were you close to Mr Garcia?'

'No.'

'He did not survive the surgery.'

We went out, Pike to his Jeep and me to my car, and we headed back through the rough barren mountains toward Los Angeles. The high desert air was cold and the surrounding mountains were black walls against the sky and the desert. At first we drove along together, but as the miles unwound we slowly grew apart, Pike with his drive and me with mine. Alone in my car, I felt somehow unfinished and at loose ends, as if there was still much unsaid, and even more unrealized. I wondered if Pike also felt that way.

I pulled into my carport just after four that morning and found a message on my machine from Ray Depente. He said that James Edward Washington was going to be buried at Inglewood Park Cemetery at eleven A.M. tomorrow, which made it today. He said that he thought I'd want to know.

I stripped off my clothes, showered, and climbed into bed, but the sleeping was light and unsatisfactory and I was up again before seven. I went out onto my deck and breathed deeply of the air and thought how sweet it smelled with a hint of wild sage and eucalyptus. I did twelve sun salutes from the hatha-yoga, then worked through a progression of *asanas* that left me sweating. At five minutes after nine I called Joe Pike and told him of James Edward Washington's funeral. He said that he would come. I called a florist I know in Hollywood and ordered flowers. I thought roses would be nice. It was late to order flowers, but the florist knows me, and promised to deliver the flowers to the church in time for the service.

I ate breakfast, then showered and dressed in a three-piece blue suit that I bought six years ago and have worn as many times. Once to a wedding and five times to funerals. Today would be number six.

It was a warm, hazy day, and the drive along the Harbor Freeway to South Central Los Angeles was relaxed and pleasant. I left the freeway at Florence, then went west to Inglewood, and then through the gates to the cemetery there just north of Hollywood Park. The cemetery is broad and green, with gently sloping grounds and well-kept headstones and winding gravel roads. A dark green canopy had been erected on the side of one of the slopes to protect the casket and the minister and the immediate family from the sun. A hearse and a family limo and maybe twenty cars were parked nearby. They had just arrived, and some of the older people were still being helped up the slope. I parked near Joe Pike's Jeep and moved up the slope to join the mourners. Joe was standing at the back of the crowd, and Cool T was four people away.

Twin rows of folding chairs had been placed under the canopy for the family. Ida Leigh Washington was seated in the center of the front row, with the elderly man to her right, and Shalene with the baby on her left. Ray Depente was behind Mrs Washington with a hand on her shoulder. He was wearing a dark brown herring-bone suit with a U.S.M.C. pin in his lapel. When Ray saw me, he said something into Mrs Washington's ear, then stood and waited for me. I went to Mrs Washington, offered my hand, and told her how sorry I was. She thanked me for the flowers and said, 'Someone from the police called my home this morning, as did one of those people from the city council. I understand that the truth about my boy Charles Lewis is going to come out because of you.'

I told her that I didn't know if it was because of me, but that it was going to come out, yes.

She nodded and considered me for quite a long time, and then she said, 'Thank you.'

I offered my condolences to the old man, and then to Shalene. Marcus said, 'I remember you,' loudly, and with a big smile. Shalene shushed him. She still didn't like me much.

Ray Depente led me away from the grave and Joe Pike drifted up behind us. Cool T watched from the crowd. Ray said, 'How come that bastard D'Muere is walking around free?'

I told him.

Ray listened, his face tight and contained. When I was done, he said, 'You remember what you said?'

'Yes.'

'You said we'd have justice. You said that bastard would pay for killing James Edward. Him getting a fourteen-year-old fool to take his place isn't what I call justice.'

I didn't know what to say. 'The DA's people know what's going on. They'll keep digging for a case against D'Muere, and when they find it, they'll file.'

Ray Depente said, 'Bullshit.'

'Ray.'

Ray said, 'That bastard called the Washingtons. He said that if they open their mouths about this, he'll kill that baby.' He pointed at Marcus. 'He called that poor woman on the day of her son's funeral and said that. What kind of animal does something like that?'

I didn't know what to say.

Ray Depente said, 'Fuck him and fuck the DA, too. I know what to do.' Then he walked away.

Joe said, 'I know what to do, too.'

I looked at him. 'Jesus Christ. Marines.'

Cool T came out of the crowd and met Ray Depente and they spoke for a moment, and then the minister began the service. Maybe five minutes into it, Akeem D'Muere's black Monte Carlo with the heavily smoked windows turned into the graveyard and slowly cruised past the line of parked cars, his tape player booming. The volume was cranked to distortion, and the heavy bass drowned out the minister. The minister stopped trying to speak over the noise and looked at the car, and everyone else looked at the car, too. Ray Depente stepped out from the row of chairs and walked toward the car. The Monte Carlo stopped for a moment, then slowly rolled away. When the car was on the other side of the cemetery, the minister went on with the service, but Ray Depente stayed at the edge of the dark green canopy and followed the car with his eyes until it was gone.

Guard duty. The kind of duty where your orders are to shoot to kill.

When the service was over and the people were breaking up and moving down the slope, Joe and I stood together and watched Ray Depente help Mrs Washington to the family's limo. Joe said, 'He's going to do something.'

'I know.'

'He's good, but there's only one of him.'

I nodded and took a breath and let it out. 'I know. That's why we're going to help.'

Pike's mouth twitched and we went down to our cars.

CHAPTER 36

At two oh-five that afternoon, Joe Pike and I found Ray and Cool T together in Ray's office. Cool T looked angry and sullen, but Ray looked calm and composed, the type of calm I'd seen on good sergeants when I was in Vietnam. Ray saw us enter and followed us with his eyes until we were at his door. 'What?'

'Are you going to kill him?'

'I don't know what you're talking about.' Innocent.

'Well, there are ways to do it. Get a good scoped hunting rifle, hang back a couple of hundred yards, and drop the hammer. Another way would be to drive around for a while until you see him, then walk up close with a handgun. There are more apt to be witnesses that way, but it's a matter of personal preference, I guess.'

Cool T shifted in his chair.

Ray leaned back and laced his fingers behind his head. 'Man, do you think I just fell off the watermelon truck?'

'What I think is that you've got a pretty good life doing well by a lot of folks, and you're about to mess it up.'

Ray looked at Cool T and Cool T grinned. Ray didn't. He gave me lizard eyes. 'That's what it is to you, that it?'

I spread my hands.

'So you come down here to point that out? Maybe set me straight?'

'Nope. We came to help.'

'Well, we don't need the white man coming down here to solve the black man's problems. We can manage that just fine, thank you.'

Pike's mouth twitched for the second time that day.

Ray gave the eyes to Pike. 'What?'

Pike shook his head.

I said, 'The DA would file if they thought they could win, and maybe there's a way we can give them that. Maybe not on James Edward, but on something.'

Ray Depente waited.

'If you want Akeem, you're going to have to go to him. That means his home, and it used to be a crack house. It's fortified like a bunker. But once we're in, I'm betting we can find something that the DA can use to put D'Muere away.'

Cool T said, 'Ain't no way we can get in there. Goddamn police use a goddamn batterin' ran to get in a crack house. Where we gonna get that?'

Ray glanced at Cool T. 'There are other ways.' He looked back at me. 'If it was worth it. If it would lead to that sonofabitch getting what he deserves.'

'We won't know until we get there, will we?'

Ray nodded. 'Why are you doing this, Cole?'

'Because I liked James Edward, Ray. Hell, I even like you.'

Ray Depente laughed and then he stood up and put out his hand. 'Okay. You want to help out on this, we'll let you help.'

Forty-two minutes later Joe Pike and I cruised past Akeem D'Muere's fortified home in Joe's Jeep. We parked six houses down on the same side of the street in an alley between a row of flowering azalea bushes and a well-kept frame house with an ornate birdbath in the front yard. Ray Depente and Cool T were one block behind us, sitting in Ray's LeBaron. Akeem D'Muere's black Monte Carlo and the maroon Volkswagen Beetle were parked at the front of his house, and a half-dozen Gangster Boys were hanging around on the Beetle. A couple of young women were with them. I wondered if they called themselves Gangster Girls.

Pike said, 'Brick house across the street. Clapboard two doors down, this side. Check it out.'

I looked at the brick house across the street and then at the clapboard house. A heavy woman with her hair in a tight gray bun was peeking from behind a curtain in the brick house and a younger woman, maybe in her early thirties, was peeking at us from the clapboard. The younger woman was holding a baby. 'They're scared. You live on a street with a gang for your neighbors and I guess peeking out of windows becomes a way of life. Never know when it's safe to venture out.'

Joe shifted in his seat. 'Helluva way to live.'

'Yes,' I said. 'It is.'

A tall kid leaning against the Bug's left front fender looked our way, but then went back to jiving with his buddies. All attitude, no brains.

Pike pulled a pair of Zeiss binoculars from the backseat and examined the front of D'Muere's house. 'Windows set close on both sides of the door. Bars on the windows.'

'What about the door?'

'Solid core with a couple of peepholes. No glass.'

'Does it open outward?'

'Yep.' Pike put down the glasses and looked pleased. Dope dealers often rebuild their doors to open outward instead of inward. Harder for the cops to bust in that way. It was something that we'd been counting on.

Fourteen minutes after we parked in the alley, Cool T turned onto the far end of the street in Ray Depente's LeBaron and drove slowly toward D'Muere's as if he were looking at addresses. He stopped in the middle of the street, and said something to the kids on the Volkswagen.

I said, 'Now.'

Joe and I rolled out of the Jeep and moved through the backyard of the near house and into the next yard toward

D'Muere's. We moved quickly and quietly, slipping past bushes and over fences and closing on D'Muere's while Cool T kept the gangbangers' attention. Akeem D'Muere's backyard was overgrown by grass and weeds and thick high hedges that had been allowed to run without care or trimming. A creaky porch jutted off the back of the house, and a narrow cement drive ran back past the house to a clapboard garage. The garage was weathered and crummy and hadn't been used in years. Why use a garage when you can park on the front lawn? Ray Depente appeared from the hedges on the far side of the yard and held up a finger to his mouth. He was wearing a black Marine Corps-issue shoulder sling with a Colt Mark IV .45-caliber service automatic. He pointed to himself, then gestured to the east side of the house, then pointed at us and then at our side of the house, and then he was gone.

Pike took the back of the house and I moved up the drive along the side. The windows along the back and sides of the house were barred, and many had been covered on the inside with tar paper, but there were gaps and tears in the paper and I moved from window to window, trying to see inside. Cool T drove away as I made the front corner of the house, and then I faded back to the rear. The rear was so crummy we could probably pitch a tent back there and no one would notice. Pike and Ray and I crouched in the bushes beside the porch.

Ray said, 'Two rooms and a bath on my side. Three full-sized windows, all barred, and a half-sizer on the bathroom. Someone was in the bathroom but the other two rooms were clear.' He looked at Pike. 'Will the door work?'

Pike nodded. 'No problemo.'

'How about the front?'

'No problemo.'

I said, 'Kitchen and two rooms on my side. I made six people, four male, two female. No children.'

Ray nodded. 'Any way out the windows?'

'Not unless they can squeeze through the bars.'

Ray smiled. 'This is going to work.'

Twelve minutes later Cool T once more turned onto the street and again stopped in front of the house. This time a couple of bangers slid off the Beetle and went toward him. When they did, Joe and I moved up the drive and across the front yard and Ray Depente trotted toward them from the opposite side of the house. One of the girls saw Ray Depente and said, 'What the hell?' and then the others saw me and Joe. The second girl ran and a short guy with too many muscles clawed at his pants for a piece. Joe Pike kicked him in the head with an outside spin kick, and then Ray Depente and I were at the Beetle with our guns out. The two guys out in the street started pulling for hardware, too, but Cool T came out with an Ithaca 12-gauge and they put up their hands. Ray said, 'Down.'

The Eight-Deuce Gangster Boys went down onto their stomachs.

Ray said, 'Make noise, and I'll bleed you.'

A tall skinny kid with a Raiders cap wiggled around and said, 'Why don't you kiss my goddamn ass?'

Ray punched him one time hard in the side of the head and he shut up.

Cool T opened the LeBaron's trunk and tossed me a bag filled with plastic wrist restraints. I passed a couple to Pike, and we tied them off. We worked quickly, and as we tied I glanced at the surrounding houses. You could see faces in the windows and behind doors. Watching. Wondering what in hell these fools were doing.

Ray gave two smoke grenades to Pike, kept two for himself, then pulled three ten-gallon metal gas cans from the trunk and four six-foot lengths of galvanized pipe from the backseat. When we finished with the tying, Pike took two lengths of the pipe and trotted to the back of the house. Cool T hefted the other two and started toward the front. When he was halfway there, the front door opened and a chunky guy with a thick neck and a thick belly stepped out and fired a Beretta 9 millimeter, *bapbapbap-bap*. One of the rounds caught Cool T on the outside of his right arm. He screamed and went down, and then I had the Dan Wesson out and I was firing, and the heavy guy fell back. I said, 'Guess they know we're here.'

Ray grunted. 'Mm-hmm. Imagine that.'

Cool T scrambled behind the Monte Carlo and we went to him. Ray said, 'How you doing, Cool?'

'It burns like a sonofabitch.'

Pike examined the wound, then used part of Cool T's shirt to bind it. 'You'll be fine.'

A couple of faces peeked around the jamb, and someone in the house yelled, 'The fuck you doin'? Whatchu want?'

Ray yelled back. 'My name is Ray Depente. We came for Akeem D'Muere and we want to see his chickenshit ass out here.'

A second voice in the house yelled, 'Fuck you.' It was going to be one of those conversations.

Someone pulled the heavy guy out of the door, then a guy in a duster jumped forward, fired two pistol shots, then pulled the door closed.

Ray said, 'You think they'll call the police?'

We left Cool T sitting against the Monte Carlo's wheel and gathered up the pipe and the gas cans and went to the house. We put the pipes across the door and wedged them behind the window bars on either side. As we did it we could hear voices inside. They were trying to figure out what we were up to. Joe Pike came back around the house. 'Back door is sealed.'

'How about the windows?'

'No one's getting out.'

Someone inside yelled, 'The fuck you assholes want? Get away from here.' The closed door muffled the voice.

I stood to the right of the door, reached around, and pounded on it. A shotgun blast ripped through the door about where I should've been standing. I said, 'Hey, Akeem. It's time to pay up for James Edward Washington.'

Another blast came through the door.

'Gunfire is not meaningful discourse, Akeem.'

Another blast came through, this one very low.

I said, 'Here's the way it's going to happen. Everybody's going to put down their guns, and everybody's going to come out one at a time, and then we're going to tell the police what really happened to James Edward Washington. How does that sound?'

Akeem D'Muere shouted, 'Are you on dope? Get the fuck out of my face.'

I said, 'Akeem, I'm going to move in and set up house on your face.'

'You can't get in here. Get the fuck away.'

'It's not a question of us getting in, Akeem. The question is, can you get out?'

Ray Depente popped the top off of one of the gas cans and began splashing gas on the door and the windows and the sides of the house. The smell of it was strong and sharp in the still air.

Akeem said, 'What the fuck you doin' out there? What's that smell?'

'We're pouring gasoline on your house. You told the Washingtons that you were going to burn them out, didn't you? We thought you'd appreciate the poetic justice of the moment.'

A different voice yelled, 'Bullshit. You wouldn't do that.'

Ray Depente said, 'Watch.'

Ray finished with one can and started with another.

Pike took the third can around to the rear. We could hear banging at the back of the house, but the pipes would hold. Across the street, a door opened and a man in his early seventies came out onto his porch and watched with his hands on his hips. He was smiling.

Inside, you could hear men moving through the house, and voices, and then the tar paper was abruptly torn off the front window and someone fired most of an AK-47's magazine out into the ground at full auto. Ray Depente looked at me and grinned. 'You think they gettin' scared?'

'Uh-hunh.'

He grinned wider. 'These pukes ain't met scared.'

Joe Pike came back. 'Ready.'

Ray Depente took a big steel Zippo lighter from his pocket, flipped open the top, and spun the wheel. He said, 'Welcome to hell, assholes.' Then he touched the flame to the gasoline.

The eastern front corner of Akeem D'Muere's fortified crack house went up with a *whoosh*. Ray and Pike moved around the house, tossing the smoke grenades in through the windows. The grenades had instant fuses, and in two seconds there would be so much smoke that you'd think you were in an inferno. The fire stayed at just one corner of the house, though, and didn't spread. We'd placed the gasoline so that it would smell, but we'd also placed it so that the fire would be small and controlled. The people inside didn't know that, though. There were shouts, and more shots, and someone banged on the front door, trying to get it open. Someone else started screaming for us to let him out, and smoke began to leak from windows and from around the front door. Across the street, more people came out of their houses to watch.

I shouted over the noise. 'The guns come out first.'

'We can't get the goddamn door open.'

'The window.' The smoke was making them choke.

More tar paper was pulled off the windows, and

handguns and shotguns and AK-47s were shoved through the glass. Clouds of thick gray smoke billowed out with the guns.

Ray Depente found a garden hose, turned it on, and sprayed it on the fire. It didn't put out the fire, but it cooled it some.

Someone inside said, 'Let us out. Please.'

I looked at Ray. He nodded. He and Joe took up positions at the corners of the house.

'One at a time. Hands on your heads.'

'Man, I'll put my hands up my ass you let me out of here.'

I unshipped the pipes, pulled open the door, and two men and two women stumbled out, jostling each other to get away from the smoke and the fire. Pike pushed them down and used the plastic restraints. Neither of the two guys was Akeem D'Muere.

Ray Depente yelled, 'You wanna cook, that's up to you.'

No one answered.

Ray looked at me and I held up three fingers and he nodded. Akeem, plus two others. They'd be hard cases, and they would've kept their guns. We could hear coughing.

Pike said, 'Maybe they doubt our sincerity.'

Pike stayed with Cool T to watch the others, and Ray Depente and I went in after Akeem. We went in low and fast, pushing through the oily smoke, and found them in a short hall between the kitchen and a back bedroom. Akeem D'Muere was with a dopey-looking guy with sleepy eyes and another guy who looked like he could have played defensive line for the Raiders. They were coughing and rubbing at their eyes. They heard us, but the smoke was too thick for them to see us. The big guy shouted, 'They're inside,' and started swinging wild. He didn't see anything, he was just swinging, and his first two punches hit the wall. I stepped outside and caught the joint of his left knee with a hard snap kick. The knee went and the big man made a gasping sound and fell. I followed him down and took his gun.

The dopey guy yelled, 'I see the muthuhfuckuhs,' and started firing a Smith .40 somewhere up toward geosynchronous orbit. Akeem D'Muere pushed the dopey guy at us and ran toward the front of the house. Ray Depente slapped the dopey guy's .40 to the outside, then hit him three fast times, twice in the chest and once in the neck, and the dopey guy fell.

Ray said, 'Take his gun.' Ray was already after Akeem.

I grabbed the dopey guy's gun, then used the plastic restraints as quickly as I could. I wanted to get to Akeem D'Muere before Ray got to him, but I didn't make it. Two shots came from the living room, then a third, and I got there just as Ray Depente came up under D'Muere's gun, twisted it free just as he had taught a thousand guys down at Camp Pendleton, then threw Akeem D'Muere through the open front door out into the yard. I went after them.

Akeem D'Muere was standing sort of bent to the side in the front yard, rubbing at his eyes and spitting to try to clear the smoke from his lungs. Ray Depente went down off the little porch, peeled away his shoulder sling, and said, 'Look at me, boy.' Ray didn't wait for him to look. Ray spun once and kicked Akeem D'Muere on the side of the head, knocking him to the ground.

I said, 'Ray.'

Up and down the block, doors opened and people came out onto porches and into yards. Pike and Cool T had the Eight-Deuce Gangster Boys on the ground and out of the play.

Ray Depente went to Akeem and dragged him to his feet. Ray was a couple of inches taller, but thinner, so they probably weighed close to the same. When Ray was lifting him, Akeem tried to grab and bite, but Ray dug his thumbs into Akeem D'Muere's eyes. D'Muere screamed and stumbled back. Ray stood and looked at him and there was something hard and remote in his eyes. Ray opened his hands. 'Hit me. Let's see what you got.'

Akeem D'Muere launched a long right hand that caught Ray high on the cheek and made him step back, but when he tried to follow with a left, Ray blocked it to the inside and drove a round kick into the side of D'Muere's head. D'Muere stumbled sideways, and Ray reversed and kicked him from the opposite side, and this time D'Muere fell. I put a hand on Ray's shoulder. 'That's enough, Ray.'

Ray slapped away my hand. 'Stand away from me now.'

'Ray, you're going to kill him.' Akeem D'Muere struggled up to his knees.

Ray said, 'And wouldn't that be a shame.' He kicked Akeem D'Muere in the chest and knocked him backwards.

I looked at Pike, but Pike was impassive behind the dark glasses.

Ray walked around behind D'Muere, lifted him by the hair, and said, 'You meet James Edward, you tell'm I said hi.' He spun again, and kicked, and Akeem D'Muere snapped over into the ground.

I took out the Dan Wesson. 'Ray.'

'You wanna shoot me for a piece of garbage like this, go ahead.'

He picked D'Muere up again. D'Muere's mouth and nose and ears were bleeding, and most of his teeth were gone. Ray held him up until D'Muere could stand on his own, then Ray punched him four fast times, twice in the solar plexus and twice in the face. Akeem D'Muere fell like a bag of wet laundry. One of the Gangster Girls screamed, 'You're gonna kill'm.'

Ray said, 'You think?'

I aimed the Dan Wesson. 'I don't have to kill you, Ray. I can do your knee. Be hard to teach after that.'

Ray nodded. 'You're right. But think of my memories.'

He lifted D'Muere's head by the hair, aimed, and punched him two hard times behind the ear. Then he let the head drop.

'Damn it, Ray.' I cocked the Dan Wesson.

Pike said, 'He means it, Ray.'

'I know. So do I.'

He reached down and lifted Akeem D'Muere once more.

As he brought D'Muere up, a dark blue Buick stopped in the street by the LeBaron and Ida Leigh Washington got out. She stood in the street, motionless for a time, and then she moved toward us. She was still wearing the clothes that she had worn to her son's funeral. Black.

Ray Depente saw her and let Akeem D'Muere fall to the ground. He said, 'You shouldn't be here, Ida Leigh.'

She stopped about ten feet from him and looked at the smoldering house, and then at the thugs on the ground with their hands bound, and then at me and Joe. She said, 'I wanted to see where he lived. Is that the one killed my son?'

'Yes, ma'am.'

Somewhere far off, a siren sounded. On the way here, no doubt.

Ida Leigh Washington stepped closer and looked down at D'Muere. His face was a mask of blood, but she did not flinch when she saw it. She put a hand on Ray's forearm and said, 'What could turn a boy into an animal like this?'

Ray said, 'I don't know, Ida Leigh.'

She raised her eyes from D'Muere up to Ray. 'This man took my last son. No one could claim my hurt, or my anger. No one could have a greater claim on this one's life.' Her voice was tight and fierce. She patted Ray's arm. 'There's been enough killing down here. We have to find a way to live without the killing.'

Ray Depente didn't move for a minute. Ida Leigh Washington kept her eyes on him. Ray stepped back. He turned away from Akeem D'Muere, and as the police cars began to arrive he helped Mrs Ida Leigh Washington back to her car.

Up and down the street, the people on the porches and in the windows and in the yards began to applaud. It would've been nice to think that they were applauding Ida Leigh Washington, but they weren't. At least I don't think they were. That far away, those people couldn't have heard one woman's softly spoken words, could they?

The cops got out of their cars and looked around and didn't know what to make of it. A Hispanic cop with a butch cut looked at Pike and me and said, 'Weren't you guys at the Seventy-seventh last night?'

'Yeah. We'll probably be there again tonight, too.'

He didn't know what to make of that, either.

CHAPTER 37

When the police went into Akeem D'Muere's house, they found $82,000 in crack cocaine in the attic, along with six cases of stolen rifles. Because the police legally entered the house investigating a crime in progress, the evidence found was admissible and resulted in charges brought against D'Muere. The investigators found no copies of the videotape that Eric Dees destroyed, and Akeem D'Muere, for some reason known only to him, denied all knowledge of such a tape.

The DA went easy on Pike and me. They agreed to trade on all charges except the assault on the police guards when Pike and I escaped from the Seventy-seventh. We were allowed to plead to a misdemeanor, served three days in county jail, and then it was over.

Of the five REACT officers involved in the wrongful death of Charles Lewis Washington, only Warren Pinkworth and Mark Thurman survived. Thurman turned state's evidence and sought neither a plea nor mercy. Warren Pinkworth was indicted on five counts of murder. He attempted a plea, but none was allowed.

Sixteen weeks after the events at the Space Age Drive-In Theater in Lancaster, Mark Thurman was fired from the ranks of the LAPD, losing all benefits that had been accrued. He said he didn't mind. He said it could have been worse. He was right. Four days after that, all administrative and criminal charges were dropped against Mark Thurman due to the intercession of Mrs Ida Leigh Washington. Three members of the city council and one member of the DA's staff objected and wanted, for political reasons, to use Thurman as an example, but cooler heads were only too happy to acquiesce to Mrs Washington's wishes. Negotiations were under way in the matter of her wrongful-death suits against the city. She was suing in the names of both of her sons.

Twenty-four weeks and three days after the events in the Space Age Drive-In, after spring had moved into summer, and then into the early part of fall, I was sitting in my office reading last week's newspaper when the phone rang and I answered, 'Elvis Cole Detective Agency, we're on your case for no money down.'

Jennifer Sheridan laughed. It was a good laugh, nice and clear. She and Mark were living together in Lancaster. She had given up her job with Watkins, Okum, & Beale and had taken a new job with a law firm based in Mojave. She had taken a twenty per cent cut in salary to do it, but she said that it was what she wanted. Mark Thurman had applied for a job with both the Palmdale PD and the Lancaster PD, but had been rejected both times. He had decided to return to school and obtain a degree in physical education. He thought he might like to coach high-school football. Jennifer Sheridan was sure that he would be wonderful at it. She said, 'How do you expect prospective clients to take you seriously if you answer the phone that way?'

I gave her Groucho. 'You kiddin'? I wouldn't work for a client who'd hire me.'

She laughed again. 'You do a terrible Groucho.'

'Want to hear my Bogart? That's even worse.' You get me on a roll, I'm a riot.

She said, 'Mark and I are getting married on the third Sunday of next month. We're getting married in the little Presbyterian church in Lake Arrowhead. Do you know where that is?'

'I do.'

'We've sent you an invitation, but I wanted to call. We'd like you to come.'

'I wouldn't miss it.'

'If you give me Joe's number, I'd like to invite him, too.'

'Sure.' I gave her the number.

Jennifer Sheridan said, 'It won't be a big wedding, or particularly formal. Just a few people.'

'Great.'

'We want a church wedding. We like the tradition behind it.'

She was leading up to something. 'What is it, Jennifer?'

She said, 'I'd really like it if you gave me away.'

Something warm formed in the center of my chest, and then I felt it in my eyes. 'Sure. I'd like that, too.'

'I love him, Elvis. I love him so much.'

I smiled.

She said, 'Thank you.'

'Anytime, kid. Romance is my business.'

She said, 'Oh, you,' and then she hung up.

After a bit I put aside the paper and went out the glass doors and stood on my balcony. It was late afternoon, and the fall air was cool and nice. A beauty-supply company has the office next to mine. It is owned by a very attractive woman named Cindy. She is also very nice. Sometimes she will come out onto her balcony and lean across the little wall that separates her space from mine, and look into my office and wave to get my attention. I did that now, leaning across and looking in her office, but her office was empty. It goes like that, sometimes.

I took a deep breath and looked out over the city to the ocean and to Santa Catalina Island, far to the south, and thought about Jennifer Sheridan and her love for Mark Thurman, and I wondered if anyone would love me the way she loved him. I thought that they might, but you never know.

I stood on the balcony, and breathed the cool air, and after a while I went in and shut the door. Maybe I would come out

274

again in a while, and maybe, this time, Cindy would be in her office.

One can always hope.

All Orion/Phoenix titles are available at your local bookshop or from the following address:

Mail Order Department
Littlehampton Book Services
FREEPOST BR535
Worthing, West Sussex, BN13 3BR
telephone 01903 828503, *facsimile* 01903 828802
e-mail MailOrders@lbsltd.co.uk
(Please ensure that you include full postal address details)

Payment can be made either by credit/debit card (Visa, Mastercard, Access and Switch accepted) or by sending a £ Sterling cheque or postal order made payable to *Littlehampton Book Services*.
DO NOT SEND CASH OR CURRENCY

Please add the following to cover postage and packing

UK and BFPO:
£1.50 for the first book, and 50p for each additional book to a maximum of £3.50

Overseas and Eire:
£2.50 for the first book plus £1.00 for the second book and 50p for each additional book ordered

---

BLOCK CAPITALS PLEASE

name of cardholder .... *delivery address*
.... (*if different from cardholder*)
address of cardholder ....
....
....
postcode .... *postcode* ....

☐ I enclose my remittance for £ ....

☐ please debit my Mastercard/Visa/Access/Switch (delete as appropriate)

card number ☐☐☐☐☐☐☐☐☐☐☐☐☐☐☐☐☐☐

expiry date ☐☐☐☐   Switch issue no. ☐☐

signature ....

prices and availability are subject to change without notice